THE LAIRD'S FORBIDDEN LADY

Ann Lethbridge

MILLS & BOON

First published in Great Britain 2012
by Mills & Boon, an imprint of Harlequin (UK) Limited.
Large Print edition 2012
Harlequin (UK) Limited, Eton House, 18-24 Paradise Road,
Richmond, Surrey TW9 1SR

© Michèle Ann Young 2012

ISBN: 978 0 263 22535 8

Harlequin (UK) policy is to use papers that are natural,
renewable and recyclable products and made from wood grown in
sustainable forests. The logging and manufacturing process conform
to the legal environmental regulations of the country of origin.

Printed and bound in Great Britain
by CPI Antony Rowe, Chippenham, Wiltshire

Ann Lethbridge has been reading Regency novels for as long as she can remember. She always imagined herself as Lizzie Bennet, or one of Georgette Heyer's heroines, and would often recreate the stories in her head with different outcomes or scenes. When she sat down to write her own novel, it was no wonder that she returned to her first love: the Regency.

Ann grew up roaming England with her military father. Her family lived in many towns and villages across the country, from the Outer Hebrides to Hampshire. She spent memorable family holidays in the West Country and in Dover, where her father was born. She now lives in Canada, with her husband, two beautiful daughters, and a Maltese terrier named Teaser, who spends his days on a chair beside the computer, making sure she doesn't slack off.

Ann visits Britain every year, to undertake research and also to visit family members who are very understanding about her need to poke around old buildings and visit every antiquity within a hundred miles. If you would like to know more about Ann and her research, or to contact her, visit her website at www.annlethbridge.com. She loves to hear from readers.

Previous novels by this author:

THE RAKE'S INHERITED COURTESAN**
WICKED RAKE, DEFIANT MISTRESS
CAPTURED FOR THE CAPTAIN'S PLEASURE
THE GOVERNESS AND THE EARL
   (part of *Mills & Boon New Voices…* anthology)
THE GAMEKEEPER'S LADY*
MORE THAN A MISTRESS*
LADY ROSABELLA'S RUSE**

And in Mills & Boon® Historical *Undone!* eBooks:

THE RAKE'S INTIMATE ENCOUNTER
THE LAIRD AND THE WANTON WIDOW
ONE NIGHT AS A COURTESAN
UNMASKING LADY INNOCENT
DELICIOUSLY DEBAUCHED BY THE RAKE

And in Mills & Boon® Historical eBooks:

PRINCESS CHARLOTTE'S CHOICE
   (part of *Royal Weddings Through the Ages* anthology)

*linked by character
**linked by character

**Did you know that some of these novels
are also available as eBooks? Visit www.millsandboon.co.uk**

Lots of people are involved in getting a story
on to the shelves or up online, and I am
grateful for all their hard work. This book
I am dedicating to my amazing editor,
Joanne Grant. Thank you for your patience and
for your invaluable guidance with this project.
Without you it would never have come to fruition.

Chapter One

Scotland—1818

Why had she ever thought returning to Scotland a good idea? Lady Selina Albright eyed the wrought-iron candelabra suspended from ancient oak beams and the grey stone walls covered with ragged tapestries, great swords and rusting pikes, and suppressed the urge to flee.

Having run from two eminently eligible bridegrooms, one more would put her beyond the pale. Not even her father's considerable influence would prevent her from being gazetted a jilt.

And besides, this one was her choice. Finally.

All around her, dark-coated gentlemen and sumptuously gowned women, their jewels flashing with every movement, filled Carrick Castle's medieval banqueting hall.

'I hadn't expected it to be such a squeeze,' observed Chrissie, Lady Albright, her father's wife of only a year and the reason Selina had agreed to this trip.

Not that she would ever have been so unkind as to tell Chrissie the truth.

'He must have invited every member of the Scottish nobility,' Selina said. 'At any moment I expect to see Banquo's ghost or three witches hunched over a cauldron.' A shiver ran down her spine. 'I should have waited in London for the end of Algernon's tour of duty.'

She glanced across the huge chamber to where Lieutenant the Right Honourable Algernon Dunstan, conversed with another officer in front of the enormous hearth decorated with stag antlers. Fair-haired and slender, he looked dashing in his red militia uniform. Not quite the brilliant catch her father had expected, but he was a young man of good family with a kindly disposition. The kind of man who would make a pleasant husband.

He caught her eyeing him and bowed.

She inclined her head and smiled. He was the reason she was here: to bring him up to the mark and get her out of her father's house, where she felt decidedly underfoot.

'I think it is all very romantic,' Chrissie said, looking around her with wide-eyed appreciation.

'I feel as if I have been transported between the covers of *Waverly*. Is Dunross Keep equally enchanting?'

'Dunross is about as romantic as an open boat on the North Sea in winter.' It was hard to imagine she'd fallen in love with the keep when she first saw it some ten years before. She'd been a foolish impressionable child, she supposed. 'Nowhere near as grand as this and as cold and damp in summer as it is no doubt freezing in winter. Did Father tell you the local people hate us because we are English? They think of us as usurpers, you know.' For some obscure reason her father, the lord of the manor, wished to visit there next—something he had not told her before they left London and the real reason she was regretting her agreement to accompany him. Dunross was the last place in the world she wished to visit.

'Oh, my word,' Chrissie gasped. 'Who is that?'

Selina followed the direction of her gaze.

A hard thump of her heart against her ribs was a painful recognition of the tall man in Highland dress framed within the stone arched entry. Ian Gilvry. The self-proclaimed Laird of Dunross.

The reason she hated Scotland. A knot formed in her stomach and made it hard to breathe as her gaze took him in.

He was not the gangling youth she remembered, though she would have known him anywhere. He was virile and brawny and, despite his green-and-red kilt, exceedingly male.

His features were far too harsh and dark to be called handsome in the drawing rooms of London, and the frill of white lace at his wrists and throat did nothing to soften his aura of danger. The raw vitality he exuded drew and held every female eye in the room. Including her own.

He was the last man she had expected or wanted to see at Lord Carrick's drum. Hopefully, he wasn't here to make trouble.

His gaze swept the room and, to her chagrin, her heart raced as she waited for some acknowledgement of her presence in his sky-blue eyes. When his gaze reached her and halted, she couldn't breathe. Her heart tumbled over.

An expression of horror flickered across his face, then his gaze moved on. The sting of rejection lashed her anew. Ridiculous. She cared not one whit for Ian Gilvry's opinion. He might have been the first man, or rather boy, to kiss her, but it had been a clumsy attempt and not worth thinking about. Especially not when their families were at daggers drawn.

'Who is he?' Chrissie whispered.

'Ian Gilvry of Dunross,' she murmured. No further explanations were needed.

Chrissie looked down her nose. 'That is Ian Gilvry? What is he doing here? I thought only the real nobility were invited.'

Selina winced at the sudden urge to protest the scornful tone. 'He is a distant cousin to Lord Carrick. On his mother's side.'

'That costume is positively indecent in polite company.' Chrissie sniffed, clearly reflecting her husband's opinion of all things Gilvry. On anyone else Chrissie would have declared it romantic. 'He looks positively barbaric.'

He did. Deliciously so.

Oh, that was not the way she should be thinking about a man who held her and her family in contempt.

'It is the traditional garb of the Highlands.'

'I am surprised you would defend him,' Chrissie said with a little toss of her head.

She felt herself colour. 'I am stating a fact.' When Chrissie stared at her with raised brows, she realised she'd spoken more sharply than she intended. She shrugged.

From the corner of her eye, she watched Ian stroll across the room to greet a friend with a smile that lit his face and transformed him from stern to charming.

What, was she still fooled by his smile? Hardly. She didn't give tuppence for Ian Gilvry or his brothers. They were proud, arrogant men who would stop at nothing to put her father off land they considered their own.

As if sensing her watching, he glanced her way. Their gazes clashed for no more than a second. Heat flooded her cheeks. She swiftly turned away.

'Look, Sel,' Chrissie said, 'there is Lady Carrick. Your father particularly asked me to get to know her better and this is the first time she has not been surrounded by crowds of people. Will you be all right here by yourself?'

Selina swallowed a sharp retort. Chrissie was being her usual sweet self and she had promised herself she would vanquish her annoyance at the young woman's attempt to play the mother. 'I am perfectly content to remain here and await your return.' She gave an airy wave of her fan and hoped Chrissie would not see the effort it cost her not to show her impatience.

Chrissie bustled away with a wifely determination that brought a genuine smile to Selina's lips and a warm feeling to her chilly heart. She hadn't expected to like her father's new wife, but they rubbed along quite well, most of the time.

Unfortunately, Chrissie's unflagging solicitude and her unfailing kindness made Selina feel increasingly like a guest in her father's house. It had become a source of increasing irritation since her accident had kept her confined to the house for so many months. With time for reflection, she had decided it really was time she found her own place in the world. And the only option available was to become a wife.

Unintentionally, her gaze slid once again in Ian's direction. He seemed to be circling the room, going from group to group, drawing closer to where she sat by the minute. Her heart picked up speed. Her mouth dried. Surely he would not have the unmitigated gall to approach her? She eased her grip on her fan and kept her gaze moving in case someone noticed her interest.

And here came Dunstan to ensure she was all right on her own. He bounded up to her like a puppy who had found his new bone, after misplacing it for a while. She wasn't sure whether to pat him on the head to keep him happy, or throw him a stick to send him scampering off. Neither was appropriate, of course. Not if she wanted to keep him.

The third son of a powerful earl, he was a perfect match for the daughter of a baron, though at one time she'd been on the brink of landing the rakish heir to an earldom, had even been so bold as to follow him to Lisbon. But when he'd come up to the mark, she'd panicked and run. When it had happened again, with a viscount, she'd been labelled a jilt and become an object of fascination for gentlemen who liked a challenge. Or at least she had until her accident made her an object of pity.

She'd been right to flee that first time, though. Her suitor had later proved himself an intractable husband, according to gossip.

Dunstan was a whole other prospect. He would make the perfect husband. Malleable. Kind. And definitely besotted. She would have no trouble twisting him around her finger. She just wished he'd been stationed at Bath or Brighton instead of the wilds of Scotland. She smiled in welcome as he arrived at her chair.

'May I say how lovely you look this evening?' he said eagerly.

'Thank you, Lieutenant Dunstan, you are too kind.'

His eyes flickered down to her bosom and then

up to her face. Desire shone in his eyes as he pressed the back of her gloved hand to his lips.

A public demonstration of possession.

Again the urge to run beat in her blood, but that would be cowardly. She gestured for him to take the chair vacated by Chrissie. 'Lord Carrick's castle is a thing of wonder, don't you think?'

Again her roving gaze fell upon Ian. He was much closer now. Too close. Oh, why was he here of all places? She could not concentrate upon a thing Dunstan was saying. She shifted in her chair, turning to focus all her attention on the man at her side. But she could still feel Ian's presence, like a dark shadow looming in the corner of a room.

She forced a smile at Dunstan, who blinked.

'I think you will like Pater's seat in Surrey,' he said. 'I am to go on leave at the end of the month. I hope you and your father will do us the honour of a visit?'

Perfect. A man only interested in flirtation did not ask a woman to meet his parents. And it seemed he was no more enamoured of Scotland than she. 'We will be delighted, I am sure. And I hope we will see you at Dunross Keep before you depart for England?' It was to be her dowry. Her contribution to a convenient arrangement. He might as well see what he was getting.

'It will be a pleasure since I will have business in the area.'

'Military business?'

'Indeed,' he said heavily, his tone full of importance. But since he did not volunteer to say more, she let the matter slide. 'There are a great many people here I don't know,' she said brightly. 'I am sure you know all those of significance. I would be grateful for your insights.' If she'd learned one thing in her years on the town, it was how to make a man feel important.

The rather proud smile as he glanced around the room gave her a pang of guilt, but he seemed to enjoy the opportunity to show off his knowledge.

'The couple talking to your father is the local constable and his wife. Colonel Berwick fought at Waterloo with the Black Watch.'

'A brave man, then.' Selina memorised the soldier's face. A good wife paid attention to those who could aid her husband. And she would be a good wife. She was determined to keep her part of the bargain.

'An unruly Highlander, more like,' Dunstan grumbled. 'They give the regiment no end of trouble.' He was now staring at Ian.

Her blood ran cold. It was as if a chill wind had swept through the room. 'What sort of trouble?'

'Illegal whisky stills. Smuggling.' His gaze narrowed.

If Ian was engaged in smuggling, he was more of a fool than she ever imagined. Without thinking, she noted the way his plaid grazed the tops of his socks as he sauntered with lithe grace to a group of guests not far from her chair.

Her heart hammered so loud she was sure Dunstan must hear it. Would he speak to her? Surely not. What would she say if he did? His words at their last meeting some nine years before had been horrid. Crushing. But more recently he had responded to a written request to call his brother home with a surprising alacrity. For that at least she owed him a debt of gratitude.

Now was not the time, however. With luck, Ian would pass on by.

Luck, as ever, was not her friend.

Annoyance crossed Dunstan's face when Ian paused in front of them. Ever the gentleman though, Dunstan gestured to Selina. 'Ian Gilvry, allow me to introduce you to Lady Selina Albright.'

Ian bowed. 'Lady Selina, it is indeed an honour to once more make your acquaintance.'

The butter-soft burr of his highland brogue made her skin tingle the way the touch of his lips to hers once had. Or was it the feel of his hand on hers and the sensation of warm breath she could not possibly feel through her glove? Or was it merely his acknowledgement of recollection?

Heat flashed in her cheeks. He was the only man who had ever had the power to disturb her equilibrium. Years of careful training stood her in good stead, however, and she gave him her most brilliant smile. 'Why, Mr Gilvry, I hardly recognised you after all these years.'

Bright blue eyes regarded her coldly. His mouth curved in a bitter smile. What did he have to be bitter about? It was her pride she'd ground into the dust by asking for his help for Alice. But the Gilvrys and the Albrights had always been enemies. Perhaps she was reading more into his expression than she should.

'You have also changed a good deal, Lady Selina.'

His tone said he spoke out of mere politeness. Something to say.

Dunstan frowned, then his brow cleared. 'Ah, right. You spent some time at Dunross Keep as a girl. You must have met then.'

'Briefly,' she said.

'Once or twice,' Ian said at the same moment.

She snatched her hand back. 'No rocks in your pockets today, I hope?'

An unwilling smile curved his full lips. 'None today, my lady,' he said smoothly.

She arched a brow. 'And how is all at Dunross? Your mother is well?'

His eyes darkened to stormy grey. 'As well as may be expected under the circumstances.' A muscle jumped in his jaw. 'I understand you are to honour Dunross Keep shortly.'

Gossip abounded. But then the self-professed Laird of Dunross would know everything about the demesne he claimed as his, when it really belonged to her father. She lifted her chin, meeting his gaze without flinching. 'I believe it is on our list of quaint points of interest.' She smiled sweetly.

He stiffened slightly. Resentment flashed across his face, before it once more smoothed to bland indifference. 'Do you have many quaint places on your list?'

'A few. It is *de rigueur* to be in love with Scotland since *Waverly* came out. You have read Sir Walter Scott, I assume?'

This time real anger flashed in his eyes. 'Why would I?'

Dunstan tugged at his collar. 'I will also be visiting Dunross.'

'How pleasant for you,' Ian replied, his gaze

never leaving Selina's face. 'I am delighted you *Sassenachs* find us poor Scots of such interest.'

'La, sir, you make yourself sound like insects beneath a lens.'

He gave a hard laugh. '*Touché*, Lady Selina.'

This was getting out of hand. She turned to Dunstan. 'Lady Albright is in alt with the country. And knowing Scotland as well as I do gives it a special charm.'

'Some say familiarity breeds contempt,' Ian said, before Dunstan could respond.

She raised a brow.

'No need to be churlish, Gilvry,' Dunstan muttered.

The orchestra struck up a reel. Ian inclined his head. 'I see I should make amends. May I request this next dance, Lady Selina?'

The air left her lungs in a rush. That she had not expected. For a moment, she almost said yes. It might be her only opportunity to speak with him alone, to proffer her thanks for the service he'd rendered her friend. A dance was about as private as she'd ever dared be with Ian Gilvry. But dancing was out of the question. Did he know that? Was he taunting her, knowing full well she could not dance? It would be the sort of thing a Gilvry would take pleasure in. 'I do not dance tonight, Mr Gilvry.'

His eyes remained wintry, giving no hint of his thoughts. 'You will excuse me, then,' he said softly. 'I promised Miss Campbell I would lead her out at the first opportunity.' He executed the slightest of bows, an arrogant inflection of his neck that said he bowed to no man or woman, and strode off, his kilt swinging with each long stride, his wide shoulders square.

The feel of her arms clinging to those shoulders for dear life teased at her memory. Although on that long-ago afternoon, they'd not been quite so breathtakingly broad.

She dragged her thoughts back to the present and watched Chrissie and her father take to the floor in another set. Despite the differences in their ages, they made a handsome couple. And she couldn't help but feel glad for his happiness, even if it did mean she must depart his home.

Her gaze wandered to Ian and Miss Campbell. His whole attention was focused on his partner's face. The girl blushed in response to a murmured word and a flash of a smile.

Something tightened in her chest. Jealousy? Certainly not. A pang of envy? Perhaps. It wasn't surprising. Not because the girl was dancing with

Ian Gilvry—about that she surely didn't give a hoot. No. It was the dancing she missed.

A wry smile tugged at her lips. She was lucky it was only dancing she'd lost as a result of her recklessness. She could have lost her life.

She gave Dunstan her most brilliant smile. 'I gather your colonel gave strict instructions with respect to entertaining the single ladies tonight and since I do not dance, I shall not keep you from your duty.'

His expression held relief. 'You are gracious to be so understanding, my lady.'

'A soldier's duty must come first.' And she really needed to be rid of him for a while. Her heart still raced uncomfortably fast after sparring with Ian.

'I will escort you to supper, of course.'

'I look forward to it. In the meantime, do not worry about me. I am well entertained.'

He bowed and departed and was soon leading out a handsome young matron. Strangely enough, Selina didn't feel a smidgeon of envy as she watched him. Nor would she, she was sure, when he continued to dance with other ladies after they were married. It was the way of their world.

As the music finished, Lord Carrick took up a position on the dais in front of the orchestra.

'Ladies and gentlemen, I have a special treat for

you before supper. If you will please follow me out onto the terrace.' A buzz of excitement circled the room and people moved towards the French doors at the far end of the hall.

Ian Gilvry, she noticed, left by way of the arch through which he had entered.

With no choice but to follow the rest of the company, she pushed to her feet.

Chrissie and her father joined her. 'What is going on?'

'I have no idea,' Selina said.

A woman standing nearby turned to them. 'It is a contest. The local lads will compete for a prize for our entertainment.'

'Not boxing,' Chrissie said with a shudder.

'Och, no. Something better. Wait and see.' She disappeared into the crowd.

The Albright party joined Lord Carrick, who indicated they should sit in the front row and guided Selina to a chair beside Chrissie.

Chrissie gave her a sweet smile. 'How are you feeling?'

'Excited about the coming spectacle,' she said, deliberately misunderstanding Chrissie's true meaning.

Chrissie leaned closer and whispered something in her husband's ear. Her father smiled down fondly, murmuring something that made Chrissie giggle.

Feeling like an intruder, Selina averted her gaze and pretended not to notice.

Lit by torches and a full moon, the flagged court-yard looked positively medieval. Lord Carrick seated himself on a thronelike canopied chair carved with symbols of his clan. Clearly he was to be judge and jury of the coming contest.

To the skirling sound of bagpipes five kilted men marched into the open area from beneath a shad-owing arch, holding swords across their chests. Among them, taller than all of them, was Ian. Two of his three brothers accompanied him.

The men bent and laid their swords on the flag-stones crossed at right angles. The music ceased.

Lord Carrick rose to his feet and the five men bowed. Their chief signalled for them to begin and the piper played the opening bars. The men were going to dance for a purse.

It was a magnificent sight. Strong young men in their plaids and white lace leaping lightly over their swords, jumping higher and faster in ever more complex patterns. Ian's heavy kilt swung high, revealing strongly muscled thighs and...nothing more. Too bad.

That thought brought heat to Selina's cheeks. How could she be so wicked?

But the sight of Ian dancing, the controlled wildness in his movement, the demonstration of his male strength and grace, called to something primal inside her. The iron control in the lightness of his feet caused her to hold her breath in awe and fear. A man touched his sword, knocking it askew with a clatter. He ceased dancing immediately, bowed and walked away defeated. She could scarcely bear to watch in case Ian also failed, yet could not look away.

The music's tempo increased. Another man dropped out. And another, until only two of the older Gilvry brothers remained.

Ian and Niall. Of Andrew there was no sign. Ian leapt without effort, his feet so close to the blades he barely moved from the centre of the cross. What held her transfixed was his intensity, the hot blood of battle expressed in the position of his arms, the proud angle of his head and the fire in his defiant eyes.

Impossible as it seemed, she felt their eyes lock and in that moment, it was as if he danced only for her.

Nay, not for her, she realised. At her, rejecting all she stood for. War declared. The final leaps caused an indrawn breath from the assembled company. Yet they landed lightly, clear of the swords, each man holding position until the last note died away.

The connection snapped.

In unison the two men bowed and stood stiffly, waiting for their chief's judgement while their audience applauded and cheered.

Even Chrissie and Father leaped to their feet, clapping.

Selina had no doubt Ian would win. Yet she still felt anxious until his chieftain beckoned him forwards. He ran lightly up the terrace steps, shook the Carrick's hand and took the purse presented with an incline of his head. He did not once glance her way.

There had been no connection between them. He probably couldn't see her on the terrace in the dark. It had all been her imagination. It wasn't the first time she'd been mistaken in his interest. The only connection they had was one of mutual dislike.

Deep inside she felt a twinge of sadness. Perhaps because whoever he had danced for, he had expressed himself through movement—a freedom and grace she could never accomplish.

The two men spoke a few words, then Ian ran back down the steps and walked away. Only when he was out of sight did the sorrow inside her lessen.

She thought she had resigned herself to the future she'd charted, but for some reason, now she felt thoroughly unsettled. She rose to her feet with a slight wince.

'Is your leg paining you?' Chrissies asked.

Dash it all, the woman watched her like a hawk. 'I am just a little stiff from sitting, that is all.' And from the tension of watching Ian.

Chapter Two

Ian joined his clansmen clustered around the piper in the shadows of the gate leading out of the courtyard to the kitchens. His breathing had slowed, but his blood still ran hot—battle fever aroused by the music. There had been a time when he danced for the pure joy of it. Now he felt like little more than a performing bear on a chain performing for these *Sassenachs*. He swallowed the anger. It had pleased Carrick and the coin would bring much-needed relief to his people. Lord Carrick could easily have spent his money on entertainment elsewhere.

He emptied the prize purse into his palm, first paying the piper his due, then dividing the spoils equally. 'Well done, lads.'

'What is that?' Logan, his youngest brother, asked, gesturing to the other pouch Carrick had slipped into Ian's palm.

'You've sharp eyes, young Logan,' Ian grumbled. 'Carrick wants us to make another run to France.'

'I thought we had all the salt we need,' Niall said, glancing up from the pamphlet he'd been reading by the light of the torch.

'He wants brandy,' Ian said. 'He will have used up most of his supply by the end of this ball.'

'Brandy is asking for trouble,' Niall said. 'It is bad enough running the whisky over the border to England.

Ian quelled him with a glance. 'How could I refuse after all he has done for us? Besides, his money will help pay for this autumn's barley.'

Niall shook his head. 'Admit it, you like the danger.'

Did he? Long ago, he'd wanted to be a soldier, but when his father died, he'd shouldered the duties of Laird without a second thought. It was his responsibility.

Straying from that duty had never resulted in anything but trouble, for him or his family. And smuggling was a necessary evil. Part of the job, if he wanted the clan to survive. And he did, desperately. It was all he thought of, day and night.

'What say we go down to the tavern and celebrate?' Tammy McNab said, jingling the coin in his hand.

Ian jabbed at Tammy's shoulder. 'Would you spend your money on drink when your babes are hungry?'

A red-haired man of twenty-five who already had three children to his name, Tammy hung his head. 'Just thought to have a wee bit of fun.'

'Why pay for it, when Carrick has food and drink for you all in the servants' hall?' Ian said.

Tammy cheered instantly. 'You'll be coming too, Laird?'

Ian shook his head. 'I've a ship's captain to meet now I have this new errand. Enjoy yourself on Lord Carrick's coin. You've earned it.'

The men moved off towards the servants' entrance in the low-slung thatched buildings abutting the castle. Ian turned to leave by the drawbridge. Logan caught his shoulder. 'Did you see who was watching? The Albrights. I'd recognise Lady Selina anywhere.'

Because she was just so damned lovely. Even lovelier as a woman than she had been as a child of sixteen. And just as much trouble as she had been then, too.

'I met her inside.' He curled his lip. 'I asked her to dance as Carrick ordered. She refused me.' He hadn't known whether to be glad or insulted.

During the sword dance, he had felt the intensity of her gaze. Had lost himself in her beauty in the final bars, drawing strength from her shining eyes and parted lips. He'd gone back in time, dancing for the girl who had roamed freely among the heather that long-ago summer. He'd been enchanted by her pretty face and spirit, until he came to his senses and remembered just whose daughter she was.

Something he'd do well to remember now, too. Selina Albright had caused his family nothing but trouble. And he, like a fool, had helped.

'I'm no surprised she wouldna dance with you, Ian.'

He stiffened. 'Aye. Albrights have always been a touch above the Gilvry clan.'

'She might think so, but I doubt she can dance, not with that limp.'

Stunned by a sudden stab of dismay, Ian whipped his head around. His eyes narrowed as he watched the progress of the dark beauty in the white gown as she crossed the terrace on her father's arm, the hesitation in her step cruelly obvious in the torchlight.

She had refused him for a reason different from the one he'd assumed. He felt an odd surge of relief.

He turned and pushed Logan after the others.

He called Niall back and lowered his voice. 'Keep an eye on young Logan. He's developing an eye for the ladies and Carrick has too many of them in his kitchen.'

Niall sighed. 'You are as bad as our mother, always worrying about the lad. You'll make him worse.'

'Our mother has lost one son.' Because he'd let his fondness for a pretty face overrule good sense. 'I don't plan to let her lose another.'

'Then perhaps you should think twice about smuggling.'

'Now who's worrying too much?' Ian snatched the paper from Niall's hand. 'You can read this later.'

'Give it back,' Niall said, his voice dangerously low.

Ian tossed it to him with a grin. 'Keep it in your pocket, then, and concentrate on what is going on around you for once.'

Niall grimaced, his eyes turning serious. 'Make this trip to France the last one, brother, or we'll all find ourselves at the end of a rope.'

Ian clapped his brother on the shoulder with a confidence that seemed to stick in the back of his throat. 'It will be fine.'

Against his will, he looked back at the terrace,

his gaze seeking the girl whose eyes spoke to him in unexpected ways. She was gone. Just as well. He had work to do.

Topaz needed no urging to canter. Selina guided her off the road and across open ground, exhilarated by the speed and the edge of chill on the breeze against her cheeks. At last she could breathe. And on horseback she could forget her incapacity.

The scent of heather filled her nostrils. Sweet, like the honey they made from the bees in this part of the country, yet earthy, too. She filled her gaze with the beauty of hills of smoky purple. Wild, unforgiving terrain, but so grand it made your heart ache.

She'd forgotten how easily the child in her had fallen in love with this place the first time she had seen it. Forgotten deliberately. Remembering only brought back the pain of loneliness and betrayal. Something she would never suffer again.

She smiled at herself. Such maudlin thoughts had no place in her mind on such a glorious day. Live for the now, plan for the future and let the past belong to the devil. Lord knew there were enough mistakes in her past well worth forgetting.

* * *

Thirty minutes later she was wishing she'd stayed on the track. After months of inactivity, her muscles were complaining at being forced to keep her steady in the saddle when as a girl she'd ridden the rough terrain astride, without effort. Riding astride was not an option for the woman she'd become. She rubbed at her thigh with a grimace at the reminder she was lucky to be riding at all. Lucky she hadn't killed herself or someone else. She slowed the animal to a walk and turned him around.

A black-and-white collie flashed out of the heather. Barking, it snapped at Topaz's heels. The horse reared. Off balance, Selina clung to his mane.

The animal landed with a thud on its forefeet, jolting her again. 'Steady, boy,' she cried out, fighting with the reins as he tossed his head and spun around, trying to watch the dog. He kicked out with a back hoof. Dislodged by the jolt, Selina had no choice but to free her foot and let herself slide to the ground.

She landed on her rump with a groan. 'Blasted dog,' she yelled. She stared up at the wild-eyed Topaz. Dash it. She'd never be able to mount him again. She'd have to lead him home. Her first chance to ride in months had ended in disaster.

She stretched out an arm to catch Topaz's reins. 'It's all right, boy,' she said softly. The nervous gelding tossed its head and pranced farther away.

Double blast.

Her thigh throbbed a protest. Surely she hadn't broken it again? The thought made her stomach roil. No. She hadn't heard that horrid snapping sound and it was her rear end that was bruised, and her pride, not her leg. Breathe. Calm down. All she had to do was get up and catch Topaz. It was a long walk home, but she could do it.

She forced herself to her knees.

'Lady Selina! Is that you?'

Inwardly, she groaned. Of all the bad luck—it would have to be that well-remembered deep voice she heard. She looked up.

Kilted and wild-looking, his black hair ruffled by the breeze, Ian Gilvry looked completely at home among the heather-clad hills as he strode towards her. He always had.

To a girl of sixteen, he'd seemed heroic and romantic. Especially since the first time they met he'd carried her home and then kissed her, a shy fumbling thing when he set her down at the gate. Utterly besotted, she'd plotted every which way to meet up with him again. And again.

In her innocence, she'd assumed he liked her.

'Are you hurt?' he said when he came close, concern showing on his face, a large suntanned hand reaching out to pull her to her feet.

She ignored it and sank back down into the springy heather, primly covering her feet with her riding habit. 'I'm fine.'

He drew back, putting his hands on lean hips, his head tilted. 'You fell off your horse?'

She glanced at Topaz, who was now happily cropping at the grass just out of reach. 'I dismounted rather more quickly than I expected. The horse was terrified of your dog.'

The smile on his finely drawn lips broadened. 'What, an excellent horsewoman such as yourself put to grass by a wee dog?'

'The dog should be leashed. The horse could have been injured and that would have cost you a pretty penny.' What was she doing? She had no wish to enter into verbal sparring with the man. She should just get up and walk away.

His eyes, as blue as the sky above his head, narrowed. 'Gill is still in training. I apologise if he upset your animal.'

Her jaw dropped. Gilvrys didn't apologise to Albrights. It was a point of honour.

'Apology accepted.' She stared off into the distance, willing him to leave.

'Allow me help you back on your horse,' he said, his voice no more than a murmur.

Kind. Full of pity. Like everyone else. She gritted her teeth in frustration.

A year ago, it would have been easy to leap to her feet and let him toss her up in the saddle. Right now, getting back on that horse and trying to control him with her aching muscles was out of the question. She should not have ridden so far.

She gave him her brightest smile and had the satisfaction of seeing his eyes glaze a little. 'I think I will stay here and enjoy the scenery for a while. No need to trouble yourself.'

Dark brows drew down. He muttered something under his breath in Gaelic. A curse, no doubt. She felt like cursing, too.

'Then I bid you good day, Lady Selina. Come, Gilly.' He gave her a stiff little bow and strode up the hill.

The dog lay down at her side.

'Go,' she said and gave it a push.

It stared at her with soft brown, laughing eyes.

Ian whistled without looking back. The dog remained where it was.

With a heavy sigh, Ian turned, walked back, pulling a rope from his jacket pocket. 'Once more I must apologise for my dog's bad manners.' He looped the knotted rope over the animal's head and gave a sharp tug.

The dog pulled back with a whine. It pushed its nose under her hand where it rested on her thigh.

'Go,' she said, desperate for them both to be gone, so she could limp home with a shred of her pride intact.

His blue eyes suddenly sharpened. 'Can you get up?'

He knew. Of course he did. He'd seen her at the Carricks' ball. 'I'm not ready to leave. Why don't you and your dog just go away?' She certainly wasn't going to give him the satisfaction of watching her hobble after her horse.

Ian stared down at the petite dark-eyed beauty sitting at his feet in the heather and didn't believe a word coming out of her mouth. The tautness around her mouth spoke of pain and more than a dash of humiliation.

'I'll go when I've seen you safely home.' He stuck out his hand to help her up.

She gave an impatient sigh, placed her small hand in his and he tugged. The quick indrawn breath of pain as she rose caused a painful twinge low in his gut. Damn stubborn female. He gently lowered her back down and crouched down beside her. 'I knew you were hurt.'

He glanced down at where her riding habit had rucked up over her ankles, showing a pair of sturdy riding boots. 'Is it your leg?'

Her cheeks flushed red. 'Partly, if you must know. But mostly it is because this is the first time I have ridden in a very long time. I stayed out too long. I am sure I will be fine in a little while, but I thank you for your concern, Mr Gilvry.'

Once he'd been plain Ian and she'd been a hoyden who one summer had roamed the hills around Dunross and fought a running battle with his younger brothers, the Gilvrys and the Albrights being mortal enemies.

He'd been away at his Uncle Carrick's most of that summer. He'd returned home for a few days before he went back to school in Edinburgh and met her by accident late one summer afternoon. He hadn't known who she was at first, and he'd come to her rescue when she twisted her ankle in a rabbit hole and carried her home.

Along with her pretty face and burgeoning womanhood, he'd found her *joie de vivre* and her artless chatter captivating. She'd treated him like a man, not a boy, and there had been hero worship in those warm brown eyes—a welcome change from schoolbooks and lessons in stewardship.

They'd met several times after that, until they'd been discovered at Balnaen Cove by his brothers. That had not gone well.

'So it seems I must carry you home again,' he said, wondering if she also remembered, then wanted to kick himself as shadows darkened her sherry-brown eyes. Of course she remembered. But no doubt she remembered his harsh words, too.

Like a fool, he'd tried to make up for his cruelty, the next time she asked for help, even though years had passed. Too soft-hearted, his grandfather had always said. Drew had paid the price for that bit of softness. Well, he wasn't soft-hearted any more. Too many people relied on him now.

But nor could he in all conscience leave her here. He reached for her again.

'It wouldn't be seemly,' she said, batting his hand away. 'I can manage perfectly well by myself. I just need a moment or two.'

The lass always did have spirit to the backbone. And now she was utterly lovely. She looked like a feast for a starving man laid out in the heather.

He shook his head at himself. He did not have the time or the inclination for romping in the heather.

He'd always left that to Drew. And because of Ian's weakness over this female, Drew was no more.

A good Gilvry would leave her here and let Albright have the worry of a missing child, but a true Highland gentleman would never leave a woman in distress. Not even his worst enemy's daughter. He glowered. 'You know I can't leave you here. And nor can I let you walk home in pain.'

'I will manage, thank you.'

He put his hands on his hips and grinned at her. 'Then climb aboard your flea-ridden nag and ride away.'

'When I'm ready,' she muttered.

Ian sank cross-legged beside her. The faint scent of roses filled his nostrils. Roses and heather. Never had he inhaled such a heady combination, although he suspected it was more to do with her than the perfume of the surrounding vegetation.

He folded his arms across his chest. 'And I will sit here until you do. Or until you come to your senses.'

She rolled away from him onto her knees, presenting a view of her curvaceous bottom that sent a jolt of lust to his groin. Thank God for his plaid and his sporran or she'd be thinking him no better than an animal.

Gilly ran around her and licked her chin. She

pushed him away, struggling with her skirts and the dog. With a small grunt, she got to her feet and took a couple of halting steps towards her horse.

Ian sprang up, putting a hand beneath her elbow. 'Ach, lass, will your pride no let me help you?'

She lowered her head, until all he could see was the top of her dark green velvet bonnet and the silk primroses adorning its green ribbon. 'It seems I have no choice,' she said in a low defeated voice. 'I cannot ride any more today.'

The anguish in the admission knocked the wind from his lungs. Damn it to hell. 'This is all my fault. I should never have let the dog off the leash.'

Her head shot up. Dark brown eyes, soft as velvet, met his. 'The fault is mine. I should not have left the track.'

'Well, it looks as if there is only one answer to our dilemma.' He put an arm around her shoulders and one carefully beneath her knees and scooped her up.

She gasped. 'Put me down. I will not let you carry me all the way to Dunross.'

'I don't intend to,' he said, looking down into those soul-deep brown eyes and feeling as if he might drown. This was not a reaction he should be having, not to this woman.

He gritted his teeth and grabbed her horse's bridle. The dog followed closely at his heels like the best-trained dog in Scotland. Naturally.

'Then where are we going?'

For no apparent reason the fear in her voice caused him a pang in his chest, though he was damned if he'd let her see it. 'To find a less objectionable mode of transport.'

At that she laughed. It was as if the sun had come out from behind a cloud and he couldn't keep from smiling, just a little.

Chapter Three

Selina held herself stiffly, trying to maintain some sort of distance between her and his chest. Impossible, when she was in his arms. Strong arms wrapped around her back and under her knees. The steady beat of his heart vibrated against her ribs. A feeling of being safe made her want to slide her arm around his neck and rest her head against his brawny shoulder.

Safe? With him? Had she banged her head when she fell?

The Gilvrys were wild and unruly. The last time she had seen him he'd ganged up on her with his brothers, calling her *Sassenach* and thief. And he now was their leader. A man who would do anything to be rid of her father from land he considered his. While she could not refuse his help, she must not trust his motives.

At the bottom of the hill they came across a

winding cart track. His steps lengthened as he followed the deep wheel ruts round a sweeping corner to where a long narrow loch glistened like beaten steel in the weak sun. Beside it lay a collection of rough stone buildings.

The old water mill. It looked different—not so derelict—and the pagoda-looking chimney at one end looked new. 'I didn't think you Gilvrys worked the mill any more.'

'My father didn't. I do.'

'And added a chimney?'

'Aye.'

Talk about taciturn. 'Why does the mill need a chimney?'

He hesitated, his expression becoming carefully neutral. 'To keep the miller warm in the winter.'

A lie. Though it sounded logical enough. What did it matter that he didn't care to tell her the truth? She didn't care what the Gilvrys did with their old falling-down mill.

He carried her into the barn and set her down on a hay bale. Immediately, she felt the loss of the strength around her body, and his seductive warmth, whereas he looked glad to be rid of her. Had she not a smidgeon of pride?

Apparently some part of her did not. The childish naïve part that had admired him from the first moment she saw him. The part of her she'd long ago buried.

Silently, he tied Topaz to a post, while Gilly curled up at her feet.

Her thigh wasn't hurting nearly as much as before. She'd given it a jolt and the bones that had knit badly had decided to protest the rough treatment. But even though the ache had subsided, she doubted she had the strength to manage her horse. She would have to settle for his alternative mode of transport.

The only occupant of the barn was a small dun-coloured pony, which he led from its stall and proceeded to hitch to a flat-bedded wagon.

'Your chariot awaits, my lady,' he said wryly.

She rose to her feet, but he gave her no chance to walk, simply scooping her up and depositing her on some empty sacks he'd laid across the bare boards.

He was unbelievably strong, so unlike most of the gentlemen of the *ton* who defined themselves by their clothes, not their manly attributes. So unlike the elegant Dunstan.

Oh, now that really was being disloyal.

She shifted until her back was supported against the wooden boards along the side. The smell of barley wafted up. A sweet dusty smell.

He frowned. 'There are no blankets, but I can give you my coat.'

No. She would not go home wrapped in his coat. It was bad enough she had to suffer his help. Wasn't it?

'This will do.' She picked up a couple of the sacks and covered her legs with one and put the other around her shoulders. She flashed a smile and fluttered her lashes in parody. 'How do I look?'

'Like a tinker's wife,' he said, a twinkle appearing in the depths of his eyes, making him look more attractive than ever. A twinkle she knew better than to trust.

She kept her voice light and breathy, her smile bright. 'The first stare of tinker fashion, though, surely?'

The corner of his mouth tipped up as if it wanted to smile more than was seemly. 'Top of the trees, my lady.'

Something about his bantering tone made her feel warm and her smile softened.

They grinned at each other the way they had on those long-ago summer afternoons, before he had turned his back on her so cruelly.

His gaze dropped to her mouth.

Her heart lurched. Her breath caught. Many men had looked at her with heat since her come out.

Not once in that time had her heart tumbled over in such a ridiculous fashion. She broke hearts. Men did not touch hers. Ever. That was the way to get hurt.

And besides, she was as good as betrothed to a very worthy man who was utterly besotted.

She turned her face away. 'We should go.'

'Aye. I'll tie your horse on behind.'

She swallowed against the feeling of loss as he walked away, trying to blot out her stupid reactions to his smile by thinking about Father and his reaction when he learned she'd been carted home by a man he despised. Father would not be pleased.

Horse dealt with, Ian leapt easily into the driver's seat with such agility, he made her feel more clumsy and awkward than she usually did these days.

He half turned in the seat, one foot resting against the footboard, his plaid falling away to reveal his knee and the start of a firm muscled calf dusted with dark hair before it disappeared in his sock. So very male. So very intriguing. So very out of bounds. She forced her gaze away.

'The track is rough,' he said. 'I will take it as easy as I can.'

'I'm not an invalid.'

'I never said you were.' He clicked his tongue

and the pony started walking. Gilly jumped up over the side of the cart and landed beside her. He lay against her legs.

'Off,' Ian said.

The dog flattened his ears, but didn't move.

'Leave him,' Selina said. 'He's keeping me warm.'

'Lucky him,' he muttered.

Her jaw dropped. Had he really said what she thought she heard? Or was he being sarcastic? He was staring morosely at the road ahead.

'What happened to your leg?' he asked. 'I saw you walking at the ball.'

So much for her efforts to glide smoothly. 'My carriage tipped over and fell on me.'

He winced. 'I hope the idiot driver was suitably punished.'

'I was. I broke my leg.'

His cheekbones flushed red. 'Oh. I didna' mean—'

'The accident was my fault. I was driving too fast and not looking where I was going.' Thinking about her recent male conquest if the truth be told. 'I was lucky I was the only one hurt by my stupidity. It doesn't hurt much any more, but the bones didn't set quite right.'

'I'm sorry.' He sounded sorry. But then once he'd

sounded as if he liked her, until his brothers caught them together.

Sassenach. Thief. The taunts danced in her head. The war between the Scots and the English might be over, but their families would battle until no one remained to swing a verbal sword.

The track had joined the main road where the jolts were less and their pace improved. Soon they were driving through Dunross village where a group of ragged boys were kicking a pig's bladder back and forth across the lane. When they saw the cart, they came running over. 'Laird, Laird,' one of the boys shouted, then said something in Gaelic.

Ian replied in the same language. He half turned to her. 'They want me to play with them.'

One of them spotted her in the cart and his eyes rounded in his grimy face. He pointed at her and yelled something. The boys all sniggered.

Ian grinned and replied, clearly in the negative.

She squared her shoulders, set her face in untroubled calm while inside she curled in a tight ball. 'What did he say?'

Ian laughed. 'Boys. They have one-track minds. They want to know if you are my woman. I told them, no, that you are a lady and to be treated with respect.'

She relaxed, looking back and seeing the boys had returned to their game. 'Shouldn't the children be in school?'

'Aye.'

Could he not say more than one word at a time? 'You call yourself Laird—why do you not convince their families to give them an education?'

He glanced back at her, his brows lowered, his eyes hard. 'They call me Laird, because that is what I am. The nearest school is fifteen miles hence.'

'Why not start a school in the village?'

'Where?' He sounded frustrated.

She subsided into silence. Father should be the one to open a school. He owned almost everything except the old mill and the Gilvrys' farmland.

'I will speak to my father about setting up a school. Perhaps in the church hall.'

Now he looked surprised, and heaven help her, pleased. 'It would be a grand thing for the families hereabouts,' he said. 'There are children up in the glens who would come, too, when they weren't needed for chores. It would give them a future.'

She cast him a sly smile. 'And keep them out of mischief.'

He chuckled. 'Perhaps, my lady. Me and my brothers got up to all sorts of mischief, despite having a tutor. But it is true that we had less time to get into trouble.'

A feeling of warmth stole through her, the feeling they had begun to talk like friends again, rather than enemies. She liked the way it felt.

As they approached the tavern in the centre of the village a youngish man sweeping the cobbles doffed his hat at their approach. He grinned at Ian. 'Good day to you, Laird.'

Ian acknowledged the greeting with a nod.

Then the man's gaze fell on Selina and all traces of good humour disappeared from his ruddy face. He spat on the ground. 'That's Albright's get. You should be dropping her in the nearest peat bog and letting her drown, not driving her around the countryside. It would serve Albright well to see what it is like to lose something.'

'Enough, Willy Gair,' Ian said. 'You know that is not the Highland way of it.'

The young man glared at him. 'Highlanders look after their ane, not the English who have no business here. You are a traitor to your clan, Ian Gilvry, if you have aught to do with them up at the keep.' He started towards them, giving Selina a look filled with such hatred that her mouth dried and her heart picked up speed.

'I'll speak to you later, Willy,' Ian said grimly and urged the pony into a trot.

She bit her lip. Nothing had changed over the years. 'Why is he so angry?'

'He was evicted last month,' Ian said flatly. 'His family had been crofters on Dunross land for generations. When he couldn't pay the rent, he had to leave. He is one of the lucky ones. His brother-in-law owns the inn and is able to give him a little work and a roof over his head.'

'Father said nothing about evictions.'

His expression said how would she know what her father did.

'Why would he?'

'Sheep.'

Another one-word answer that was as clear as mud. Clearly he wasn't going to say more. Well, she would just have to ask her father.

'Almost there,' Ian announced.

Beyond him, Dunross Keep jutted up into the blue sky.

The last time he'd carried her home he'd been nothing but a gangly boy, but to her he'd seemed like a knight in shining armour, and she his lady. Childish romantic nonsense.

He turned his head slightly, still looking ahead. 'Angus McIver is heading this way on foot.'

She winced. 'I said I'd be back in an hour.' She raised herself up and peered over his shoulder. A severe-looking Angus with a knobby walking stick was striding towards them. She waved.

Ian's lips pressed tight. He drew the cart up when he came abreast of the big Scot.

'My Lady. Laird.' Angus touched the bonnet perched on his head. 'Thank ye for bringing the lassie home.'

Selina let go a breath. No yelling. No harsh words. A simple grim politeness, but then the Highlanders were known for their impeccable manners. Some of them.

Jaw set, Ian nodded. 'I'll drive her in.'

'Best not. I'll take her and the horse in through the gate.'

'Angus,' she gasped.

'I've no wish to enter the keep,' Ian said harshly. He clicked his tongue and the horse moved onwards. 'Not while it belongs to another.'

The whip of his words caught her on the raw. She was wrong about him. He resented her just as much as he always had.

And there was something she'd been putting off saying. She'd forgotten until just now. She'd have to hurry if she didn't want Angus to overhear.

'I never thanked you for calling your brother Andrew home after I wrote to you.'

He stiffened, his face turning granite hard.

'My friend, she is happily married now. It…it all turned out for the best.'

'Did it now?'

'It was good of you.' His granite expression made it hard to continue. 'I just wanted to thank you.'

His lips twisted into a bitter line. 'And one good turn deserves another. You'll no mention the changes at the mill to your father.' The cart lurched to a halt beside the stone arch.

Her stomach dipped. It was hardly the kind of response to her thanks she'd expected. He was waiting for her answer. She straightened her shoulders. 'No. I won't say a thing.'

Then Angus was there, reaching into the back of the wagon to help her down.

The dog lifted his lip and growled low in his throat.

Selina laughed, albeit the sound a little brittle, but true to form, and Angus noticed nothing. 'You'll have to get past my protector, Mr McIver.'

Angus glanced up at Ian. How odd. She'd meant the dog.

'Gilly,' Ian growled. 'Down.'

The dog put its ears down and thumped its tail, sending up a puff of dust. Angus lifted her down.

'Can ye walk, lass?' He handed her his stick. A solid, gnarled length of hawthorn.

She gave him a grateful smile. 'This will certainly help.'

The old Scot untied Topaz, grasped him by the bridle. Together they walked towards the gate

At the sound of the cart pulling away, she glanced back and met Ian's dark gaze. He nodded, a slight movement of his head, yet it seemed to say *I trust you not to betray me.*

And she wouldn't. She never had.

Her heart was pounding as if she had run a mile, when really she had only walked the few steps from the manse. It was excitement causing her heart to beat faster, not the fear of seeing Ian again. Or the prospect of seeing his pleasure at the news she brought.

Dry-mouthed, she knocked on the door of his house. One of the few not owned by her father. Some long time ago, Ian's grandfather had married well, giving the family the house, some land and the mill, according to her father. And they'd been a thorn in the side of every Albright since.

If they would just work together… Perhaps they

could now, if Ian's pride would let him accept her offer. Half-afraid she might turn and run, she knocked again. Breath held, she listened to the sound of footsteps on the other side.

The door swung back and Ian stared at her, his mouth dropping open. He was in his shirtsleeves and waistcoat. His throat was bare, where he had not donned a cravat. He looked thoroughly rakish and disreputable. Inside she winced. Clearly, she should have warned him of her intended visit.

He rubbed at his chin with an ink-stained thumb as he clearly tried to recover from his surprise. 'Lady Selina?' He glanced over his shoulder, then stepped outside to join her on the front step, pulling the door almost closed behind him, as if he did not want whoever was inside to know she was there.

Heat rushed to her cheeks. A bright smile formed on her lips. It always did when she was nervous. She nodded regally. 'Good afternoon, Mr Gilvry.'

The wary look on his face remained. 'What are you doing here?'

'I have something to show you.'

'What sort of something?'

Always suspicious. She pulled the key from her reticule. 'This.'

'Who is it, Ian?' a woman's voice called from inside the house.

'No one, Ma,' he called back. 'Wait here a moment,' he said to Selina. He shot back inside and closed the door.

He definitely didn't want whoever was inside to know who had called. Most likely she was his mother. The minister had told her and Chrissie that Mrs Gilvry had been ill for some time. Selina walked down the short garden path to the lane. She didn't want her presence to cause him any embarrassment. Nor did she want to be caught on his front step by one of his younger brothers.

A few moments passed before he joined her, properly dressed in his coat with a belcher knotted at his throat.

'I'm sorry for keeping you waiting,' he said politely.

'Not at all.'

'What is this about?'

The way he said 'about' made her toes curl in her sensible half-boots. 'It is a surprise.'

'A pleasant one, I hope?'

She cast him a glance from under the brim of her chip-straw bonnet. 'I believe even you will think so.'

They walked in silence for a few minutes, towards the manse, then she turned onto a narrow lane with stone walls on either side that led around the back of the church.

Excitement bubbled up in her chest again. He had to be pleased. He could not turn down this gift of hers. Well, hers and Chrissie's. They had plotted it all out for two days, talking and explaining, until Father had thrown his hands in the air and told them to do just as they pleased, because they were going to anyway, with or without his permission.

Chrissie had happily left to her the duty of telling the Laird of their intention.

She stopped at a gap in the wall. The track to the ancient building before them was overgrown with weeds.

'The tithe barn?' he said. 'Is this your surprise?'

'Yes.' She picked up her pace and instead of going in by the double-wooden barn doors, she made her way to a small door at the far end, carefully avoiding thistles and stinging nettles, some of which grew as high as her shoulders. She unlocked the door and threw it wide open, revealing a dusty empty room with a counting desk and a set of wooden shelves with pigeon holes against one wall.

'It hasn't been used for years,' she said.

'A tithe of nothing is nothing,' Ian said. 'The

vicar takes his due from the collection plate. What is it you wanted me to see?'

'Wouldn't this make the most perfect place to hold a school for the local children?'

His eyes widened. 'Are you telling me the vicar agreed we could use this building for a school?'

'The barn is on Father's land.' She bit her lip. She should not have mentioned who owned the land. 'He has agreed it can be used for a school.'

He stepped inside and turned in a circle, glancing up at the roof and staring at walls, much as she had done the previous day. He swung around to face her. He didn't look particularly pleased, but nor did he look annoyed.

'You don't think it would work?' she asked, fighting her disappointment with a smile.

'It is a fine room. We could build trestle tables, find some stools.'

'There are funds set aside by Lady Albright for a teacher. We could send to Edinburgh. What to do you think? Will you support the idea?' she asked. 'The clan members won't send their children if you speak against it.'

He stared at her. 'Why this concern now? We don't need your charity.'

His suspicions were like a blade sliding between

her ribs. 'Would you prefer the children to run wild, with no chance for an education?'

He stepped closer, too close, looking down at her, his eyes flaring hot. Anger, she thought. Then wasn't so sure. The blue in his gaze was so intense, the heat so bright with his body only inches from hers, it crashed against her cool skin. Her heart banged against her ribs, the sound loud in her ears. Breathing became difficult, as if the only air in the room belonged to him.

The strangest sense that he was going to kiss her tugged at her, drawing her closer; she could swear her body was leaning into his with a wild kind of longing.

He jerked back. She could have sworn she gasped at the shock of it, yet her ears heard no sound. It was all in her imagination, the connection, the physical pull.

'It won't make them think any better of your father,' he said, his voice harsher than usual, his breathing less steady than before.

She shrugged, feigning indifference to the obviously dismissive words. 'I didn't expect it would.'

'Niall will teach them. Two mornings a week.'

Did this mean he supported the idea, after all? 'He can apply to the vicar with respect to his pay.'

'He will not require payment.'

Apparently, his pride would not permit Albright money to be spent, but he would begrudgingly accept the loan of the building.

'Are you sure Niall would be willing to work for no pay?'

'The children will not come to a stranger. And they need someone who speaks the Gaelic.'

'The children would obey you.'

A small smile curved on his lips. 'Aye.' He brushed by her and out of the door. He stopped and looked back. 'Thank your father for the use of the barn. I'll have Will Gair set to making some tables and trestles. Him, your father can pay.'

No wonder he looked so pleased with himself. He had found a way for Father to right what he saw as a wrong. 'You are welcome, Mr Gilvry.'

His cheeks flushed a little red. 'Thank you, Lady Selina.' He strode away.

A proud man, but even so she had managed him quite nicely. And so what if he took it upon himself to provide the teacher and charge her father for the furniture? The children would have their schooling.

That was all that mattered. A feeling of satisfaction filled her. A sense of a job well done, despite his reaction. Perhaps the people of Dunross would recognise her father's generosity, even if their Laird would not.

And as for thinking he was going to kiss her, well…that was all in her imagination. More likely, he had wanted to tell her to go to hell, but had put the welfare of his people ahead of his own preferences.

Two days later, a fine drizzle hung over the hilly landscape like mist. It was almost as if the clouds, having brushed against the heather-clad hills, wanted to linger. There was no thinking about setting foot out of doors, not even in the carriage, so Selina stretched out on the sofa in the drawing room with a book to while away the hours until supper.

The drawing-room door opened and Chrissie bounced in. 'You will never guess who is here.'

Selina put down her book. 'Who?'

'Lieutenant Dunstan.'

Her heart took an unpleasant dive. She hadn't expected him quite so soon. But the sooner the better, surely?

'Is he here to see me?'

'He is with your father in his study.' Chrissie clasped her hands together. 'I am sure he is here to propose.'

Good news—then why did she feel a kind of panic? She wanted this. It had been all her idea. A new beginning after her accident. 'Did Father send for me?'

Chrissie frowned. 'No. But I am sure he will want to see you when they have concluded their business.'

Chrissie was as anxious for the marriage as Selina was herself. She hadn't said anything, but she and Selina had occasionally disagreed on household matters. Until Father had finally told Selina it was no longer her concern.

It had been a painful truth.

She swung her feet to the ground and set her book aside. She patted her hair and smoothed her skirts, a pomona-green muslin. 'Should I change, do you think?'

'You look lovely,' Chrissie said with a smile. 'You always do.'

'Thank you.' Before her accident, she had taken her appearance for granted. More recently, she had felt unsure. She took a deep breath and tried to keep her steps as even as possible.

The antechamber to the study was empty. Mr Brunelle, her father's secretary, must be inside with her father, taking notes, recording agreements. Should she knock and go in, or wait for them to come out?

As she dithered, the door to the study opened. She pinned a smile on her face.

'Lady Selina!' The lieutenant sounded surprised.

She glanced at her father.

He frowned. 'Did you want something, daughter?'

Blast. It seemed she wasn't expected, or wanted, which meant they had not been discussing the betrothal after all. A feeling of relief swept through her, even as she realised they were waiting for some sort of explanation.

Heat bloomed in her cheeks as her mind raced. 'I heard Lieutenant Dunstan was here and came to bid him welcome.' She hoped she didn't sound too feeble. 'To ask him to take tea with Lady Albright and me in the drawing room.'

Dunstan's face lit up. 'Very kind of you, Lady Selina, I must say. I fear I cannot take advantage on this occasion. I have urgent business in the neighbourhood and came to discuss it with your father as local magistrate.'

'Trouble?' she asked.

'Selina,' her father said in a warning tone.

'Smugglers,' Dunstan said at exactly the same moment.

'Oh, my goodness, are there really such villains abroad around here?' she said with a hand to her throat and a gasp. She gave him a glance that said in her mind he was a hero.

'Don't worry, Lady Selina, my regiment won't let them escape us, I can assure you. You have nothing to fear.' The paternalistic tone made her grit her teeth. But he was only trying to soothe the feminine nerves she had put on display and there was nothing in his manner she should resent.

She fluttered her lashes. 'I am so glad you are in charge, then.'

He bowed, took her hand and kissed it. 'Until we meet again.'

His touch left her cold, calm, uninvolved. No wild flutters invading her body—just as she preferred.

'Lieutenant Dunstan is engaged to us for dinner next week, Selina,' her father said. 'There will be lots of time for chatter then.'

Next week. Her future would be settled next week. The delay felt like a reprieve from the hangman's noose, when she should be impatient for it to start.

'I will look forward to it,' she said, giving him her most brilliant of smiles and watching him blush with a sense of foreboding. Had she made a mistake in this man? Was he weaker than she had thought? She wanted him malleable, it was true, but not spineless.

It was too late for second thoughts. Too late to change her mind. She had made her choice and must abide by it, or be deemed beyond the pale.

Dunstan turned back to Father. 'This will be the end of them, I promise you. I bid you good afternoon, Lord Albright.'

With a sharp bow, he strode from the room, his spurs jingling with each booted step on the stone stairs leading down to the hall below.

'The end of whom?' Selina asked.

Her father waved her question aside. 'You sounded over-anxious. You have done well to catch a man from such an important family. We don't want to scare him off.'

'Scare him off? I hardly think so,' she drawled, hiding her hurt.

'Two jilted suitors are enough to make any man think twice.'

It seemed the *ton* had a long memory. 'I will be more circumspect next time he calls, Papa,' she said, dipping a curtsy.

'Good.' He rubbed his hands together. 'If this thing goes well tonight, I believe I will have a buyer for Dunross, too.'

She gasped. 'You are going to sell Dunross?'

'Dunstan has no need of a keep in the wilds of Scotland. You don't want to live here. With the proceeds, he can buy a country house close to his parents in Sussex and a house in town, just as you wanted.'

For some reason, she never thought Dunross would be sold. It was her dowry. She thought it would be settled on one of their children.

She frowned. 'What does success catching the smugglers have to do with selling Dunross Keep?'

'Ian Gilvry has been nothing but a thorn in my side and a deterrent to any serious purchaser. With him gone, we should get a good price.'

Her blood ran cold. All she could do was stare.

'Well?' her father said.

'I… Nothing. I really should go back to Chrissie and tell her we are not expecting the lieutenant for tea.'

'Never mind. I will join you instead.'

Blast. Now she needed to let the housekeeper know to deliver a tray to the drawing room, when what she wanted to do was be alone to think.

Chapter Four

Selina thumped at her pillow, sure someone had put rocks in it instead of feathers. She tossed onto her back. If Dunstan's plans came to fruition, Ian would find himself behind bars, or worse. The fool. How could he risk his life with so many relying on him?

The cottages in the village were in terrible shape—certainly much worse than when she'd left seven years ago. The children playing in the street hadn't just been ragged and dirty, they'd been painfully thin. The people were slowly starving. He should be helping them sell their crops, not seeking wealth from criminal activities.

Potatoes and barley were the only crops suited to the poor soil in the Highlands. And they used the barley to make whisky instead of bread. It was one of the reasons her father despised them so—their preference for hard spirits over food.

The Highlanders swore by their whisky, attributing healing properties to the malted liquor. They even gave it to babies.

And it wasn't only illiterate crofters who held fast to the old ideas. The nobles did it, too. A school, education, would bring them into the nineteenth century, but it wouldn't get off the ground if Ian ended up deported or worse. Didn't he realise that, by taking risks with his own life for a few barrels of brandy, he was risking their futures?

Or was he smuggling in order to put food in their bellies? Because her father cared not one whit for the people on this land.

Her blood ran cold. She didn't want to believe it, but her father was completely ruthless when it came to money and power. It was what had made him so successful.

He'd be delighted to see the Gilvrys out of his way.

The memory of Ian's strong arms around her shoulders, beneath her thighs, haunted her as if she was still some besotted schoolgirl. Only worse, because other sensations tormented her too, little pulses of desire she couldn't seem to control.

And the way he had looked at her in the tithe barn had only made them worse.

Hot and bothered, she slid out of the bed and

walked to the mullioned window. Clear. The rain clouds gone. Stars twinkled teasingly.

The perfect night for smuggling.

The perfect night for a trap.

She gazed in the direction of the village. Was it her imagination, or could she see men leading strings of ponies across the heather between here and the village?

Imagination. It was too dark to make out anything except the dark shape of the distant hills against the sky.

Was Ian out there? About to be caught in the hated Revenue men's net? She should have gone to warn him this afternoon, instead of telling herself it was none of her business. She owed him more than a thank you for helping Alice. And even if Dunross's people hated her, she had this strange feeling of responsibility. Dunross Keep might be her dowry, but Ian Gilvry was their laird. She would never be able to live with herself if she didn't at least try to warn him.

A clock struck eleven. What had felt like hours was only a single turn of the hour hand. It might not be too late to tell them. It wasn't as if everyone didn't turn a blind eye to smuggling.

Good Lord, her own father had a cellar full of smuggled wines in London. As long as those responsible didn't hurt anyone along the way, smuggling, while a crime in the eyes of the law, was seen as more of a game.

A game Ian should have avoided with her father in residence at the keep.

Hands shaking with the need for haste, she sorted through the clothes in her press. Stays. How would she lace her stays without her maid? She lifted up a gaudy skirt she'd worn to a masquerade in Lisbon. She'd played the part of a Portuguese dancer. Somewhere she had a peasant blouse and an overbodice, which laced up the front.

But if she wanted to ride Topaz, she would need breeches, because she'd have to ride astride. She dug out a pair she'd worn on her childhood adventures when Father had left her with servants and hadn't cared what she did most of the time. Tonight she would wear them under her petticoats.

Anyone seeing her, such as the Revenue men for example, would take her for one of the village girls in such attire.

As long as she didn't run into Dunstan.

Her stomach rolled in a most unpleasant way. If she was caught, it would be the end of all her hopes for a good marriage.

She would just have to make sure he didn't see her. She was only going to the village and back.

He would be waiting on the shore for the smugglers. Hopefully in vain.

She finished dressing swiftly, throwing an old woollen cloak around her shoulders and hurrying downstairs in bare feet, carrying her shoes. She put them on at the side door and went out to the stables.

Blast. A light shone from a window above the stalls where Angus lived. He'd hear her and stop her if she tried to take Topaz.

Then she'd walk. The gate, of course, was locked and barred. Anyone would think they were at war, the way they locked up the keep at night.

There was another way out. The old sally port—an escape route for if the keep was ever besieged. Long ago it had been her route to freedom and a few secret meetings with Ian.

Hopefully no one had blocked it up in the meantime. She took the stairs down to the ancient undercroft. In medieval times the kitchen was located here; nowadays the space was used for storage.

The next flight of stairs was barely wide enough for her feet and twisted in tight circles. She wished she'd thought to bring a lantern. Damp and musty-smelling air filled her lungs and tainted her tongue as she felt her way down in the dark until she reached the door at the bottom.

The last time she'd been down here she'd hidden the key up on the lintel. She groped around and shuddered at the clingy touch of spider webs. Her fingers touched a metal object. She grinned. It seemed her old way out remained undiscovered.

The key turned easily in the lock and she slipped it in her pocket and entered the tunnel, a dank place, smelling of earth, dug into the hillside. It came out among a pile of rocks some distance from the keep.

Once outside, the air was fresh and even felt warm compared to the dank chill below ground. As she hurried down the hill to the village, the stars gave her just enough light to avoid the worst of the ruts and it wasn't many minutes before she was standing outside Ian's house.

A light in both ground-floor windows gave her hope she was in time. She banged on the door.

From inside she heard the sound of coughing, but no one came to the door.

She banged again.

'Come in,' a woman's voice called out and the coughing started again. Mrs Gilvry. Did that mean Ian had left already?

What should she say? Accuse this woman's son of being a criminal? No doubt that would be well received. Perhaps she should just leave.

'Come in,' the voice called again, stronger this time.

She could hardly leave the woman wondering who had knocked on her door and fearing for her safety. She pressed the latch and the door swung open.

'In here,' the voice said through an open door on her right.

Selina entered the chamber, expecting a drawing room, and instead found a large four-poster bed containing a pallid-faced woman with greying hair tucked beneath a plain cap propped up against a pile of pillows.

'Mrs Gilvry?'

'Aye.' Pale fingers tightened on the sheets under her chin. A pair of eyes the colour of spring grass regarded her gravely. Andrew and Logan had inherited those eyes. Ian must take after his father. 'And who is it who comes calling in the dead of night?' Her voice was wheezy, breathless.

'Selina Albright. I am looking for your son, Ian. Is he home?'

The woman's eyes widened. 'Ian, is it? And what would Albright's daughter be doing looking for him at this time of night? Hasn't your family done enough to our people?'

The sins of the fathers were still being visited upon the children. 'I need to give him a message.'

The green eyes sharpened. 'Is there trouble?'

Selina nodded. 'The Revenue men are out to-night.'

The woman in the bed twisted her thin hands together. 'I told him not to go.'

'Ian?'

'No, Logan. My youngest. He was supposed to stay with me, but he couldna' resist. He followed his brothers not more than a half-hour ago. He'll no listen to me any more. Am I to lose all of my sons?'

Selina's heart ached for the torture she heard in the woman's voice. 'Do you know where they went? I…I could warn them.'

The woman looked at her with suspicion in her gaze. 'Why would you do that?'

She shrugged. 'Ian is a friend.' It was true, if not quite reflecting the nuance of their relationship. An uneasy friendship.

The woman turned her head upon the pillow, staring at the fire, her mouth a thin straight line. Then she turned back to Selina. 'It goes against the grain to trust an Albright. If you play me false, I will curse you for all of my days, however few they are.'

Selina recoiled at the bitterness in the woman's eyes. 'Tell me where they are.'

'Balnaen Cove.'

The name tore at a scar she thought long ago healed, yet was now raw and fresh. Ian had taken her there once, the last time they'd met. They'd shared a kiss, a moment full of magic and dizzying sensations and walked the sand hand in hand, until his brothers had come across them. Then he'd heaped scorn on her head.

She forced herself not to think of that day, but the task at hand. The cove was at least three miles from the village. She would not reach it by midnight. 'Do you have a horse?'

'There's one in the stables. Take it if you must,' Mrs Gilvry croaked. 'But 'tis no a friendly horse and there's no one to help.'

Of course it wasn't. Nothing about the Gilvrys was friendly or helpful.

'I'll manage.'

'Go through the kitchen and out of the back door.'

The directions took her straight to the stable where a lantern flickered above the door. She took it inside with her and found three empty stalls and one full of a large black stallion. It shifted uneasily as she entered.

A small shadow came out of the gloom, wagging its plumed tail. 'You,' she said, staring at her nemesis of a dog. 'I might have guessed you'd be along to cause trouble.'

She hung the lantern on a beam, found a bridle and bit and took them into the stall. The horse showed her the whites of its eyes. Not a good sign. Nor were the bared teeth.

'Easy,' she said softly. 'I'm not here to hurt you.' She patted its cheek and ran a hand down its wither. The blasted dog came wandering in. Troublesome creature. The dog sat at her feet and leant up against her leg.

The stallion eyed it, then lowered its head. Nose to nose, the creatures greeted each other.

The stallion calmed.

She patted the dog's head. 'Well, now, is this some sort of formal introduction to your friend?' It seemed so, for while the dog sat grinning, the great black horse allowed her to put on a bridle. But would he accept her on his back? Or was she just wasting time here? She might have walked a good way along the road by now.

No time for a saddle. Nor could she do it by herself. A blanket she found over a rail would have to do. Riding a horse bareback? She wasn't even sure she could. But she had to try. She led the stallion out to the mounting block in the yard and lunged onto its back, one hand gripping the reins, the other grasping the long black mane before it could object. It shifted, but didn't bolt.

The dog barked encouragement and shot out of the courtyard and into the lane. The horse followed.

She kept the stallion at a trot. She daren't go any faster through the village in case she attracted unwanted attention. The dog ran alongside.

The bouncing made her teeth clack together and jarred her spine. As they passed the last cottage, she urged the horse into a gentle canter. Its long stride smoothed out and she felt a lot less like a sack of potatoes. Perhaps she really could make three miles without falling off.

At the crossroads she hesitated. The right fork led to the path along the cliffs and a long gentle slope down to the cove. Straight ahead and she'd have to cut across country. The way down to the beach there was difficult and steep. It was quicker.

Nose to the ground, the dog dashed straight ahead. The horse followed. It seemed as though her decision was made. Shorter and quicker was better.

She let the stallion have his head and concentrated on retaining her balance and watching out for danger. After ten minutes or so, the dog veered off towards the sea. If there was a path, she couldn't see it, but she urged the horse to follow and in no time at all, she could hear the steady roar and crash of surf. Salt coated her lips and she licked it away, inhaling the tang of seaweed. 'Tangle', the locals called that smell.

If she remembered correctly, the rest of the way was rocky. Dangerous to a horse. She brought the animal to a halt and slid down. Her bottom was sore, but her injured leg easily held her weight. Riding astride, even bareback, was apparently easier on her leg than a ladies' saddle.

'Where are they, boy?' she asked the dog, looking around warily. One thing she did not want to do was run into the Revenue men or, worse yet, Dunstan's company of militia.

The dog set off at a trot. She followed, leading the horse. Would she be in time?

The dog circled her as if to assure her everything was all right. Or was he, in the nature of his breed, trying to herd her in the direction he wanted her to go?

Stumbling on the rough ground, Selina followed Gilly, hoping he would lead her to his master and not on a rabbit hunt.

A dark rift in the rocks where a small burn ran

in a gully down to the sea told her she had re-membered correctly. She'd climbed down beside the stream to the beach on one of her forbidden explorations.

A sound behind her. Cracking of twigs. She whirled around, hand to her heart.

A large figure loomed out of the low brush off to her left, an outline against the empty sea and starry sky. It lumbered towards her.

'Hold,' a male voice whispered loudly.

Why hadn't the dog warned her? Friend or foe? Could she take a chance?

She turned to flee.

The man threw himself at her legs and flung her down.

Pain. Her shoulder wrenched. Her cheek scratched by heather. She cried out.

He cursed.

A hand came over her mouth. Heart racing wildly, she kicked out. Missed. Kicked again.

A brawny arm lifted and set her squarely on her feet. 'Hist, now,' he said in a low murmur. Scottish, she thought.

'Silence, man,' someone whispered from not far away. 'What the hell are you doing?'

'Ah,' her captor said. 'It seems I have caught myself a spy.'

Chapter Five

The taste of salt was strong in the back of Ian's throat. He stared into the dark, catching the occasional glimmer of foam-crested waves. The steady crash and hiss of waves breaking on sand and the louder roar of water pounding the rocks filled his ears.

But his mind kept wandering. Hell. He had almost kissed Selina back in the tithe barn. The urge to taste her full lips, to feel her body pressed against his, to explore her soft curves with his hands had run hot in his blood. And if he wasn't mistaken in the way those lips parted and her gaze had softened, she would have let him, too.

The attraction between them had not diminished over time. Indeed, if he wasn't badly mistaken, it had increased exponentially. Damn it all, he had betrayed his family for her once. He would not do it again.

To be so distracted at such a time as this was insane. He forced his mind back to the job at hand. This last run of brandy would give him the money he needed to buy all the copper required for the still.

Everything was ready for the boat. Nothing could possibly go wrong.

He glanced at the man standing at the very edge of the promontory with a lantern at the ready. 'Any sign of her?'

Gordy, the signalman, shook his head. 'Nought.'

Ian grimaced. Time was wasting. He narrowed his eyes to look back across the rocks and the strip of beach into the gully where the men and ponies awaited the signal. They would come out on to the open beach only when the boat was almost aground. Well versed in their respective tasks, they would unload a boat and have the goods travelling back up on to the cliffs in less than ten minutes.

He scanned the cliff tops. No sign of his guards. And nor should there be. But they were there, ready to warn of intruders. He smiled grimly. As usual they'd outwitted the gaugers. Everything was going according to plan. Except the damned boat was late.

Hairs stirred on the back of his neck. The sensation had nothing to do with the stiff breeze hurling itself off the waves. He tried to shake off the feeling all was not well. Over the years, he'd learned to trust his instincts. Why would he ignore them now?

He glanced out to sea. Still no light from the ship. 'I'm going up top to take a look around.'

Gordy nodded without turning, then stiffened, pointing. 'There!' he whispered. He fumbled with the lantern cover. 'The light dipped beneath the waves, but...yes, there she is.' Ian, too, could see the faint twinkle far out on the water.

Gordy flashed four times. Two flashes came back.

'That's them,' Ian said. 'Guide them in, lad. Any trouble, flash two long and two short, out there and up towards the cliffs, as well.'

'I ken my job, Laird.'

Ian slapped him on the shoulder. 'That you do, lad. Just reminding myself. I'll let the men know we've sighted the ship.' Then he'd climb the cliff to check on his guards.

He clambered across the rocks guarding each side of the small bay, keeping to the shadow. Once in the gully, out of the light of the stars and sheltered from the offshore breeze, he smelled the ponies. Manure and the smell of hardworking horse. And hardworking men. A familiar pungent smell.

It had surrounded him most of his life. That and the danger. But the joy had gone out of it since Andrew had gone. His brother had loved the adventure of it.

This would be the last run. There was enough money in the coffers to buy the new still. A still that would be legal anywhere else in Britain but here in the Highlands.

'Tammy,' he called in a low voice. The man rose up from a rock. 'She's coming in.'

'Aye,' Tammy said. He nudged the man beside him. 'Pass the word.'

'I'll be back down before she lands.' Ian walked past the line of horses and men. Men he had trusted with his life more than once. Good men, who trusted him and who'd lose their homes if they didn't bring this off safely. One or two of them muttered greetings as he passed.

At the end of the line, he passed a slight figure holding the bridle of an ass. Ian frowned. That made nine men. He'd thought there were eight. Was this the source of the troubled feeling he'd had out on the point? The man had a cap pulled down over his eyes and was trying to hide on the other side of his wee beast. Another thing that wasn't right. They used ponies because they were more docile.

Ian reached over the animal and grabbed the man by the collar. A familiar face grinned up at him.

'What the hell? Damn it, Logan, you are supposed to be caring for our mother.'

His brother shrugged him off. 'It is a woman's job,' he said sullenly.

Ian closed his eyes in silent prayer for patience. 'You know what Mother will do if anything happens to you. Make sure you stay out of trouble.'

'She knows where I am. I'm no child to be left at home. You were out here at eighteen and I'm near twenty.'

'That was different.' In those days there hadn't been anyone else to go. The clan had relied on him and Andrew to help them get through the winter. But for all his slight stature, Logan was right, he was old enough. And another pair of hands wouldn't hurt.

'Fine,' he said. 'But if the gaugers come, you are to run. I'm relying on you not to get caught. You'll need to warn the village.'

Logan grinned, his teeth a quick white flash in the dark. 'Aye. I'll run like the wind. You can count on me.'

Ian knew he could. And if he tried to protect him, Logan would rebel and go his own way as

Andrew had. 'See you keep that damned beastie quiet.'

A dog whined. It jumped up at Logan, who pushed him down.

'What in the devil's name is Gilly doing here?' Ian asked.

'I dinna ken. I locked him in with Beau. He must have escaped.'

'Carelessness,' Ian said. 'Keep the damn animal quiet.'

Logan glowered and made a grab for the dog. It darted out of reach.

The man next in line chuckled.

Ian smothered a cursed and left his brother to it.

The prickles on his neck had not subsided. If anything, they were worse. He climbed the steep path up the wall of the gully instead of following the track beside the burn tumbling down to the sea.

As he raised his head over the brow, a whiff of pipe smoke tickled his nostrils. 'Damn it, man. Put that out. It can be seen for miles.'

Davey had brawn, but no brain. He knocked the bowl on his heel and stamped on the embers. ''Tis all right for them down in the gully. The wind's damn cold up here, Laird.'

'It'll be hot in hell if you get yourself shot.' Ian

swept his gaze around the surrounding country-side. 'Hear anything?'

Davey gave a smug laugh. 'Aye, I heard something, all right. At first I thought it was a rabbit. I walked back along the path a ways.'

'And?'

'I caught a lass creeping up on us. Ranald has her.'

What had been a faint unease across his skin was now a full-fledged alert in his gut. 'A woman?'

'A *Sassenach* by her voice.'

This really wasn't good. 'Stay here and keep a sharp look-out.'

'Aye, Laird.'

Ian strode along the stream bank, until he came to the place where it disappeared underground. 'Ranald?'

The burly innkeeper rose up out of the heather. 'Here.'

'Davey said you caught a wench spying.'

'Aye, Laird, I have her tied up over there beside the horse.'

Definitely not good. And yet something lightened inside him. It was the oddest sensation. Shoving it aside, he strode to the cluster of rocks indicated by Ranald. He held up his lamp and looked into a pair of very angry brown eyes.

'Lady Selina. I might have known.' He knelt beside her and undid her gag.

'Your man is an idiot,' she hissed. 'I told them I had a message for you. I told them to fetch you, but they wouldn't listen.'

He pulled out his knife and sawed at the ropes around her wrists. 'What message?' He started on her ankles, keeping his gaze fixed on the job and not letting them stray to her shapely calf. Or at least, not much.

'The Revenue men know about tonight. They have set a trap. You have to leave here right away.'

So, his instincts had not played him false, curse it. If they left without the goods, it would be another year before he could set his plans in motion. And Lord Carrick would not be best pleased. 'How do you know this?' He cut through the last of the rope and helped her to her feet. God, she was small. The top of her head barely came to his shoulder.

She rubbed at her wrists. 'Never mind that. You have to go. Now.'

'Where are they waiting for us?'

'Surprisingly enough, they didn't give me any details.'

The sarcasm in her voice made him want to laugh. 'How did you get here?' And then he saw for himself. Beau. And no saddle in sight. 'You rode bareback?'

'I couldn't saddle him myself.'

He shook his head. It seemed there was still something of the spirited girl inside the sophisticated woman.

She pulled her cloak around her. 'I'll go now.'

'No.'

'Why not?'

'Because I said not.' Gaugers weren't above firing their muskets at shadows, let alone at a fleeing horse. 'Ranald,' he called softly.

The innkeeper appeared like magic. Obviously, he'd been standing close by, listening. 'Keep her here. I'll go warn the men on the beach and return to take her home. And, Ranald, not a word of this to anyone, understand?' Ranald nodded.

Ian glanced at the stubborn set of Lady Selina's jaw. 'Whatever you do, keep her here.'

What they needed now was some sort of diversion.

Selina glared at Ranald. 'I told you he would want to hear my message.'

The man mumbled something under his breath, then covered his lantern. Selina blinked furiously to adjust her vision to the gloom. She should leave.

She could be home in bed before anyone noticed her departure, her conscience clear.

What Ian did on his own account was his concern. But if she was caught aiding them Father would be mortified. And furious. If Dunstan discovered she'd warned the smugglers, after he'd let fall information about his mission in her presence, he'd call off their betrothal. If nothing else, a man expected loyalty from his wife. And that meant she'd have to start looking for a suitable husband all over again. Unless the scandal ruined her completely. It probably would.

But she'd known the risks when she set out. And she would do it all over again if required, because she was honour bound to help him as he had helped her when she'd asked. Not to mention that she did not like the thought of him being sent to prison.

Only now she needed to go home. She rubbed her cold hands together and looked at the horse and then at Ranald. 'Let me go. I'll return the horse in the morning.'

'Ye'll stay put,' the burly man said. 'The Laird said so.'

'The Laird is an idiot.'

'Take one step and I'll tie you up again.' The tone of voice made it clear he meant it. She huffed out a breath. Men. They always wanted to rule the roost.

The minutes lengthened. She watched Ranald, waiting for him to lose interest, to give her a chance to slip away. At any moment the Revenue men could be upon them, or, worse yet, Dunstan and his militia.

That really would be her undoing.

The sound of booted feet on rocks brought her head around. Men. Coming up from the shore at a run, leading a couple of ponies with muffled hooves and ladderlike carriers on their backs. Empty carriers. They guided the beasts to the path along the cliff top towards the village. What on earth were they doing?

Another pony emerged from the gully. This one was laden with tuns and turned away from the village and disappeared into the dark. Blast the man. He had taken absolutely no notice of her warning and was continuing as if nothing was wrong. She was a fool to have thought she could help.

A shout rang out on the headland in the direction the first two ponies had gone. A flash. A loud bang. Clearly a shot. Then more flashes and bangs, getting closer.

They were shooting at the men he'd sent along the headland. Someone was going to get killed. Was Ian mad?

The train of loaded ponies continued on, one

after another, while she bit her knuckles to stop from giving voice to her fears. The men leading the ponies passed by at a run, heads down and faces covered with mufflers. Then there were no more. Like ghosts, they had disappeared.

Where was Ian? She peered into the gloom, moving closer to the rocky path.

Shouts came from farther along the cliffs. The sound of men fighting hand to hand. Ranald muttered a curse, clearly impatient to be gone. Could Ian have somehow slipped past her to join in the fray now that the smugglers had departed with their booty?

Another figure emerged from the path up from the beach, cursing and swearing as he pulled on the leading rein of a resisting animal. It squealed indignantly. Its handler threw an arm over its nose to muffle the sound. The ass snorted a protest.

Selina understood just how it felt.

Then the damn thing surged forwards as if terrified. The man holding it cursed again. A flash of white at the animal's heels told Selina all she needed to know. 'Gilly,' she whispered.

The handler halted the ass and stared at her. 'Lady Selina?'

'Logan Gilvry. Another idiot. Where is Ian?'

He shook his head. 'He'll be up shortly. He's

helping the boat to shove off. Giving us a chance to get clear.'

'Then go,' she said.

'Aye. Gilly, set him on.'

The dog nipped at the ass's back hoof. It jerked forwards and set off at an awkward run with Logan at its head and Gilly close behind.

The sounds along the cliff had ceased. The smugglers—a decoy, she guessed—must have run for it. No doubt the Revenue men and the militia would soon realise they'd been tricked and make their way along here.

She had to leave before they caught her.

Ranald also hopped from one foot to the other, looking worried.

'Go,' she said.

'The Laird said I was to watch you. Here.'

'The soldiers could arrive at any moment. I'll ride and warn Laird Gilvry, while you follow your men. Help me up on the horse and then you can leave.'

Ranald scratched his head. 'You'll go to him?'

She nodded.

'All reet, my lady, but I am trusting you to keep your word.' He tossed her up on the big stallion's back and led the horse to the top of the pathway.

'Watch your step. It is verra steep.' He touched his forelock and took off after the others.

She urged the stallion down the rugged slope and hoped to goodness the animal wouldn't stumble as she let him have his head. Miracle of miracles, the horse seemed to know his way down the rock-strewn path. Ian must have ridden him down this way in the past.

It was a small lonely patch of beach along a rocky shore, known to few but the locals. Or that's how Ian had described it that long-ago day. A place where they could be alone. She realised now that he had been ashamed to be seen with her.

At the bottom of the incline she found Ian walking up the beach towards her; behind him a row-boat was steadily pulling out to sea. He glared at her as she drew up beside him.

'What the hell are you doing here? I'll have Ranald's—'

'Hush. The Revenue men are close behind me.'

He frowned. 'They followed you? Damn it. What game are you playing?'

'They didn't follow me. They know exactly where they are going and they will be here any moment. While they come down this way, we can ride up the path on the other side.'

He pressed his lips together. 'Aye. Hang on tight, then.'

She grasped the stallion's mane. Ian took a few steps at a run, then leapt up behind her. Impressive.

The sound of men in heavy boots echoed off the gully walls along with curses as they slipped and slid on the tricky path.

'Time we were gone.' He leaned forwards and they were off.

The feel of his hard thighs cradling her buttocks was positively indecent. So was his arm around her waist. But locked in that strong embrace, she felt perfectly safe, when she should be feeling terrified.

A cry went up behind them. The Revenue men must have heard the beat of the horse's hooves on the sand. It also meant they weren't far behind, but a man on foot was no match for this horse, even carrying two riders.

She set the horse's head towards the zigzagging path at the other end of the cove. A gentler climb up to the headland. They were halfway there, when a stream of men poured onto the beach from that direction.

'A pincer movement,' Ian yelled. 'That's how they meant to catch us.' He yanked the horse's head around. The beast turned in a circle while Ian scanned the cliffs and the men coming at them at a run from both sides at once.

'Look's like we've only one option,' he yelled. 'Keep your head down.' He set the horse running at the sea.

Her mouth dried. Her heart thundered. What could he be thinking? They'd drown. From horseback, the sand looked very far away. Too far to jump off. At this speed there was nothing she could do but hang on.

The wind whipped her hair out of its pins and it flew wild in her eyes. She leaned low over the horse's neck so Ian could see where they were going.

Where were they going?

Surf splashed up around them. Ian didn't slow the horse's pace. The water hit her face like icy needles and soaked her legs through the clinging fabric of her skirts and then the wool fabric of her knee breeches all the way to her waist. She gasped.

A howl of dismay went up from the men running after them.

'Load.' The terrifying shout came from the behind them. They were going to shoot!

The horse tried to turn back as its feet lost contact with solid ground.

Ian slid from its back into the water. 'Come on,

Beau,' Ian yelled. 'It's all right, lad.' The horse's ears pointed forwards, its body low in the water, its breathing fast and laboured.

A volley from the beach kicked up spurts of water all around them. Selina closed her eyes, waiting for the pain. Nothing.

'Hang on,' Ian shouted. 'We are nigh out of range.' He struck out strongly, with the horse trailing behind. Laying along the stallion's back, her skirts a tangle around her legs, Selina clung to the horse's neck for dear life. Waves hit her in the face with a salt-laden slap, making her gasp and blink to clear her stinging eyes. It was impossible that this horse could swim very far.

Another volley. Selina glanced over her shoulder to see the waterspouts a few feet behind and, if her eyes weren't deceiving her, the men were already waist-deep in the sea. Surely they didn't stand a chance of hitting them now. She prayed she was right and concentrated on holding on to the pitching beast.

Ian slowed and swam alongside. 'Come on, old fellow, you can do it.' He directed the horse to swim parallel to the shore, heading south.

How Ian kept swimming in such chilly water she didn't know. Her hands and legs were numb, her teeth chattering. She tried to remember how far it was to the next beach and wondered if they would get there before they drowned. Or perished from cold.

It might be better to drown than be caught with a known smuggler. Father would never forgive her and even the placid Dunstan would never marry her.

When she'd finally found the perfect man and plucked up the courage to take the matrimonial plunge, she'd ended up up to her neck in the sea instead.

She just had to make it home without anyone finding out.

Chapter Six

The cold seeped into Ian's bones. He wanted to turn over on his back and float as what little heat he generated from motion was leached away by the chill of the sea. With an effort he glanced over at Beau and his passenger. The lass had heart and no mistake, but it was clear she'd not last long. And the horse was snorting and blowing hard, starting to tire.

He peered through the spray at the top of each wave, searching the shore, seeing only the faint phosphorous glow of sea breaking on rocks. There. A dark patch. He veered towards it, praying there were no watching eyes up on the cliff.

Unlikely. It would take those on the beach too long to make the climb, and surely they'd be more interested in chasing the contraband.

It had seemed like eons before he felt sand under his feet and heard the gentle hush of surf on sand.

Not that there was much of a beach. A sliver, only revealed at low tide. But it was enough. The horse passed him, eager to be clear of the water, and pranced up onto the dry ground like a colt, while Lady Selina clung on for dear life.

Ian dragged his weary legs through the surf, weighed down by his kilt and grabbed at the bridle. 'All right,' he soothed, patting the sodden neck. 'You did it, old fellow.'

He reached up for the girl. She fell into his arms a dead weight. Dear God, don't say she was hit. He didn't think the shots came anywhere close. 'Selina. Are you injured?'

'J-just c-c-cold.' Her teeth clattered together.

He had the answer for that, if she could hold on long enough. 'Can you walk?'

'C-c-can't feel my legs.'

Oh, hell, what had he been thinking? It was all right for him to swim in the ocean, he'd been brought up on it, swimming in the cold lochs in the hills when there was nowhere to bathe, but this delicate creature wasn't used to such hardship.

He swept her up in his arms.

'No. You must be tired.'

'Aye.' He was. But he was used to battling on, no matter how exhausted. Hardship was a fact of life in the Highlands.

He staggered up the narrow beach, clicking his tongue for the horse to follow. Rocks jutted out from the cliffs, forming a natural inlet invisible from the overhanging cliff top. From the sea at high tide, one needed a boat, but right now, the entrance to the cave was a gentle slope into the dark. A cave wrought by seawater and an ancient underground river.

He ducked inside.

The sound of the waves became a muffled roar— a bit like listening to a shell up against your ear.

The fragile body in his arms vibrated. Shivers. He was feeling chilled himself, but out of the wind it wasn't so bad.

Beau shook himself, water drops flying. He obviously approved of the dry and followed Ian willingly.

The incline got steeper, rockier. The horse's hooves slipped here and there, but the animal kept close behind, trusting. God, the whole clan had trusted him to bring this off tonight. And now he was stuck here with no idea what was happening.

If not for the girl, he'd probably be dead. And now she lay lifeless in his arms, her dark hair hanging like seaweed over his arms, her body cold and suddenly still. He should have called the whole thing off the moment he saw her. Got the men away. Ignored the boat.

Either that or given himself up instead of plunging into the sea. Please God, he could get her warm and dry before she succumbed to the cold.

The cave was black as pitch and freezing, but he knew it as well as he knew his own bedchamber in the dark. His senses told him when the passage opened into the cave proper. That and the light touch of air rushing by his cheek. He set the fragile female in his arms down on the sand. She struggled to a sitting position and he felt relief flood through him at the sound of another round of clattering teeth.

'Wait there,' he said and felt his way to the corner where he found several oilcloth-wrapped parcels.

It wasn't long before he had candles lit, tinder and peat laid out for a fire and blankets spread on the floor. He lit the kindling from a candle and nursed the fire to life, gently blowing on the embers until flames flared up and beat back some of the darkness.

'W-w-what is this p-p-place?' Her voice was an echoing whisper.

Thank God, she was alert enough to talk. ''Tis an old cave used by fisherman.' He kept his voice matter of fact. No point in letting her know how much he had feared for her. He strode to her side. 'Sit by the fire. There are more blankets. We'll get you out of these wet clothes.'

He helped her to her feet. Made to pick her up.

'I can walk,' she said. She staggered a few steps, but, unable to stand the sight of her weakness, he picked her up and carried her to the warmth of the fire.

'I'm cold too, lass. I've no wish to be waiting a week for you to get yourself by the warmth.'

He put her down on the blankets and handed her another. 'Put that around you and take off your wet things.'

He turned his back, more and more aware of the sodden cloth clinging to his legs and dripping onto the floor. He grabbed Beau by the bridle and led him to an iron manger some enterprising ancestor had attached to the rock wall. There were oats and hay in a sack, waiting for just such an occasion as this: a need to hide from the authorities or to save a fisherman caught out in a storm.

It hadn't been used for a good long while, as far as he knew, but one of the local fishermen had the job of keeping it stocked in case of a wreck.

After emptying the hay into the manger, he used the sack to rub the horse down, then went farther up the tunnel on the landward side, to the rain barrel. The water was peaty-tasting, but clean and fresh. He filled a small pan for the horse and a couple of leather flasks.

Busy work, because all he could think of was her slipping out of her clothes, baring her lush body. He gritted his teeth. He was not the adolescent he'd been that long-ago summer, fancying himself in love with a girl he should have nothing to do with. None the less, the images were certainly warming his blood. And that wasn't such a bad thing.

By the time he got back, Lady Selina's clothes lay near the fire and the blanket was wrapped tightly around her delicious curves. She looked beautiful. Pale, her lips a little blue, strands of damp hair curling around her face, sticking to her skin. A legend come to life.

He grinned. 'You look like a selkie.'

'A sea witch? I feel more like a bit of jetsam washed up on the shore.' The brave smile on her lips as she dragged her fingers through her hair caught at his heart.

'Are you warmer?' he asked.

She nodded. 'What about you? Shouldn't you…?' Her words trailed off and she looked away, embarrassed.

Noble lasses like her didn't think about men taking their clothes off. Indeed, they probably didn't think a man had anything beneath his clothes. Clothes made the man, if the strutting peacocks in Edinburgh were to be believed.

Well, he wasn't going to stand here and drip to save her sensibilities. 'Aye. There's a spare kilt here, but nothing fit for a lady to wear. You'll have to dry your clothes before we leave.'

He grabbed the supplies put there for men prevented from landing their fishing boats at the quay during a storm. Or smugglers forced to flee the long arm of the gaugers.

He moved out of the light of the fire, wrapped a blanket around him and stripped off to his coat and shirt, using another blanket as a towel.

When he turned back she was eyeing him from beneath lowered lashes. She probably didn't realise the light from the fire, while distorting her features with flickering shadows, did not hide her expression of interest.

Heat travelled up his neck to his face.

Blushing like a lad. Surely not?

'What the hell did you think you were doing, coming down to the beach?' he said, his voice gruffer than he intended. 'What you did was brave, but foolhardy.' There, that was less ungrateful if still grudging.

'You are a fool, Ian Gilvry,' she said scornfully. 'All that danger for brandy.'

Stung, he glared at her. 'The brandy pays for other things.'

She gazed at him blankly.

He shrugged. What would a privileged lass like her know or care about the hardships his people faced? All her father cared about was the hunting and the grouse. 'As soon as your clothes are dry I'll get you home.'

Her gaze wandered to his horse. 'I have never seen a horse swim that way.'

'I lost a horse in a river once. He went in at a ford and got confused. I swore I would never lose another horse to the water.'

She rested her chin on her knees. 'I can see why. They become like friends…' She hesitated. 'Your mother gave me permission to ride him.'

'Did she know who you were?' He sat down beside her on the blanket. The fire's warmth was painful to his icy skin.

'Yes.'

That did surprise him. His mother had always been opposed to everything English—it was a point of honour. If she ever learned Ian had sent Drew off to America at the behest of Albright's daughter, she would never forgive him.

He'd done it for the memories of a short time when he'd felt happy and carefree, when he'd forgotten his duties and responsibilities. Very selfish reasons wrapped around youthful dreams and wishes. Reality in the shape of his brothers' shock at seeing them together had brought him back to earth, but he'd never stopped feeling guilty for the hurt look on her face at his rejection and cruel words spoken in parting. That guilt had sent Drew to his death. He would not let her influence him against his family again. But she had made up for it in part, at least, with tonight's warning.

'Thank you for coming tonight. Without your warning we would have been caught. I wish you had not come down to the beach, though. I would have handled it.'

She sighed. 'I thought the Revenue men would follow the goods and we could ride up the path on the other side.'

He was surprised by the resignation in her voice. 'How did you know of their plans?'

'Through my father. I should have sought you out earlier in the day.' She sighed. 'I was almost too late.' She shook her head. 'Why risk lives for a few tuns of brandy? How will the women and children survive without their men?'

She was lecturing him? After all her father had

done to destroy their way of life? 'They can't live on fresh air.'

'Well, they can't live on brandy.'

'You are a *Sassenach*. What do you know about what my people need?'

She flinched and he felt like a brute. His rough direct ways did not suit a drawing-room miss. Not that she'd seemed much like a lady riding bareback to his rescue.

'It brings money to purchase what they can live on,' he explained. More than that, though—it was an investment in the future.

After a few moments' silence, she turned to face him. 'Do you think we were recognised?'

He shook his head. 'They were too far away.'

She breathed a sigh of relief. That small little breath, that mark of gladness, sparked warmth in his chest. Foolish warmth. She was the daughter of his clan's worst enemy. He'd do well to keep that in mind.

But she had risked a great deal tonight and he would not have her suffering for it. 'The sooner we get you back to the keep, the better,' he said, 'before you are missed. Hold up your clothes to the fire so they will dry.'

She did as he bid and they both sat toasting her

clothes, watching the steam rise from them to mingle with the smoke from the fire.

'Why do your people try to turn back the clocks? Bonnie Prince Charlie is never returning.'

She understood nothing. 'My people were here long before the English. Yes, they need to move with the times, but not give up who they are, their traditions or their homeland. All the great landowners are turning their land over to sheep. Or using it for sport. They are leaving nothing for the clan members. If you take away their livelihood, then they need other work to replace it. Instead of that, they are being left destitute, labouring in the kelp fields or smuggling whisky. Hundreds of them have shipped off to America. Soon there will be no Highlanders left.'

She frowned. 'Don't the crofters earn enough to pay their rents?'

'The rents keep going up.' He combed his fingers through his almost-dry hair as he sought for a way to explain without giving away his plans. 'The old ways, such as crofting, are no longer viable, but I believe other ways can be found to keep the people here. In Scotland. But the English, men like your father, pass laws that make it impossible for us to earn a living. Those are what need to be changed.'

Her silence said she wasn't convinced. Hell, he

was barely convinced himself that changing the law would make a difference. Yet some men were making a go of it, but they were men who owned their estates, who had the power to decide the best way to proceed. If Albright decided to clear his lands, in the end there was little Ian could do about it.

'Must we swim back?' she asked.

At last a question he could answer with confidence. 'No. The cave has a back door. Or a front door, depending on your point of view.'

'Then we should go. I cannot be found missing from my bed when the maid comes to light the fire.' She shivered.

Instinctively, his arm went around her. He touched her cheek. The skin was warm and alive beneath his fingers, her mouth so deliciously inviting. Her back was frigid beneath his arm. No wonder she had shivered.

'We have to get you fully dry first.'

'I am much warmer than I was.'

'Aye, but not warm enough.' He lifted her easily and set her between his legs, so her back was against the warmth of his body, her round little bottom nestled between his thighs. He almost groaned with the pleasure as his body hardened and he prayed she could not feel it through the blanket. He forced himself to ignore the delight-ful sensation and instead focused on the feel of her cold back permeating through her blanket and his. He pulled her close up against his chest.

'What are you doing?' she asked breathlessly.

'Body heat. The closer we sit together, the warmer we will both be. Something I learned on cold nights when out on the hunt with the men of the clan.'

She leaned back and hummed her approval. The sound struck low in his gut. His arousal swelled painfully. He forced himself to breathe and to think. This woman was not for him.

She laughed a little.

'What?' he said through gritted teeth.

'I'm thinking about a bunch of men snuggled together.'

'Not pleasant, believe me. Men stink after days in the hills. But it saved us from freezing to death or returning empty-handed.'

'The clan always protects its members.'

'Aye.'

'One of them gave you away tonight.'

'Possibly.' A traitor in their midst. The thought gave him a cold feeling in his gut. It would have to be addressed, though. As soon as the hue and cry died down. 'You didn't hear who spilled the beans?'

'No.'

Of course, it wouldn't be that easy, would it?

He rubbed her finely boned arms with his hands, taking care not to hurt her. Heat blossomed beneath his palms.

'That feels good.' She sighed.

He wanted to do more than warm her arms. He wanted to take her with him to the stars and back. A boy's long-ago dream. It was no more right today than it had been then.

The sooner he got her home, the sooner he could be rid of temptation. It would lead to nothing but trouble for all of them.

The thought of her leaving made the fire seem to blaze less brightly and the cave seem more cavernous and empty. Not since Drew's departure had he enjoyed one of these night-time adventures, he realised, or shared his worries about the future.

How much more disloyal could he be to his brother's memory? Probably a whole lot more when it came to this woman, unless he was careful.

He was always careful. Always in control. Tonight was no different.

Chapter Seven

Selina let the blessed warmth of Ian's body at her back and the heat of the fire in front gather her up and set her adrift. The feel of his arms around her made her feel safe, protected from the world beyond their cave.

Men usually made her nervous. They had to be watched and judged and kept at a distance. If you let them get too close, they found a way to hurt you.

Ian had taught her that lesson when she was an impressionable schoolgirl. How could she forget that about him now?

Or was it the schoolgirl who had once more taken over her mind and her body reminding her of those old foolish longings?

Certainly not. She knew what this was, what it had always been: forbidden desire. A fragile woman always brought out a male's urge to protect. And thus she held the upper hand, as long as she didn't allow herself to be drawn under its spell. Under those conditions, there was nothing wrong with a little bit of mutual lust. Provided it didn't go too far.

A lady had to be careful of her reputation, especially if she hoped to marry.

Then why this pervasive sense of well-being wrapped in his arms when tonight she had risked everything?

She turned her face up, looking at his hard square jaw covered in stubble. Her gaze traced the shadow of his cheek and the carved cheekbone. And the longing inside her seemed to increase with the expansion and contraction of his ribs at her back. A silent sigh, yet she felt it with every bone in her body.

'I never forgave myself for what I said to you, that day at the beach,' he murmured low in her ear. 'Children are cruel, but I was old enough to know better. I had an overabundance of pride in those days.'

Surprised, she twisted in his arms to better see his expression, to assure herself he wasn't mocking.

Indeed, his lips did smile, but it was a lovely generous smile, youthful, touched by regret, his eyes gleaming with firelight.

Her insides drew tight, pulsed with a sensation that made her eyelids droop and her body soften.

Looking down at her, he inhaled a swift breath. The glimmer in his eyes burst into searing flames.

The air crackled and warmed. All around them heat conspired to make them short of breath and wordless. His arms tightened around her body, his head dipped until his mouth was close enough to brush her lips. The soft caress of each exhale tickled her lips, the scent of him, salt and sea air, and something very male filled her senses.

'It seems we are destined to rescue each other from time to time,' she said on a breathless laugh. Though it must never happen again.

Without thought, she put her arms around his neck, tipped her head and kissed his cheek, much as she had as a girl. 'I'm glad I reached you in time.'

A groan broke in his throat. 'Me, too.' His hand came to her jaw, cradling her chin, angling her head the better to kiss her back.

His lips firmed over hers, testing and teasing. His lips parted and his tongue licked her bottom lip. Thrills ran amok in her body, making her gasp with shock at the pleasure of such an intimate touch.

Heavenly sensations coursed through her veins and turned her bones liquid.

His parted lips matched hers and, open-mouthed, their lips melded and moved in a harmony she hadn't expected. Tentatively, she tried a taste of her own. Their tongues met and danced and played, at first gently, carefully, and then with wild fervour.

Dizzy, breathing hard, she lay in his arms. The magic of his kiss took her out of her body. Whereas she'd been floating before, now she was flying, soaring, released from the chains of the world.

Inside she trembled.

Never in her adult life had she lost her sense of self so utterly as now, as if some part of them had fused and become something different altogether. It exhilarated. And terrified.

Fear made her struggle.

He drew back, breathing hard, looking into her face with a jaw of granite, with eyes the colour of midnight, hot and demanding.

'We must not,' he said, gravel-voiced.

'No,' she agreed, gazing up at his hard expression. Yet longing was there, in the way his gaze devoured her face, in the way his hands trembled where they touched her cheek, light and gentle as a butterfly. Forbidden wanting. Or was it only her fevered blood making her wish it?

She closed her eyes against such traitorous thoughts. She'd made her choice.

When she opened her eyes she saw anger in his. Perhaps even revulsion. Yet it did not seem so much directed at her as directed at himself as he stood up, leaving her cold and bereft.

'You must be warm by now,' Ian said, matter of factly.

Warm? She was burning. 'Yes. Thank you.' There, didn't she sound equally calm? Equally unaffected?

'Here.' He handed over her skirts and her bodice. 'These are dry.' He frowned when her breeches fell to the floor.

'For riding,' she said defensively. 'What about you?' She glanced at the blanket he had wrapped around his waist and then at the still-steaming mass of his kilt. It would take hours to dry. A small shiver ran down her back at the thought of hours of temptation in this cave.

'There are spare clothes here.' He picked up one of the packages and unwrapped it.

Fascinated, she watched him. 'You would spare your maidenly blushes if you will look away now, Lady Selina.' The mockery was back in his voice.

Maidenly blushes. After that kiss he no doubt suspected they were nothing more than a front.

Her cheeks hotter than the fires of hell, she whipped her face away and fluffed the billowing fabric of her skirts. Yet for all her good intentions, she could not help but cast a glance from the corner of her eye as he let the blanket fall silently to the floor.

At the edge of the firelight the gleam of his skin was like marble. The image of wide sculpted shoulders tapering to lean waist and firm flanks, the swell of firm lean buttocks and strong thighs seared her vision. Her body clenched at his sheer beauty.

So large and so male. Lithe and perfectly formed. Athletic and sure in his movements as he bent to adjust the cloth. So opposite to her small stature and rounded curves and the awkwardness of her halting gait.

The silhouette of his erection made her gasp. Had he heard and guessed she was watching? If so, he gave no sign. She ducked her head and busied herself with her clothes. Swallowing against the dryness in her mouth, she kept her gaze fixed on her task.

The fire was hot and the light cotton fabric dried quickly. She concentrated on holding her breeches

out to the flames. She glanced up when he returned bare-chested. Another delicious clench of
her insides. He picked up his shirt and held it to
the warmth. The trousers were on the tight side
and too short and made his thighs look huge. Not
that she was measuring. She wasn't. But a woman
would have to be blind not to notice how strong
his legs were and that his feet were large, just like
his... She forced the thought to be gone.

But never would she forget the image of his body,
the way he looked in profile. Different. Glorious.

'Time for you to dress now,' he said, 'if we are
to get you home before dawn.'

She jumped at the sound of his voice. He was
right. They really should not linger. 'Turn your
back while I dress.'

An eyebrow flickered up—no doubt she had
sounded too harsh, but he walked away, went to
his horse with clearly no interest in spying on her.

So they'd kissed. A moment of passion after a
wild escape. Whatever had happened between
them had been the result of shock. Mutual comfort. Nothing more.

She pulled her hair back from her face; it felt
matted and still damp, but she didn't care. She
made a rough plait to hold it, then dressed be-

neath her blanket, not because she feared he would look, but to ward off some of the chill of the cave. Dressed, she turned back to find him rubbing the horse down with the blanket he had discarded earlier.

She picked up her shawl, still saturated from the sea, and folded it up. A blanket would make a better cloak and be warmer, though heaven knew what her maid was going to say. She wrapped it around her shoulders and tied it behind her waist as peasant girls did, then gathered up his kilt, folding it to give her hands something to do while she waited for him.

'Are you ready?' he asked, leading the horse towards her.

She nodded. It was a lie. A knot formed in her stomach. The thought of returning home made her feel the way an escaped prisoner must feel about the return to prison. A prison of her own making. Which didn't make a bit of sense, not when she was about to marry the man she had chosen for herself. She held out his kilt. 'You will want this.'

He used one of the ropes to tie it, then rested it across the horse's withers. 'We'll mount up outside.' He picked up a bucket and emptied it on the fire. Choking smoke filled the cave.

Selina coughed and rubbed at her streaming

eyes. 'You idiot. Couldn't you wait until we had left?'

He chuckled. The next moment, he was behind her, lifting her onto the horse. 'We need to make haste, now.' He jerked on the bridle and led the big black into the tunnel, holding a torch up so they could see ahead of them. They climbed upwards through the narrow space. Sometimes, when the surf was quiet, she could hear running water— what was left of the stream that had carved its way through the rock and out to the sea, no doubt. And then they were out in the cold night air.

He doused the torch, tossed it over the cliff and continued leading the horse, back towards the road.

She clung on to the stallion's mane and prayed they would make it home in time.

A good few yards from the keep's entrance, Selina directed him across country. 'There is an outcropping of rock on the back side of the hill,' she murmured quietly.

'I know it.' Why had he never suspected it might hide an entrance? As lads, his brothers would have been delighted. The thought of the trouble they might have caused made him shudder.

They needed to hurry. Dawn was already changing the eastern sky from black to grey. Beau shied as a figure rose out of the heather. Ian jerked the horse to a stand.

'Angus,' Selina cried.

'Shh,' Angus hissed. 'What by all that is holy are you thinking, Ian Gilvry?'

'What are you doing here?' she asked.

Ian had a sinking feeling in his gut. Who else knew to expect Lady Selina?

Angus shot a glance up at the keep. 'Do you think I don't know every nook and cranny of my master's house, my lady? So it is true.'

'What are you insinuating, Mr McIver?'

Never had Ian heard her sound so haughty. So much like the stuck-up noblewoman Andrew had described on his return from London.

'What is happening, Angus?' Ian asked, jumping clear of Beau.

'That young lady has been missed from her bed and her fiancé is crying foul, that is what is happening.'

'Fiancé?' His gut slipped sideways. He glared up at Lady Selina. Had she been playing some sort of game with him back there in the cave, the sort of flirtation engaged in by ladies of the *ton*, according to what Andrew had told him?

'Nothing has been formally announced,' she

said, sounding defensive. She slipped down off the horse and stood at his side.

'It may not be official,' Angus said, 'but he is verra angry. Threatening to ruin your reputation and that of your father. Interfering in official business makes you an accomplice under the law.'

'He can't know for certain,' she said heatedly. 'No one saw me.'

Ian had the feeling she had her fingers crossed when she said the last. 'Did someone see her?'

'I'm no privy to that information. I do know that young Dunstan is beside himself with anger. No doubt he expected a bit of glory out of tonight's affair. Instead...'

She winced. 'Father knows I knew what was planned for tonight and he thinks I betrayed him.'

'Well, you did, didn't you?' Angus muttered, his deep voice turning into a low growl of frustration. 'Lady Albright is in tears, speaking of ruin and disgrace. Your father...' He shook his head.

Ian stiffened, but for all the anger he felt, he had to acknowledge that if word of her escapade got out Lady Selina would be ruined. Helping a Gilvry escape the gaugers would not be seen as heroic by her people. They also might ponder why she had helped him, and not to her credit.

'I'll just have to face the music,' Lady Selina said

in a small breathless voice. 'It is no one's business what I was doing tonight and so I will tell him. Father will forgive me, eventually.'

'I advise against such a step,' Angus said, his voice as dry as dust. 'That young man won't be satisfied until you admit where you were tonight and give evidence against the Laird. If he persuades your father he is right, you'll have a hard task standing up to them.'

Ian's fists clenched at the thought of her being bullied.

'And once they have what they want,' McIver continued, 'the Laird will be convicted.'

'But what else can I do?' she said.

He gave her a sharp look. 'According to that maid of yours, it wouldn't be the first time you'd gone off on a whim in the middle of the night. All you have to do is disappear for a while and turn up somewhere else safe and sound.'

'So Mary has been gossiping, has she?' she said icily.

'Mary is worried out of her wits that she will get the blame.'

Lady Selina's shoulders sagged. She shook her head. 'Surely, Father would not blame a servant for my actions? Besides, he knows I don't do that sort of thing any more.'

'Who's to say what maggot gets into a woman's head?' Angus said. 'There has to be somewhere you could go, some friend you could visit who could vouch for your whereabouts?'

She turned to Ian, her face full of worry. 'There is Alice. Lady Hawkhurst as she is now. Hawkhurst is a formidable man. He might be able to convince them I left before all this occurred. Father would listen to him.'

'You'll have to be careful,' McIver warned. 'They'll be searching the glens for you both by morning.'

Ian stared at McIver. 'Are you proposing I escort her there?'

'Aye. Unless you have a better idea.'

A curse sprang to his lips; he swallowed it. 'Perhaps if you bat your beautiful eyes at them, Lady Selina, and tell them you were out for a walk, they'll believe you.'

'I'm willing to give it a try,' she said with a defiant little toss of her head.

'Laird, if I might have a word with you in private?' Angus said. He looked up at Lady Selina. 'Clan business, you ken, my lady.'

'I suppose you are afraid I will tell them your secrets,' she said. 'Well, I'm not so poor spirited.

However, speak privately if you must.' She walked a few steps away.

Ian drew closer to Angus. 'What is it, man? More bad news?'

'It depends on your point of view.' Angus gripped his arm hard. 'I ought to beat you to within an inch of your life for involving her in your doings.'

Anger rising in his craw, Ian stepped toe to toe with the man. McIver was big, but Ian was taller and fitter. He clenched his fists and pitched his voice low. 'Speak your piece, man.'

'Marry the lass.'

The words hit him like a punch to the jaw. Words would not form for a moment or two. More shocking yet was the deep sense of longing filling his chest, as if some hitherto-unrecognised hope had been forced to the surface. No doubt the wrong part of his anatomy doing the thinking. 'Are you mad? She's Albright's daughter.'

The child of his family's enemy. That was why he'd driven her off all those years ago, when he realised he was in danger of losing himself in her velvet-brown eyes. When he'd felt the stirrings in his blood and in his heart—and seen his brothers' horror.

Albright would never have countenanced their friendship, let alone anything closer.

And Andrew. Andrew would haunt his every moment if he did such a thing. If not for Selina's request, and his lingering guilt at the way he had treated her, Drew would still be alive. Instead, he'd forced his brother to leave London and his pursuit of the heiress, his answer to the clan's financial troubles, who just happened to be Selina's good friend. Not only that, Ian had shipped the furious Andrew off to America, where he'd been killed. How could he marry a woman who had twisted him around her little finger to the detriment of his brother? He certainly didn't deserve the surge of happiness the thought of it brought him. 'You are out of your mind.'

'I'm being practical, laddie. Marry her and even if they badger her until kingdom come, her word is no good in a court of law.'

'I don't believe Lady Selina would give evidence against me.'

'She might do her best to hold out, but she's made a complete fool of that young *Sassenach*. Let her go in there now and you might as well go in, too, with a noose draped around your neck. It'll be the end for the folks around here. With you gone there will be nothing to stop them from clearing the land. As I said, Dunstan is threatening retribution against her and against her father. Who do you think she will choose, once you are hiding out in the hills?' His grey brows drew together. 'Think about it, Gilvry. No matter what happens, she is ruined. I just can't see her letting her father be implicated, too.'

Damn it to hell. It was too hard a choice for any daughter to make. She owed Ian nothing and her father everything. But marriage? 'There must be another way.'

Angus looked grim. 'Your brother Andrew cut a swathe through the lasses in every glen from here to Edinburgh, but you are the Laird and she is a lady. Have you no honour?'

Resentment at the distaste in the other man's tone fired his temper. 'I haven't touched the lass.' He flushed red as he recalled their kiss and was glad of the poor light. But it was only a kiss. 'I didn't ask her to follow me tonight.'

McIver sighed. 'But she did. Will you let her suffer for trying to help? You are not the man I thought, if you do not do the right thing.'

He squeezed his eyes shut, trying to focus, to see his way clear. He needed time to think. Time to plan. 'I will take her to her friend, but that is all I will do.'

McIver shook his head as if disappointed. 'Think on what I have said, lad. In the meantime, travel as far as you can from here before it is light. You'll find a welcome in the glens until you get far enough south. Do not dally. There will be a price on your head by morning.'

Reeling with the conflicting thoughts in his head, Ian returned to Selina with McIver on his heels.

'Well?' she said.

Ian gave her a rueful grin. 'I will take you to your friend.'

She turned to McIver. 'Are you sure this is the only way?'

Angus nodded. 'Go with Gilvry or your help will have been for nothing.' He plucked a saddlebag off the rocks where they'd first seen him. 'There's water in here, oats and supplies, some coin. Enough to see you on your way. Get a message to your brother, Laird, when you have things in hand.' He emphasised the last word with a hard look.

Ian didn't like McIver's glibness. He seemed to have thought everything out, as if he had some purpose of his own. But he couldn't see any alternative.

Certainly not marriage.

He looked up. Dawn was reaching into the sky and he could see Selina's features more clearly and the anxiety in her eyes.

'We need to go. Now,' he said.

Wearily, she nodded her agreement and let him throw her up on Beau. She clung there looking down at him with worry and trust.

If anything, it made him feel worse. Somehow he had to find a way out of this mess. For them both. He mounted before her and looked down at Angus. 'Tell Niall I will send word.'

He turned Beau around and dug in his heels.

Chapter Eight

Selina had no choice but to cling to the firm waist of the man before her as he turned across country. A dull ache filled her chest. In trying to help Ian, she'd ruined her own future. If only she'd stayed in London, none of this would have happened.

And Ian would have been caught.

It was all the fault of that stupid man Ranald. If he would have just taken her warning to Ian, she could have gone home and no one would have been the wiser.

She looked back over her shoulder at the keep, its outline already distinguishable against the sky. Was she now doing the right thing in going with Ian?

While her heart had said 'yes', which was why she hadn't given them too much of an argument, her head thought it a huge mistake. She had learned a long time ago not to listen to her heart. A cold feeling sank into the pit of her stomach as she realised she was putting her faith in a man she barely knew and had absolutely no reason to trust.

But if Dunstan was threatening to charge her with complicity in smuggling, she needed an alibi. Someone who could vouch for her presence elsewhere.

Alice had been the only person she could think of. But her husband, Hawkhurst, might well not approve. Selina had always had the feeling he didn't like her very much.

They travelled west, away from the sea and the keep. After an hour or so, Ian slowed the horse to a walk. The beast's head hung low, foam white around the bit.

He threw one leg over the horse's withers and jumped down. He lifted her off. 'We'll walk for a while.'

She rubbed at her thigh, easing the stiffness that always beset her after sitting for too long. It felt good to be off the horse and on her feet. The doctors had advised lots of walking to strengthen the muscles in her leg, though nothing would cure the hesitation in her step. She was lucky Dunstan hadn't cared that she was no longer a diamond of the first water, no longer the perfect pocket Venus, but then money solved many problems.

'Where are we headed first?' she asked.

He grinned and grabbed the bridle. 'Into the glens. Where the Scots always go when plagued by the English.'

She matched his pace. 'That I know. But where?'

'There is a place I know where we can spend the night, if we can reach it before nightfall. It is a long hard walk, so save what you can of your breath.'

She stumbled on a rock hidden in the heather.

He caught her arm before she fell. 'Be careful. I always forget what a little bit of a thing you are.'

'I'll try to be taller.' She took bigger steps.

He laughed. 'You are a surprising woman, Lady Selina. Any other lady of my acquaintance would be twisting her hands together and bemoaning her fate.'

'If hand-wringing would do me any good, be assured I would put it to good use.'

He glanced over his shoulder. 'We are far enough from Dunross that we can slow our pace, I think.'

'I'm not an invalid. I am perfectly capable of walking.'

'I see that.'

Still she couldn't help but be aware that he had adjusted his stride to match hers. She decided there was no point in saying anything. It clearly wouldn't do any good. He saw her as crippled, no matter what she said.

After what felt like hours, with the sound of the curlews and the wind the only noises, he stopped by a stream. 'We will let the horse drink and then ride for a while.'

She tried not to sigh with relief at not having to walk as she sank down and she scooped up water in her hands and enjoyed the cold trickle down her parched throat.

He drank, too, once he had seen to the horse, then crouched down beside her. 'It would be better, if we meet anyone, if you do not give your real name.'

A pang tightened her chest. Of course he would not want it known he was in her company. She smiled brightly. 'Who shall I be? Mary Queen of Scots?'

He frowned. 'The cousin of a friend, on her way to her family. I don't suppose you speak any Gaelic.'

'A word or two, but I can speak with a Scottish burr,' she said in broadest Scots.

He nodded. 'Och, I remember you doing that

before. It was days before I realised you were English.'

'I'm like a chameleon,' she said with a laugh that was a little more brittle than she intended. 'I fit in with my surroundings.'

It wasn't true. She fit in London. Not here.

'We can say you have been away to school in England and lost the Gaelic. Come, we must keep moving.'

'How long do you think it will be before they give up looking for us?'

He shrugged. 'For you? Until you send them word you are safe, I assume.' He bent and laced his fingers together beside Beau.

'And you?' she asked as he tossed her up.

'With no evidence, there will be no point in them looking.'

Once more she found herself clinging to Ian's waist, thoughts churning around in her head.

She just wished she could be sure she was doing the right thing running away with Ian instead of seeking out her father and denying it all. Unfortunately, that kind of blatant lying was not her forte.

If only she could think of a logical explanation for being gone in the middle of the night. Something that would not leave them suspecting her of betraying what should have been a confidence, though no one had specifically asked her not to speak of it.

Unfortunately McIver was right—the smugglers' escape and her disappearance were just too much of a coincidence. She wasn't even sure that Hawkhurst could, if he even would, give her the alibi she needed.

On the other hand, no one but the smugglers had seen her.

She stared at Ian's back. One of his own men had betrayed him; if that person had seen her, it wouldn't matter what kind of alibi she had, there would be a witness against her.

Was that why McIver had drawn Ian aside? Did he know who had betrayed them to the Revenue men?

She bit her lip. Perhaps it was better not to know. The thought gave her a horrid churning feeling in her stomach. Surely Ian wouldn't... Smugglers were known to be exceedingly dangerous if crossed.

Oh, dear. Had she gone from the frying pan into the fire? She could not, would not, believe Ian would do her any harm. He was simply trying to help her escape the consequences of her folly, because she had helped him. Nothing more.

'Do you have any idea who gave you away?'

His back stiffened. 'I have been thinking about it, to no avail.' He gave a short laugh. 'No doubt he was forced to it by circumstance.'

'What do you mean?'

His shoulders rose and fell. 'Who knows what people keep hidden? It could be debt. Or illness. Or fear of being turned out. There are many ways to make a man betray his loyalty.'

And it depended on where you stood as to what was or was not deemed loyal. 'Which means we can't trust anyone in your clan.'

He didn't answer for a long while. 'Let us put it this way. There are people I know I can trust and people I am not sure of.'

'What about me?' She winced. Did she have to ask? How could he possibly trust an Albright. A *Sassenach.*

'I trust you.' He sounded almost surprised. 'But I have to be honest, I also believe your first loyalty is to your father.'

She could not deny it, though Father might not exactly see it that way at this moment.

They kept moving all day, sometimes riding, sometimes walking, the hills becoming higher and steeper with every passing hour. They travelled in silence, saving their breath for travelling. And always she felt his urgency, though he never gave a sign he thought she was holding him back. He didn't have to—she knew she was. Often she had the feeling he only stopped because she needed to rest.

The farther away from Dunross they got, the more she began to fear that her running away was not the right answer. Surely she could have bluffed her way out of the mess. Batting her beautiful eyes, as Ian had said.

He thought her eyes beautiful. When he had said it, she had been too worried to let the words sink in. Now strangely, they made her feel warm inside.

On foot once more, she lifted her gaze and became aware of her surroundings. It was all so wild and beautiful. Misty hills stretched in every direction, their outlines softened by heather and scarred by the odd outcrop of ancient granite. She'd been enchanted by it all that long-ago summer when her father had brought her here after her mother had died. He'd been desolate and had wanted to return to the place where he had spent his honeymoon. Then he'd run off to Inverness—for business reasons, he'd said—leaving her to mourn alone.

Later, he'd admitted that she reminded him too

much of her mother and he just couldn't bear it, but at the time she'd felt abandoned. By them both.

Sixteen and utterly lonely, she'd been ripe to fall in love with the first handsome young man who came her way. Naturally it had to be the worst possible person. Had Ian actually suggested she run away with him then, she would have said 'yes' in a heartbeat.

He'd been a knight in shining armour the day he carried her back to the keep in his arms. He'd made her feel soft and feminine. A rush of longing for that feeling filled the empty place in her heart she'd refused to acknowledge.

She shouldn't be noticing now when they had so many more important things to think about.

'Do you think we will make it to this place you know of by nightfall?'

He glanced up at the sky. 'Yes. It is not more than a mile or two now. You've done very well for a *Sassenach* lass. Far better than I expected.'

Praise indeed, though she could have done without the reminder that she was English. Even so, she found herself smiling. He grinned back. How odd to feel happy in such peculiar circumstances.

'How long do you think it will take to reach Hawkhurst from there?'

'Once we cross the border and pick up a stage-coach, it shouldn't take more than a couple of days.'

They crested the rise of a hill and, as nothing but hills stretched before them, the enormity of the distance they would have to travel became real.

'What will you do, after?'

He shrugged. 'Come back and continue on as before.'

'More smuggling, I suppose. Until they finally catch you.'

He shot her a look that was both devil-may-care and world weary. 'They won't. And what else can we do until the law punishing us for supporting the true king is changed—the one separating the Highlands from the rest of Scotland and making it impossible to survive?'

Such bitterness. 'Can the law be changed?'

'Who will take our part in Westminster?'

Not her father. He had no interest in his Scottish estate, except for sport and a means to political advantage. 'Lord Carrick?'

'He does what he can, but Carrick is one voice among many. Highlanders are not popular with the English aristocracy.'

'It shouldn't be a matter of what is popular. The laws should be fair.'

He grinned at her. 'So they should. But since they are not, then we deal with them our own way.'

There was more than a smidgeon of pride in the way he spoke. Clearly it would irk a man like Ian to be begging for help. But if he had brought his case to her father, might he not have tried to assist?

She stopped and looked at him. 'Did you ask my father?'

'Albright? Ye jest.'

The bitterness and scorn in his voice cut like a knife.

A shot rang out, the sound bouncing off the hills.

Ian jerked and clutched his arm with a cry, then spun around. He grabbed her arm and drew her down to the ground. 'Keep your head low.'

'They were shooting at us.' The shock of it left her dizzy.

'Aye.' He got up on his knees and looked down the hill they'd so recently walked up. He cursed. 'Soldiers. It won't be long before they are upon us.'

Crouched low, he ran the few steps to the stallion, whipped the blanket from the animal's back, rolled it up and tied it lengthways along the horse's back.

'What are you doing?'

He shot her an impatient glance, then began talking in a low voice into Beau's flickering ear. To her shock, he whacked the horse hard on its rump. It took off at a gallop.

Lying flat in the heather, she stared after the horse in dismay. 'Why did you do that?'

Crouching low, he picked up the saddlebag and reached out to take her hand. 'Buying time. Keep your head down until we get over the brow of the hill.'

And then they were running, at first at a crouch, then, once they had crested the rise and were going downhill, at full tilt.

Her heart thumped against her ribs. Her breath came in short little gasps. She skittered along after him, trying to keep her head down, imagining at any moment a bullet slamming into her back, all the while wanting to lie flat on the ground and put her hands over her head. She sensed she wasn't going fast enough for Ian. Breath rattled in and out of her lungs. Her legs, already tired, felt as heavy as lead. She really could not go any farther.

She let go of his hand and sank into the heather, gasping for breath. 'Go. Leave me here.'

The look he gave her from beneath his brows was fierce and uncompromising. Before she realised what he was about he swept her up in his arms and tossed her over his shoulder. He took off, in an awkward jolting run.

With each step his shoulder dug into her belly and pushed the air out of her chest. The blood rushed to her head where she hung over his back.

She didn't know which was worse, the pain under her ribs, or her difficult breathing, but she bore it in silence, glad he hadn't abandoned her to save his own skin. He didn't seem to even notice her weight. He was as lithe and sure-footed as one of the deer that roamed these hills, but after a while even his breathing became harsh and laboured.

They crested two more hills and then he stopped. 'Get your head down.' He threw himself flat and she did the same, lying on her back, trying to catch her breath.

'If I tell you to run, head for the burn at the bottom,' he instructed, his voice a rough rasp. In a crablike crawl, he went to the top of the rise behind them and once more lay flat, looking out. She tried to listen, but all she could hear was the blood rushing in her ears. She kept her gaze fixed on Ian, ready to run should he give her the signal. Or at least try to run. She wasn't sure she could take another step.

He sauntered back to her with a grin on his face. He actually looked as if he was enjoying himself. She wanted to shake him. She pushed to her feet. 'I assume they took the bait?'

'They did that.' His grin widened. 'If we are lucky, Beau will beat them back to Dunross.'

She couldn't help an answering grin.

His expression turned serious. 'We are not out of the woods yet. They no doubt have a glass and, if they realise there is no rider, then they will circle back. We must hurry.'

'Hurry where?'

He grinned. His blue eyes danced. 'Over there.'

This time he directed her across the hillside, rather than down. He seemed to be searching the ground, for what she couldn't imagine. There was nothing here.

He dropped to his knees and parted the heather around a large boulder. 'Ah, here it is.' He pulled aside what had looked like twisted clumps of dead heather on solid ground, but was really more like a thatch covering a deep scoop in the side of the hill.

'In you go.'

A quick breath of fresh air and she crawled in. A strange smell filled her nostrils. Peat smoke and something else. Trusting he knew what he was about, she turned around and waited.

He followed, pulling the undergrowth back in place. It wasn't completely dark inside. As her eyes adjusted, she realised they were in some sort of earthen room and that daylight came in through chinks in a roof made of brush.

The space, a sort of earthen cave, contained a couple of stools, a rotten straw pallet in one corner and a rusted metal object standing on the remains of a fire. A twisted piece of metal hung down beside its chimney. 'What is this place?'

He drew her close and placed a finger to her lips. 'Listen.'

Over the thud of her heart, she heard a different kind of thud. Horses. The sound vibrated up through her feet. They sounded very close. Would they trample over what was a very flimsy roof and end up falling in on top of them? The sound of her breathing and her heartbeat filled her ears.

She could only imagine what was happening outside. Without thinking, she drew close to his large protective form. Strong arms went around her, holding her firmly. She snuggled closer, listening to the strong steady beat of his heart instead of the sound of nearby horses, drawing strength and courage from his warmth and his closeness, wanting to burrow deeper every time they came so close she could hear the laboured breathing of the horses.

Slowly the sounds receded.

'Whoever is in charge has a brain,' Ian murmured into her hair. 'I'm thinking the rest of the group followed Beau, but he sent a couple this way just to be sure. No doubt they will be back the moment they discover they were tricked.'

'How comforting,' she said, easing away from him. It seemed to her that he was reluctant to let her go, as if he had drawn some comfort from having her in his arms.

What an imagination she had. The sooner they left here the better.

She patted her hair, smoothing her skirts, hoping she did not look as if she had just huddled against him like a frightened child.

He hissed in a sharp breath. One of pain.

She recalled his jerk and the cry right after the shot. 'Did they hit you?'

She felt sick. Nauseous. Her father wouldn't have ordered him shot. He wouldn't.

'A scratch. The ball was spent.'

Her knees went weak. 'I should look at it.'

'It is fine.'

She wanted to believe him. 'Perhaps I should look at it just to be sure? It's too dark in here to see anything. We should go outside.'

'Not yet. Not until we are sure they are not coming back. It will be hard for them to return to this exact spot. Since they will expect us to run, we will stay put. We'll move on in the morning. More carefully.'

'What of Beau?'

'He's used to these hills. He'll go home.'

'And if they catch him?'

He shrugged. 'They will eventually. Either on the hoof or at my house. He was an army horse before I bought him. He'll probably be happy to rejoin.'

But Ian wasn't happy. She could hear it in his voice.

She once more looked around the cave. The smell had an underlying musty scent. 'What is this place?'

His mouth tightened as if he preferred not to say. She stiffened her spine against the hurt of his distrust. 'It was an illegal whisky still.'

He had trusted her after all. Something inside her softened. She sat down on the stool, looking up at him. 'How did you know it was here?'

He grinned, his teeth flashing white in the gloom. 'Just brimming with questions, aren't you, Lady Selina?'

'How do you know the soldiers don't know about this place?'

'No one does.' He crouched down and poked around in the fire. 'It hasn't been used in years. It was my father's.'

No wonder he hadn't wanted to say where they were headed. In a strange way she felt honoured.

'Is your arm really all right?'

'It stings like the blazes.'

She winced. 'You could have been killed.' Or she might.

'Aye.' He picked up the saddlebag and sorted through it, setting out its contents on the floor. 'Flint. A couple of candles. Oats. Bannocks wrapped in cloth. A flask.' He shook it and something gurgled inside it.

'What is it, water?'

He opened the stopper and sniffed. 'Something better. Whisky.'

She huffed out a breath. 'Water would be better.'

He chuckled and the sound was warm and low and easy. 'There's clean water in the burn, lass.'

'So now we just sit here and wait for morning,' she said with a sigh. 'Do you have somewhere we can go next?'

'I've a friend to the south and east of here. Captain Hugh Monro. He has contacts. He might lend us a horse. Or even a cart.' He looked at her. 'The thing is, I am just not sure he would see my side of it. He's a law-abiding man. I doubt he'd approve of smuggling, no matter the reason behind it. And he is more than a day's walk away.'

More walking. And worrying about being shot at.

'We'll make ourselves as comfortable as we can tonight,' he said. 'When it gets dark, I'll fetch water from the stream. We will eat the bannock and we will soak the oats for the morning.'

'It sounds most appetising,' she murmured.

He cracked a laugh. 'A banquet.'

She rubbed her arms. The warmth she'd gained from walking and running had faded. Chill now seeped into her from the surrounding damp earth. In a while, it would be dark and much colder. 'Do you think we can light a fire?'

'If we hadn't been seen, I'd risk it, but they might come back once they catch Beau.'

They would have to make do without heat, then. They had one blanket between them. Sadly, the other had gone with the horse. Although he did have his kilt, which had dried over the course of the day.

'Why did your family abandon the still?'

He grimaced. 'The gaugers get wind of them and destroy them. See, the kettle's been split with a hammer.'

She stared at the odd-shaped stove. 'How does it work?'

'This metal kettle here is a wash still, and when it is heated up over the peat fire, the steam containing the alcohol passes up the chimney and then down the worm, the coiled pipe there, and into a spirit still. All that's left here is the first part of the process. Father used to prepare the mash in a local farmer's barn and then bring it up here to turn it into whisky. Good whisky, too. We've a dram or two left in our cellars.'

There was pride in his voice. Over illegal whisky. It was a world in which she was a foreigner. The thought made her feel rather dismal.

'We should eat now, while we can still see.' He glanced upwards and she became aware of just how much the light had faded.

He unwrapped the bannocks and handed her one. They were surprisingly tasty. Or was she so hungry that anything would have tasted good? There were six altogether. She ate two. When he had wolfed down three of them he eyed the one remaining. 'Do you want it?'

'Oh, no,' she said lightly. 'I couldn't eat another bite. You finish it.'

He didn't speak.

She looked up to see him watching her. It was hard to fathom his expression, his eyes looked so dark. 'Is something wrong?'

'Why do you do that?'

'Do what?'

'Lie to me in that stupid little voice. Eat the bannock.'

She flashed hot. 'You need it more than I do.'

'Right, and I am the kind of man who takes the food out of the mouths of women and children.' He stood up and bent to rake around in the rubbish in the corner. A grunt of satisfaction told her he'd found what he was looking for. When he stood up, she saw he had an old and bent metal pot in his hand. She couldn't understand why he looked so pleased.

He must have sensed her puzzlement. 'I recall using it the last time I was here. If it had been gone, we would have had to use the flask for water.'

'And thrown out the whisky,' she said.

'Never.'

'You'd rather do without water, than waste the whisky. I should have guessed.'

'*Uisge-beatha*, lass. The water of life.'

She watched him leave, a smile on her lips, then tackled the last of the bannocks.

Chapter Nine

By the time he returned with water, their dwelling was pitch black and a chill permeated the air. Perched on the stool, wrapped in her blanket, she really wished they could light a fire. She forced her teeth not to chatter, though stilling her shivers was harder.

The sound of Ian's breathing filled the small space. She sensed him fumble around, heard the clang of metal on rock and guessed he'd set down the pan of water. 'I'd forgotten how dark the night can be out here,' he muttered.

And how cold, she wanted to add. She shivered. 'Are you sure we can't light a fire?'

He hesitated, then sighed. 'It would be a mistake. I think we can light one of the candles, though. Its flame is too small to be seen at any great distance.'

The sound of steel striking against flint only made her think more of warm fires. Yet when the wick caught and the small light flared, putting shadows in the corners of their small den, it did seem a bit warmer.

Then she noticed his grimace and the way he flexed his left hand.

She got up from the stool. It was a rickety old thing and did not sit flat on the ground, but it was all they had. 'Sit down and let me look at your arm.'

'Getting a little bossy, aren't you?'

'Sit.'

He sat.

She took a deep breath. 'Perhaps you should take off your jacket, so we can see how bad the wound really is. It won't help us if you become ill.'

'Aye, I suppose you are right.'

'I wish we had some basilica powders.'

Looking surprised, he eased first one arm out of his coat and then, wincing, drew it slowly off the other arm. The fabric was dark with blood.

She gasped. Her stomach rolled. The blood seemed to drain from her head and the small space spun around. His coat had hidden the extent of the wound.

'Oh, Ian,' she whispered, 'you need a doctor.'

'It is not as bad as it looks,' he said through gritted teeth as he pulled the fabric away from the wound. He cursed softly.

Throat dry, she swallowed. 'We should clean it.'

Looking up, he raised a brow. His eyes gleamed with amusement. 'We?'

She took a deep steadying breath. 'Me, then. Look, it is bleeding again. Take off your shirt.'

Now he really looked surprised. 'All right.' He fumbled at his collar with his good hand.

She brushed his hand away. 'Let me.' Standing this close to him, with the light coming down from above making every sinew and bone as sharp and clear as a portrait as each breath expanded and contracted his chest, she could feel his warmth against her skin. Unnerved, she felt her hands tremble. Indeed, her very bones shook with a force she couldn't quite grasp. When she breathed in to steady herself, it was like breathing in his air, his essence.

A shock jolted through her. How could that be?

It couldn't. She was being stupid, just as she had been as a girl. In real life, they stood on the opposite sides of a line drawn on a map.

She forced the inappropriate sensations aside. The man was hurt and patiently waiting without complaint with his chin raised for her to undo the darned knot.

It came free and she cast the cloth aside and went to work on the buttons. Undressing a man—never in her life had she done anything so daring.

The collar fell open with each button she freed from its mooring, slowly revealing the hollow of his strong throat, his collar bones, a wedge of chest lightly furred with dark crisp curls that brushed against her knuckles as she released the final fastening, enticing to her fingertips and her gaze.

Such feelings led in only one direction. Down a path that would do her no good.

She let her hands fall to her side and stepped back. She glanced up to find his gaze fixed on her face. Intense. Heated. He was breathing faster than before.

He also felt desire.

It hung between them, hot and heavy. Terrifying. With effort she made a small gesture with her hand. 'You should be able to take your shirt off now.'

The fire deep in the blue of his eyes flared, then died.

'Aye. I can do that.' He pulled the shirttails free and with his good arm pulled the shirt off over his head, unveiling the body of a Norse god she'd only dared to peek at in the sea cave.

The muscles of his arms were carved and hard,

his chest vast and sculpted beneath its smattering of hair. In the face of such magnificence, breathing was nearly out of the question.

But breathe she must. 'Hold out your arm.'

She knelt close to his knee. He held his arm steady with his other hand, bending his head to look at the wound.

Their foreheads collided.

A nervous giggle escaped her lips. Heat fired her face. The schoolgirl was back. She felt giddy, and not from the sight of his blood.

He grunted. 'It doesn't look too bad.'

'I can't see.'

He leaned sideways.

A nasty gash scored his arm. Bile rose in her throat.

She swallowed it down. 'You are right, it seems to be nothing more than a flesh wound.' She controlled a shudder. 'I will clean it and bind it.'

Blood from where he'd pulled the shirt free of his skin trickled down to his elbow. She grabbed up the flask. 'If I recall correctly, this is better than water for a wound.'

'A terrible waste, lass.'

'I'll save you a drop. Give me your knife.'

He eyed her aslant. 'Why?'

'Unless you have a nice clean handkerchief, I

need some cloth to pad the wound. We will use your stock to hold it in place.' She looked at his shirt. He'd need to put that on again, bloody sleeve or no. She lifted up her skirt and looked at the hem of her petticoats. The lace of the top one was in tatters after being soaked in seawater, straddling a horse and dragging through heather. Now it would serve to staunch the blood.

He pulled his dirk from his sock and handed it to her, hilt first.

She shook her head. 'I'll hold the fabric taut while you cut. I am sure you will do a better job than I.'

An eyebrow shot up and he looked at her rather oddly, but he bent to the task. It felt a little strange with his face so close to her legs, even though he must be able to see little more than her shoes, since there were two more layers of cloth beneath the first petticoat. Portuguese women adored petticoats.

He soon had a long strip cut from around the bottom.

'Cut it in two,' she said, 'and I'll use one piece as a rag for washing.'

A frown creased his forehead. 'Where did you learn such skill?'

'I wouldn't call it skill. I hate the sight of blood.

But my friend, Lady Hawkhurst, convinced me to volunteer at the hospital she funds for injured seamen. I read to them and roll bandages.' She soaked one of the rags with whisky.

'So you have no experience in binding wounds and such like?'

'None at all,' she said cheerfully, 'but I have seen it done.' No point in telling him she'd thrown up in the nearest chamberpot when she'd looked at the wrong moment. Instead, she gritted her teeth and dabbed the cloth at the ragged cut.

He hissed in a breath and she waited for a spewing of swear words.

He remained utterly silent.

Impressed, she continued dabbing. If he could put up with the pain, she could put up with the sight. Although if anything the dizziness of earlier was growing worse. She continued dabbing and wiping until all the dried blood was gone.

The wound looked nasty—ragged edges and fresh welling blood.

Black edged her vision. She felt herself sway. She squeezed her eyes shut, regaining her balance and fighting the sickness.

This wound was nowhere near as bad as the one to her own leg. One brief glimpse of that and she had passed out cold.

Jaw clenched, she tried to remember what Alice had said about the symptoms of spreading infection. Redness? Yellow pus? No sign of anything like that. Yet.

She looked away and drew a deep breath in through her nose. 'There is not much more I can do, except bind it.'

'I am glad to hear it,' he said wryly.

Her gaze flew to his face. His mouth was set in lines of pain. She'd been so busy trying not to pass out that she hadn't thought about how much she must be hurting him, because he hadn't made a sound.

Because he was strong and she was weak.

'Hold still,' she said gruffly. She placed the pad over the wound, then wrapped his neckcloth around it, tying it off with a knot.

He flexed his hand and she watched, fascinated by the way the muscle in his upper arm bulged against the bandage. He did it again. This time something happened to his chest; it seemed to grow firmer and develop more definition. It almost made her forget just how ill she felt, until her gaze fell on his torn and bloody shirt.

The room wavered in and out of focus. Her knees buckled and the shadows leaped out from the corners to take over the room. And she was falling.

'Selina?' he asked as though from a great way off.

A strong arm banded around her waist. It pulled her against something warm and hard. She collapsed against it, her stomach heaving as the candle refused to remain in one place.

'Selina.'

Ian. Ian had hold of her. She closed her eyes and waited for the horrible sensations to pass. Slowly she became aware that she was sitting on his knee, cradled within his arms. He was stroking her back. She opened her eyes and was glad to see that nothing was spinning.

'Feeling better?' he murmured, his voice low in her ear, the roll of his 'r' a sweet comforting sensation in the pit of her stomach. She always seemed to feel better when he had his arms around her. Too bad he couldn't keep them there.

'I'm such a coward,' she said, trying to sit up, but he held her against his chest and she realised he was rocking gently back and forth.

'No, you are not. You have been very brave. I promise everything will be all right,' he whispered. 'I'll get you safely to your friend and we will sort it all out.'

She half groaned, half laughed. 'I'm not worried about that. The sight of blood always makes me feel ill.'

His rocking ceased briefly, then continued. 'Then I am all the more grateful, lass.'

Oh, that wonderful deep velvety voice, so close to her ear. She was melting, burning up with a fever of longing and desire.

'You must think me completely useless.'

'You are braver than anyone I know, because you knew how it would affect you.'

But she hadn't been thinking. She'd acted on instinct. She never seemed to think straight around him.

A prickle of awareness made her look up at his face. A slight curve to his mouth and the twinkle in his eye caused her heart to clench.

She couldn't resist the temptation. She reached up and put her hands on his nape and kissed him full on the lips.

He groaned softly.

His lips parted against hers. His tongue traced the seam of her lips. It felt delicious. Her spine tingled, her hands cradled his head, feeling the soft curl of his hair between her fingers.

His hand came to her cheek, his fingers shaking with the power of this moment between them.

Never had her heart raced so fast or her body grown so warm with such a whisper of touch.

He was a big man, huge in comparison to her, and for him to tremble at the mere touch of her lips was heady indeed.

Many men had desired her over the years, lusted for her and declared their love, but they'd only ever seen what she wanted them to see. The perfect nobleman's daughter. The diamond of the first water. The impeccable manners. The flirtatious wit. This man knew her weaknesses, and yet he trembled.

The knowledge melted her bones.

She parted her lips and let him into her soul. The kiss wasn't all one-sided. Oh, no. Her tongue slid wantonly along his, tasting whisky and earthy man, while she inhaled the scent of horse and leather and fresh air tinged with peat smoke. Sensual sensations rippled through her body with every beat of her heart.

She arched against him, pressing her breasts against his hard wall of a chest, wound her arms around his neck and submitted to her hunger.

He growled deep in his throat, shifting beneath her, making her aware of the male part of him that pressed against her thigh through her layers of clothing.

She breathed his scent, revelled in his heat and

the feel of hard muscle and sinew beneath her exploring hands.

Breathing hard, he slowly pulled away, looking into her face. Could he see in her face the awe and wonder rioting through her body? Could he feel the heat burning in her belly, in her breasts, flowing through her veins?

Helpless with need, she gazed up, waiting.

'You'd tempt the devil himself, Lady Selina.'

She didn't want the devil. She wanted him. She gazed back at him with longing and desire and a sweet softness that made her insides feel open and yearning.

He reached around to catch her hands clinging around his neck and tore them free, holding them fast in his. 'This must stop,' he said harshly. He disengaged his hands from hers.

'Don't you want me?' she asked, feeling suddenly bereft, even knowing the question was unfair. She felt his desire, insistent, rampant against her bottom.

'Not want you?' he growled. His mouth descended in a punishing kiss, full of ardour and passion and heat. Her mind refused to form a single thought. Her hands, freed from his grip, wandered his broad sculpted chest and floated over his back, measuring the width and strength of him.

Lacking air, they slowly parted, their chests rising and falling in perfect harmony as he nibbled and licked at her lips, her chin, her jaw. He teased the tender place beneath her ear, breathing against her neck. 'I want you. But if we do this now there will be no going back. We will have to be married.'

The words were like a splash of cold water. Have to be married? Clearly it was not something he wanted, any more than she did. Did she?

He groaned and rose to his feet with her still in his arms. He set her back on the stool, wrapped the blanket around her and cleared the opening to the outside.

'Where are you going?' To her chagrin, panic edged her voice.

'I'll be right back.'

'That wasn't an answer,' she said. Too late. He was gone.

Shame at her cowardice roiled in her stomach. Why would he abandon her here? It didn't make any sense, but the fear was real enough. The fear of being left as her father had abandoned her the year he'd brought her to Dunross. For years, she'd worried that he would forget about her again, when she was at school, when he was away on business. Even now, when she knew the reason why, she hated knowing that people important to you could just walk away. It was better if you did not allow them to become important, then you didn't have to worry.

And Ian hadn't left. He sounded as if he was searching through the heather. Hunting?

Then he was back, pushing something ahead of him. The smell of fresh-cut vegetation filled the cave. Fuel for a fire?

But, no, he didn't go to the hearth. He spread it out in the corner. 'Give me your blanket,' he said.

'Why?' The thought of losing even the little amount of warmth it provided was unwelcome.

'We need it to make a bed.'

'A bed?'

'Aye. We can't sleep sitting up. The heather is springy enough that it will do us for one night. With a blanket beneath us and my kilt for a quilt, we'll be warmer than toast. Drew and I did it all the time as lads.'

A bed. With him, and after her wanton behaviour? She blushed from head to toe. Now was really the time she should object. Somehow the words wouldn't form. She stood up and handed him the blanket. He laid it across the shrubbery.

'Lay yourself down,' he said. His voice was grim and when she peeped at his face, she saw his mouth was set in a stern line.

What was the matter with him? She settled herself down on one side of the makeshift bed, looking up at him.

His hands went to his belt, then glanced at her. He picked up his shirt and drew it over his head. 'Close your eyes.'

'A bit late for modesty, isn't it?' she asked, stifling the urge to giggle.

He turned away, uttering a sound between a curse and a laugh of his own.

A huff of his breath blew out the candle and a moment or two later came the sound of him unfastening his belt. Her unruly mind travelled right back to the scene in the cave, him standing there dressing. Now he was undressing. She didn't need a candle to see.

Cursing silently, she tried not to envisage what was taking place.

A moment later, she felt his warmth along her side and the weight of the thick wool of his kilt settle onto her body. It retained some of his warmth.

She'd slept on softer mattresses, been covered by finer linens, but given her state of exhaustion she could not say that any had felt better than this bed of heather.

'Thank you,' she said.

'You are welcome.'

She shivered.

Ian's arm came around her shoulders and he pulled her towards him, tucking her against him so her head rested on his chest. Instantly, she felt warmed by his heat, by the feel of his hand on her waist. But more than that, she felt safe. Protected.

It felt wonderful.

She snuggled closer. 'Body heat,' she said, laughing softly, feeling wicked and a little giddy suddenly from lack of breath. 'Goodnight,' she breathed and tipped her face up to kiss his cheek. At least she was sure that was what she had intended, but she found his mouth instead.

He kissed her back, long and deep until her senses swam. He rolled her on her back, plundering her mouth with his tongue, gently cupping her breast, tenderly pressing her legs open with his firm thigh.

She moaned as her feminine centre responded to the pressure. Her hips arched upwards as she accepted Ian's deepening kiss.

Suddenly, he jerked away as if stung and uttered a curse. He rolled away from her and she could hear the sound of his ragged breathing in the dark.

'Ian,' she said tentatively.

'Go to sleep, little *Sassenach*. I'll no be touching you and you'll no be touching me. Are we agreed?'

It seemed that what to her had been a moment of bliss to him had been…well, something inconvenient.

He lay perfectly still beside her, slowing his breathing, pretending to be asleep, no doubt. Unbelievable. She was lying next to a nearly naked man, out in the wilds of Scotland, a man she found hugely attractive and who had just kissed her senseless, and he was acting as if he was her brother.

Perhaps the idea of making love to a cripple was more than he could stand. It was hard to blame him if that was the case. She had to admit the scars were pretty ugly and the limp was far from alluring. She was lucky Dunstan had been willing to overlook her flaws. Her stomach sank. Dunstan had done it for the money. He was also a nice man. Kind. Sweet.

A thought, crystal clear and dreadful, came out of nowhere. For the first time since they'd left the keep, her mind seemed sharp.

She shoved at his shoulder.

'What now, lass?' he mumbled as if he was really asleep.

'My father will guess I have gone to Alice. I always do.'

'So?' Ah, now he sounded more awake.

'What if he gets to her first?'
'What if he does?'
'Then the alibi won't work.'

Chapter Ten

The next morning, they turned south. As she strode along beside him, she noticed that her leg barely ached at all. The doctors were right—walking was good for her, though they had not envisaged her tramping through the heather for days. Even so, she needed all her concentration not to trip over the clumps of heather and rocky outcroppings.

While they walked, Ian continually scanned the hills, ahead and behind, especially before they crested each hill. Each time he signalled for her to duck down, her heart rose in her throat. He was clearly intending not to be surprised as they had been the day before.

The next hill they crossed brought them to a valley so small it was more like a crevasse. A cottage snuggled against its craggy cliff. A tiny croft with a peat-covered roof neatly held down with a spiderweb of ropes weighted with boulders. Two people conversed outside the front door, an old crone and a ragged child with a basket over her arm. Rust-coloured chickens were picking about in the dirt at their feet.

'Let's hope Grannie has a stew pot over the fire,' Ian said. 'And whisky on her table.'

Selina's stomach growled at the thought of hot food. She quickened her pace.

Ian stayed her with a touch to her arm. 'Wait here. I'll make sure things are what they seem.'

Whereas she would have charged in and devil take the hindmost. It was a good thing one of them had some sense. Sighing with relief at the chance to rest, she sank down on a rock and watched him stride down the hill.

Such a braw laddie he looked in the sunlight. Her heart lifted at the sight of his broad shoulders and the way his kilt revealed his strong calves and manly knees. He looked at home and very much in command.

The chickens scattered with clucks and squawks at his arrival. The old lady shielded her eyes from the sun. The girl stared up at him with awe.

The old woman beamed, obviously recognising him. She might have been welcoming the Prince

Regent, so effusive was she as she gestured for him to enter, bridling like a girl in her eagerness.

The child curtsied.

The charming smile on Ian's face would make any female bridle. He looked so handsome when he smiled. He glanced in her direction, indicating he had a companion. Once more the woman put a hand up to shield her face. In an instant, her demeanour changed. She waved her arm first in one direction, then in another. An argument seemed to ensue. Selina could hear the old woman's raised voice, but not the words. She ended her diatribe, waving an admonishing finger in his face.

The child fled.

How very odd. Highlanders were known for their courtesy, especially to travellers, even if it was only a dram of whisky and an oatcake to see them on their way.

To her surprise, the woman disappeared inside the croft and slammed the door. The sound reverberated off the rocks and crags and faded in ever-quieter echoes.

Ian stomped back towards her. As he drew closer, she could see the glower of anger on his face and behind it worry.

She pushed herself to her feet. 'What happened?'

His mouth flattened to a thin line. 'The soldiers were here.'

Her heart picked up speed. 'Looking for us?'

'Aye. She sent them off with a flea in their ear.'

'I thought she was going to let you in.'

'Aye.'

'Then she realised I was with you.' The rejection stung.

'I told her you were my cousin, but, given what the soldiers told her, she refused to believe it.'

'And because I am an Albright she doesn't feel the need to offer hospitality.'

'Her son was transported for poaching on your father's land.'

'Oh, dear.'

'Her son was one of the lucky ones. Tearny shoots first usually.'

Tearny was the land agent. 'Not on my father's orders, I can assure you.'

He shrugged. 'Be that as it may, we have no choice but to go on.'

She glared at him. 'If Mr Tearny is shooting people on Albright land, he will be punished.'

He cocked his head on one side. 'All right. You will speak to your father. Let us leave it at that. We will walk many a mile before we find another house where we can request food.'

'And no doubt they will turn us away, too.'

'Not everyone is as bitter as Grannie.'

Hopefully not, or it would be a long hungry walk to the mail coach.

He looked off into the distance. 'I think I will speak to Niall before we go too much farther. Find out what the soldiers are doing. I may have to go to Dunross myself.'

A feeling of panic ran down her spine. 'You can't leave me out here.'

'Laird.' The high-pitched voice came from behind them. 'Laird.'

Ian glanced back.

Selina turned right around. It was the girl who'd been at the old lady's door, hurrying after them, her basket held out to the side as if she feared whatever was in it would break.

'Wait,' Selina said to Ian, who seemed inclined to keep walking. 'Don't make her run.'

The girl arrived, bright-eyed and panting. Russet curls escaped from beneath the ragged shawl she had pulled over her head and her dark green eyes darted over Ian and Selina in several wide-eyed passes. Her cheeks flushed scarlet.

'Well,' Ian said when she didn't speak, 'what do you want, Marie Flora McKinly?'

'Ian, you will scare her. Give her a chance to catch her breath.'

Still the girl didn't speak. She curled her toes around a stem of heather, watching her foot, peeping up at Ian as if he was some sort of ogre.

Ian said something in Gaelic in a gentler tone.

The child took a deep breath and gabbled away for a minute or two.

He shook his head at the child and again spoke in Gaelic.

The child's chin went up. Her eyes flashed.

'What have you said?' Selina said. 'Why is she angry?'

Ian muttered a curse. 'She's offering us food at her father's house a couple of miles from here. I don't want to put them in danger.'

'There's only Da, miss,' the child said in a lovely Scottish brogue. 'And me and my two brothers. My Da would never forgive me if you didna' take a dram with him, Laird. He's been dying for some company and news for weeks. We've food in the larder.'

Selina looked at Ian. The child looked at Ian. The frustration on his face was evident. Not only did his people have a duty to him, not to accept an offer of hospitality would be an insult.

'Very well. We'll visit with your Da for an hour or two and then be on our way.'

Marie Flora gave a pleased little hop and a skip. 'This way.'

She started up a hill that seemed steeper than all of the others they'd come across. Instead of heading south, she was going west.

Selina took one look at the miniature mountain and groaned.

'Do you think you can make it?' Ian murmured and took her arm to help her. 'It might be better if we didn't use your last name with these folks.'

'Doesn't she know it?' She indicated the child.

'Grannie McLeod guessed immediately, but didn't speak your name. And nor did I.'

'McLeod. I remember her, now. She used to live in the village.'

'Aye, until a year ago when she didna' pay her rent and was evicted. That was her son's place. When her son was shipped off, she cursed the Albright name all seven ways to Inverness.'

She flinched. 'I'm not surprised she was angry.'

'She's an evil auld woman. She cursed the factor, too,' Ian said. 'He came down with an enormous boil on the end of his nose the day after he barred her door.'

He was teasing her. Had to be. 'Served him right.'

''Tis no laughing matter. She cursed auld Willie McLaughlin and he died within the week.'

A year ago was when she had had her accident. The thought of the old crone's curse being responsible sent prickles racing across her shoulders. 'Superstitious nonsense.' Yet she shivered.

'Believe what you will, my lady.'

She huffed out a breath. Now he'd gone all stiff and starchy again. She glanced up ahead and saw they'd reached the top of the rise. Her aching calves and thighs were looking forward to a downhill incline.

In the valley below them, a croft sat beside a small burn, longer and lower than the one they'd just left and as small as a doll's house. They had a good distance yet to go and Marie Flora was waving at them impatiently.

Worry consumed Ian. Its cold breath licked at his brain, at his gut, deep in his chest.

You abducted Albright's daughter, Grannie had said, repeating what the soldiers had said. *Are you mad? He'll hang ye and anyone helping you.* The old witch had shut the door in his face. A face that probably looked guilty, because while he hadn't abducted her, he had spent the night with her in his arms. And he would have liked to do a hell of a lot more than that, after their kiss.

The force of what he had felt for this *Sassenach* girl was quite different to anything he'd ever experienced in his life—and he and Drew had sampled their share of females in their wild youth. Women far more experienced in tempting a man than Lady Selina. Hell, he'd even considered marriage to a warm comfortable widow he'd been seeing for years, until Selina's letter had arrived and turned his life upside down.

Thank God, he'd had enough control not to ruin her last night.

But she was ruined. Somehow the soldiers knew Lady Selina was with him. Or they suspected it, anyway.

The only way to avoid it was to marry her. Acknowledging the truth was like taking a fist to the gut. He didn't want to think about it.

The very idea left his head spinning. He couldn't afford a wife, certainly not one of her calibre, a woman used to nothing but the best. And Albright's daughter, to boot. But he was beginning to feel as if there might be no other option, just as Angus had suggested.

The cottage at the bottom of the glen drew ever

closer. William McKinly was a proud, stiff-necked man. If he would take payment for their lodging instead of seeing it as charity, Ian wouldn't feel so bad about accepting food and drink. But he wouldn't and that was that.

Before he realised what she was about, Selina left his side and cut across the side of the hill, heading for a burn. Cursing, he followed, watching as she stood on the bank, looking down at the water. What the hell was she about now?

Did she have any idea how delicious she looked in her wild gypsy skirts, with her dark hair hanging in a tangled mane down her back? She looked like a lass well bedded, that's what she looked like. Even if she wasn't.

The constant arousal that he'd been dealing with since she'd kissed him of her own free will and a night spent curled around the softness of her curves, her scent filling his nostrils, hardened to rock.

He wanted to reach out and pull her into his arms, kiss those lovely lips and plunge into her heat. Know her, the way a man wants to really know a woman. And if he was honest, it seemed it might be only a matter of time before he gave in to the torment of lust.

Well—apparently he'd made the decision. He could only imagine what she was going to say.

'Don't fall in,' he said, reaching her side.

She gave him a mock glare. 'I'm not that clumsy.'

She wasn't clumsy at all. She was graceful, even with the small hesitation in her step that appeared when she was tired. Small and delicate like a wee faery. And all he could think about was getting her in his bed. And there was only one way to accomplish it. Marriage.

It seemed that the seed planted by McIver had taken root.

He watched her balance on a rock, crouch and scoop the water in her cupped palms, sipping delicately as water trickled through her fingers. A sylph who had used her magic to capture him. She shook her hands, wiped them on her skirts before jumping clear.

This was the way he'd remembered her as a girl. A free spirit wandering the hills. Sneaking out of the keep to meet him day after day until he'd been thoroughly enchanted. But she wasn't a sprite. She was the daughter of a powerful man. His enemy. And if the man had hated his family before, this was going to make things worse.

She looked over. Caught his gaze and smiled. 'It tastes lovely.'

Hellfire and brimstone, he'd been staring like some besotted calfling. 'If you are done, we'll get along or McKinly will think we are no coming at all.'

He hadn't meant to growl, but it was better than grinning at her like an idiot.

The smile left her lips. She climbed up the shallow bank. He turned and walked down the hill, leaving her to make her way as best as she could. It was either that or take her in his arms and kiss her senseless.

Tonight. He'd reveal her fate tonight, after dinner.

Marriage to a *Sassenach*. And an Albright to boot. What the devil would his mother say? And the clan? Damn them all, if they didn't like it, they would have to put up with it. He was their Laird. They would abide by his decision.

Marie Flora and her father were waiting at the croft door, where the heather had been beaten back by soft springy grass. A small vegetable patch behind the cottage was bare of all but a few turnips.

'McKinly,' he said, holding out his hand as he neared the man's threshold. For once, Selina hung back. Afraid of her reception, no doubt.

'Laird,' McKinly said. His hair was copper-coloured. Darker than his daughter's and shot through with silver. The man was stooped and weathered and could have been anywhere from forty to sixty years old, but Ian knew him to be in his late thirties. Crofting in the Highlands aged a man early.

'Are you well?' he asked.

'Aye. Come in. Come in. Take a dram with me. The lass says you're in need of sustenance.' His gaze went to Selina, curiosity shining in his blue eyes.

'Aye, if you can spare it. My wife here is bone weary.'

Wife. The moment he saw McKinly's measuring stare he realised there was no honourable alternative. Having said it, he had a sense of accomplishment. She'd got herself into this mess trying to help him for friendship's sake, or out of some misguided sense of obligation, and a Gilvry always paid his debts. They didn't ruin innocent females, either.

He'd bring the clan round to his way of thinking. Indeed, it was none of their business whom he took to wife. They'd accepted his decisions up to now and they would damned well accept this one. His mother and brothers would be a different matter and so would her father. It was customary to ask a father for his daughter's hand, but it wasn't as if Albright could refuse. Not under the circumstances.

Marriage to Selina wouldn't be such a bad thing. He definitely wanted her in his bed more than any other woman he'd ever met. He'd been aching from the denial all night. And he had no doubt that she wanted him, too. It was a starting place and surely not such a bad one.

Aware of Selina's sharp stare and her prodding finger in his ribs, he glanced down into her upturned face. 'Isn't that right, my sweet?' The thought she might deny his words burned a path through his gut.

'So you are married, then?' McKinly said.

Ian looked at Selina, warning her with his gaze.

'Yes,' she said finally. 'We are married.'

And that was that. Guilt churned in his gut that he'd not discussed this with her, but there would be time enough later.

She smiled at their host. 'I am sorry to be such an imposition, Mr McKinly. We appreciate that you were not expecting us and would not wish to put you to any trouble.'

Politeness itself and no brittle society manners, no breathy little-girl voice, just a calm friendly manner with a touch of a lilt to her voice. He let go a sigh of relief.

McKinly grinned. 'Welcome, lady.'

His last-minute instinct had been right. As his

wife, she lost her status as *Sassenach*. Stranger. As his wife, any discourtesy to her was discourtesy to him.

A boy of about six wiggled his head between his father's legs. 'Is that the Laird, Da?' He turned his face upwards to look at Ian. 'Is it?' The child spoke the Gaelic.

'Oh,' Selina said. 'And who are you?'

'My youngest son, Tommy,' his father said, shaking his head at the impish face. 'Come away, lad. Let me pass. How is the Laird to get through the door with your head blocking my way?'

The head disappeared.

McKinly stepped aside and gestured for them to enter.

Ian bowed to Selina and waved her forwards.

'Thank you, Mr McKinly,' she said as she passed the man and stepped inside. 'I am honoured by your hospitality.'

He felt as proud as a barnyard cock as he followed her in. A peat fire smoked in a low stone hearth with a stew pot hung over it. The dwelling was poor, but it was clean. The small boy retreated to settle beside the fire and pulled a whittling knife from his pocket and a small piece of wood.

Ian watched the way Selina looked around the

croft, her face carefully blank, but he could imagine what she was thinking.

A pang of guilt twisted in his chest. This was not the kind of dwelling for a woman used to the luxuries of life, a woman brought up to live in the society of London. Married to him, her lot would be little better.

He would make it better.

'I am glad to see you well, McKinly,' he said in tones a little too hearty, but apparently McKinly noticed nothing wrong.

'You were lucky to catch me at home,' McKinly said as he poured drams into clay drinking cups. 'I was off to make hay in the next valley this afternoon.' He offered one to Selina. She smiled and shook her head. McKinly's eyebrow shot up, but he made no demur.

McKinly did not deserve to have his hospitality thrown back in his face. Ian's voice was harsh when he spoke. 'Take a dram with us, lady wife.'

Eyes wide, Selina looked ready to argue, then pressed her lips together as McKinly handed her the rejected cup and poured another for himself.

Selina shot Ian a look while the man's back was turned. No doubt he'd hear some words from her, but he was glad she decided to wait to get him alone before speaking her piece. She was a smart woman, no doubt about it.

'I'd no heard you were getting married, Laird?' McKinly said, his face full of curiosity. He shook his head. 'Though there's no reason why I should, I've seen no one for weeks. My congratulations to you.' He smiled albeit a little grimly. 'And to you, lady. Please be seated.'

Selina's smile as she took the wooden chair he offered was stiff. 'You are very kind, Mr McKinly.'

Marie Flora stood beside her, staring at her adoringly. Ian knew the feeling. Even here in these dreadful surroundings, and after a night spent in the worst of circumstances, she was lovely.

'To you and your bride,' McKinly toasted.

Ian tossed off his dram. Selina wet her lips and her eyes watered. At least she didn't cough and choke.

While McKinly turned to refill his and Ian's cups, Ian took hers and swallowed down the contents. She gave him a smile of gratitude and refused the refill offered by McKinly.

The man gestured for him to sit on the trestle at the table, his eyes sharp and bright. 'What brings our Laird wandering the hills on foot?'

'Gaugers,' Ian replied, seeing no reason to lie. All Highlanders despised the King's Revenue men.

McKinly frowned. 'You're a fool to be running afoul of them and you just married.'

'Aye.' Ian grinned. 'Needs must.'

'You'll be wanting a room for a night or two, perhaps?' McKinly said.

'At least one night, if you can spare it. A corner by the fire or in the byre.'

McKinly looked shocked. 'Certainly not.'

Selina looked doubtful. 'We should really be moving on.'

Ian shook his head. 'Not until we know how things stand at Dunross.'

She looked ready to argue, then shrugged. 'Then thank you, Mr McKinly.

'Not at all,' the Scotsman said. He glanced at his daughter. 'Marie Flora, put fresh linens on the bed.

The child beamed. 'Yes, Da.'

Selina smiled at the child. 'Show me where it is and I will help you.'

The lass was doing her best not to shame him. Somehow she knew this was important. His heart seemed to grow too large for his chest, as if he really was a proud bridegroom. Well, he was, really, wasn't he?

He gave her a grin of approval. She raised a brow in reply and rose to follow the child.

'I'll see you at supper,' McKinly said, rising

to his feet. 'My older lad has already left for the fields. I was waiting for the girl to return with the eggs before joining him.'

'About that older boy of yours—I've an errand for him.'

'Oh, aye.'

'I need him to take a message to Niall.'

McKinly looked grim, but nodded his agreement.

Ian had a pretty good idea of the source of his worry. 'I'll take up his scythe while he's gone. It will do me good to get some exercise.'

McKinly's face split in a grin, clearly relieved. 'Well, now, there's always plenty to do around here.'

'Can I come, Da?' the boy sitting in the corner asked.

'No, Thomas,' his father replied. 'You have your own work to do. And I need you here to take care of the womenfolk.'

The boy's scrawny chest puffed up and then he returned to his work with the knife. Ian moved closer to see what he was working on, but the lad hunched over it. 'It's not finished.'

'Leave him, Laird. The lad is a mite odd about his carvings. Doesn't let anyone see them until they are done.' He raised his voice. 'Marie Flora?' The girl popped her head out of the adjoining room. 'We'll see you at suppertime. Be sure you have a good meal waiting.'

'Yes, Da.'

Selina appeared beside the child. Ian leaned in and kissed her lips and almost chuckled at her gasp of surprise. 'We'll talk later,' he murmured against her mouth. When he pulled away he saw a blush creep up her snowy cheeks.

Because he'd kissed her in public. He wanted to do it again.

'Yes,' she said, with a tight little smile. 'We will talk later.' That sounded like a threat.

She ducked back into the chamber.

Ian shrugged and followed McKinly outside. He would just have to find a way to make her see he was right.

What a wretch, Selina thought, staring at the four-poster bed crowding the small sleeping chamber off the kitchen. Beside the bed there was a chest in one corner and a faded and patched runner on the floor.

Lies had tripped off Ian's tongue as if he was the devil himself. She should have denied it all. But she couldn't. Not without shaming him in front of his people.

'Whose room is this?' she asked Marie Flora as the girl expertly twitched the blankets off the bed and piled them on the rug.

'It used to be Ma and Pa's room,' the girl said. 'Now I sleep here and he sleeps in the loft with the boys.'

'Oh, dear. We don't want to put you out of your bed.'

''Tis a privilege and an honour to serve the Laird.' The girl smiled shyly at Selina. 'And his new wife.'

Guilt twisted in her stomach. These people would be so angry if they knew who she was. Selina took the end of the sheet at the foot of the bed and Marie Flora took the end nearest the head and they pulled it free. The mattress had seen better days, but it was clearly the best they had and Selina was certainly not going to complain.

The child pulled out linen sheets from the chest, thin and patched here and there, but spotlessly clean. Together they made up the bed. When they were done, Marie Flora patted the blanket with a smile. ''Tis a comfortable bed. Not many has one like it. Father built it when he was first married. Ma died when Thomas was born.'

'I'm sorry,' Selina said.

The girl shrugged. 'We buried her up on the top

of the hill. She liked to go up there and look at the mountains.'

There was a little sorrow in the girl's voice, but mostly acceptance.

'How many children are you altogether?'

'Four. My older brother is away south to the mines, he sends money when he can.' Marie Flora headed back into the main room and Selina followed her.

'What else can I do to help?' Selina asked.

'Can you peel tatties? We've to make the stew go further.'

'Tatties? Oh, you mean potatoes.' It was a long time since she'd heard that word used. Not since she used to hang around the kitchen at Dunross, getting under Cook's feet. 'Yes, I am sure I can.' How hard could it be?

Chapter Eleven

Marie Flora stumped in with a bucket of water and a frown on her face. 'Thomas, are you still here? Did Father not ask you to move the cow to the other pasture?'

The boy shoved his whittling in his pocket and left without a word.

'He's such a dreamer,' Marie Flora said. She put the bucket between them and went to a bin in the corner where she gathered an apron full of potatoes and put them beside the bucket. She handed Selina a knife. ''Tis sharp. Mind you do not cut yourself.'

Quite the little mother and not at all shy any more. Selina couldn't help but smile. She watched the child peel her first tatty and then began to work on her own.

'Not sae deep,' the girl said sharply.

Selina looked up.

'You are cutting too much of the flesh,' Marie Flora said. 'There'll be nothing left. Watch.'

Clearly if she didn't get this right her worth was going to go down in this young lady's eyes. She watched closely, saw how she rested her thumb against the vegetable and skimmed the skin away.

She tried again. This time she did better and the child nodded her satisfaction. She grinned to herself. This was nice, sitting here working on something useful with a companion, instead of setting fine stitches within an embroidery hoop on a piece of cloth only fit to adorn something that was already beautiful enough.

'Dig the eyes out like this,' Marie Flora said, showing her how she twirled the point of the knife in the little brown indentations. She put her finished potato in the bowl and washed another one before starting in on it with her knife.

Selina finished her first one by the time Marie Flora had done three, but she elicited no more criticism so she assumed she was doing it right, if slowly.

Thomas wandered in with a wooden bucket full of creamy milk. It sloshed over the side when he closed the door. His sister muttered something in Gaelic and leapt to her feet. The boy went bright red. She snatched the bucket from his hand, all the while scolding. The boy shot Selina a considering glance.

'Don't you have any Gaelic at all?' he asked.

'Not really.' She knew a few curse words, but it would be better not to say those. She would save them for Ian when he returned.

Married, indeed. At least he could have warned her. And now they were to share that bed in there. Her traitorous body tightened at the thought and she flushed warm all over. But it would be just like last night, she reminded herself. They would sleep. Nothing more.

The potatoes were finished and her hands were red, raw and numb from the cold water. This would be the kind of thing she would have to learn if they really were married. It would be a very different life. And fraught with danger, no doubt. A trickle of excitement flowed through her.

Marie Flora handed her a towel and turned to her brother. 'Thomas, take these peels outside, then take yourself off and cut some peat for the fire.'

Thomas picked up the bucket and heaved it out of the door. 'I'll add just these tatties to the stew and then we'll make bannocks,' Marie Flora said.

'You'll have to teach me that, too.'

'The Laird's wife doesn't know how to make bannocks?'

She winced. 'I'm afraid not.'

'Oh, aye, you'll be living in that grand house in the village. Da took me there once to sell—' She clapped a hand to her mouth.

She rushed off and busied herself at the table, cutting up the potatoes and adding them to the pot over the fire, which was already giving off a delicious aroma.

First Marie Flora put a large flat rock on top of the fire. 'The bannock stane,' she said at Selina's surprised expression. 'We don't have a *girdle*.' She meant a griddle, Selina guessed. The girl then put out flour in a bowl and mixed it with water. After turning it into a flat round bread, she carefully put it on the hot stone. 'It won't take long.'

Selina's stomach grumbled loudly.

The girl looked at her in astonishment. 'Are you hungry?'

It was then that Selina realised that she had eaten nothing since dinner time the night before, apart from a handful of oats this morning. How could she ask for food when these people had so little?

'A glass of water is all I need,' she said, taking a mug from the shelf on the wall and pouring a glass from the pitcher on the table. It would hold her until supper. Unless by some wonderful chance of fortune they ate at midday.

Marie Flora finished cleaning up from her baking and Selina smiled at her. 'What next?'

'I have some darning if you've a mind to help me. With Da and two boys there's always a muckle of mending to be done.'

Selina laughed. 'Well, that is one thing I know I can do.'

Marie Flora pulled out a basket full of what looked like rags, but as she held them up Selina saw they were rough homespun shirts and hose that had been patched and darned more than once. Immediately, she settled herself down to make the necessary repairs and while she worked she asked Marie Flora to teach her the Gaelic words for the things around them. The time flew by.

Selina didn't remember a time when she had felt more at ease within herself or had spent so pleasant an afternoon. She was still wondering at the strange feeling of contentment when a noise outside had Marie Flora leaping to her feet. ''Tis Father home for his dinner.'

She packed her sewing in the basket and took the shirt from Selina, who had just finished turning the cuff, and began setting the table.

Selina went to the window and saw a man dismounting from a horse.

Not in uniform, but still her heart began to race. Was it someone looking for her and Ian? What should she do?

'Marie Flora, it is not your father.'

The child left what she was doing and came to the window. She frowned. 'Why, it is Mr Tearny, the rent man. It is not his day to come.'

Tearny. An employee of her father's. Was it co-incidence he was here?

'The Laird and I do not want anyone to know where we are,' she said quickly.

The girl's face asked why.

'Please, Marie Flora, do not mention you have seen us.' She slipped into the bedroom listening as the girl answered the knock on the door, hearing the rumble of the man's voice, but not clearly enough to make out the words.

Her heart banged against her ribs. Her body vibrated with the force of its beating and all the while she was torn as to whether she should simply go out there and ask him to take her home.

Leave Ian without a word of farewell?

She couldn't. It would be wrong. Besides, she had no idea what sort of welcome awaited her there. She might be thrown in prison as a smuggler.

The moment Marie Flora closed the outside door Selina stepped out of the bedroom. The child's face was white; she looked ready to faint. She held a paper in her hand as if she feared it would bite.

'What is it?'

She raised her gaze and Selina saw tears standing in her moss-green eyes. 'I have not opened it. It is addressed to Pa, but Tearny said it is a notice to leave.' She held the paper out and Selina saw the Albright seal.

'Why?'

'We havena' paid our rent this quarter. Da needed a bit more time.'

Her stomach sank. What was Father about? It was wrong to throw families out of their homes. He might be ambitious, but she had never thought him cruel.

Sounds of voices outside sent Selina skipping back into the bedroom and Marie Flora running to the window.

'It is all right,' Marie Flora called out. ''Tis Father and the Laird washing up for dinner at the stream.'

Selina closed her eyes with relief, but the heartache remained. It was wrong to turn out this family.

His hair damp, his shirt wet and clinging to his broad shoulders from where he had bathed, Ian looked weary, but also mouth-wateringly attractive. Selina had trouble forcing herself not to stare.

She'd been running into this problem from the moment she had seen him at Lord Carrick's drum. It was pathetic. Where Ian Gilvry was concerned, she was pathetic.

And now she had all her hopes pinned on him being able to help this small family.

''Tis a good day's work we did today, lass,' McKinly said, his weary face wreathed in a smile as his gaze rested on his daughter. 'The Laird did young Willy's share as well as his own.'

'That's good news, Father,' Marie Flora said. Her gaze dropped to the letter on the table.

'What's this, then?' he asked.

'Mr Tearny left it but a few moments ago. I am surprised you didn't see him.'

All the joy went out of the room and the shadows in the corner seemed to encroach as McKinly picked up the paper. His gaze went to Ian, who gave a single regretful shake of his head.

Young Thomas barrelled in. 'Pa,' he yelled, 'there are soldiers riding in the glen.'

'Ah, saints give me strength. Not so soon.' He ripped open the paper. He stared at it, his lips moving as he read the words.

Ian's shoulders tensed. He looked as if he wanted

to snatch the paper and read it for himself. Instead he went to the window and looked out. 'How far away are these men?' he asked Thomas.

'They were at Grannie's house.'

His father looked up sharply. 'You ijit, boy, I thought you meant they were coming here.'

The boy looked offended. 'They might come here next. They were asking Grannie if she'd seen any travellers in the past two days.'

Ian stiffened. 'What did she say?'

The lad gave a sly smile. 'She said the only thing strange within twenty miles was the boggert she'd seen last night wandering the hills to the north. They rode off in that direction.'

Ian relaxed. 'She's an evil old woman, but she's not a traitor.'

McKinly glanced down at the paper in his hand and then handed it to Ian. 'We have a week to come up with the back rent or we must pack up and go.' Hands flat on the table, he bowed his head, his eyes closed.

'I could—' Selina started.

Ian cut her off with a sharp chop of his hand and a glare.

'We will sell the cow and the calf,' McKinly said. 'I'll take it to market.'

'But, Father,' Marie Flora said, 'we need the milk.'

Her father let go a long breath. 'You are right, lass.' He looked at Ian. 'Will you buy my barley? It will soon be ready for harvest.'

Ian's jaw flickered. 'What about bread for your children.'

What on earth did he mean?

'Happen there'll be enough coppers left after Albright is paid off to buy bread.' He looked hopeful.

Selina felt sick. How could Father do this?

Young Thomas crouched beside the hearth, his face pale, his eyes scared. A weight descended on Selina's chest. She longed to offer comfort, to reassure this small family that everything would be all right, but she couldn't. She had given up any hope of influencing her father by warning the smugglers and then riding off with Ian. And if she hadn't, she would not have known any of this. But there must be something she could do.

McKinly glowered down at the paper. 'These notices have been going out for weeks to anyone behind in their rent. Will you buy my barley before I bring it in? Will you risk it?'

'Aye,' Ian said, nodding. 'It looks like a good

crop. Too bad we didn't know about this before your boy left, he could have brought the money back with him.'

'We have a week,' McKinly said. 'I look forward to seeing Tearny's face when I hand him the money.'

Ian held out his hand with a grin. 'It is a bargain. Tomorrow we'll work on clearing the other field of rocks, so you can plant more barley next year.'

McKinly turned to his daughter. 'See what it is to have a Laird who cares about his people, lass? Now, where is that dinner I am smelling? My guts are kissing my backbone, I'm that hungry.'

The sight of McKinly acting cheerful, when he must be feeling desperate, made Selina feel worse than ever. She could only be thankful he didn't know who she was. He would surely not be inviting the daughter of his landlord to sit down at his table.

The sense of being watched made her glance at Ian and she found his eyes fixed on her, his eyes narrow, his lips pressed together, as if he was holding back words, yet his gaze when it rested on her was hot.

An answering heat flared in her body.

'After dinner, we'll talk.' His deep voice held a promise.

* * *

Supper over and the children put to bed, Selina sat beside Ian on the settle with the obligatory dram of whisky in her hand. She took a cautious sip. This time it did not burn so much. Holding the cup between both hands in her lap, listening to the men chatting idly about the weather and crops, she could almost imagine living this way for ever. Preparing food for a husband and children and then sitting companionably in the evening talking about the day. It wouldn't be an easy life, but it would have purpose.

For the first time in a very long time she felt a sense of belonging. She sighed.

Ian's hand closed around hers. Startled, she glanced up at him.

'The glass was about to fall,' he said with a smile. 'You must be exhausted.'

It was a pleasant kind of exhaustion. Not the kind one experienced after a ball, when one's head pounded and one's feet ached from being trodden upon. It felt good. She nodded. 'I should go to bed.'

'A toast before you go,' McKinly said, filling his and Ian's glass. 'To the Laird and his bride. May you be blessed with many sons. *Slàinte!*'

The two men downed their drinks in one swallow. Selina took another sip.

McKinly refilled his and Ian's glasses. Selina held her hand over the top of hers. 'No more for me, thank you.'

Ian raised his glass. 'To my host. May your sons and daughter grow straight and true.'

McKinly looked pleased and the two men downed their whisky in unison.

Ian looked pointedly at her glass.

Oh, dash it. She tipped her glass and swallowed it down, sitting utterly still as the heat travelled down her throat into her belly and she tried not to gasp.

Both men laughed, but there was a pleased look in Ian's eyes, a warmth that heated far deeper than the spirit.

'It will help you sleep,' he said.

'Aye, and keep out the chill,' McKinly said. 'There's no fire in yon room, but there's privacy.'

'Go to bed, wife,' Ian said gently enough, but there was no mistaking the command.

She bristled.

He must have seen because he raised a dark brow. 'I've a few matters to discuss with McKinly, but I'll be there shortly. You will not be lonely for long, that I promise.'

Heat rushed to her face. He was making it sound as if, as if... Well, as if they really were man and wife.

She got up with a smile and sent a narrowed-eyed glance his way so he would be under no mis-apprehension that they would indeed talk. The grin he sent back was deliciously cheeky.

The man was impossible. And incredibly hand-some.

Still, he was only playing his part—besotted bridegroom—when the truth couldn't be more different.

Ian handed her a candlestick and escorted her to the bedroom door where he raised her hand to his lips.

'I'll be along soon,' he murmured, his voice offering a sensual promise. She didn't know if she wanted to slap him, or rise up on her toes and press a kiss to his smiling mouth. She whisked into the room before she did either and shut the door behind her, leaning against it.

She heard his deep chuckle before he moved away. The sound drifted around her like smoke, weakening her limbs, making her heart open with tendrils of hope.

No.

The world had turned upside down. Her heart was lying to her. Ian was a dangerous man. He thrived on adversity. All she wanted was a pleasant husband, a house in a good part of town and a comfortable life with the people she knew in the society where she belonged.

This tramping around Scotland was like Marie Antoinette pretending to be a milkmaid in the gardens of Versailles. It wasn't real. It wasn't her life as she had planned it.

The sooner they parted, the better it would be for her peace of mind.

Running from the keep had been madness. She could have handled her father's anger. And she would not have buckled under any amount of badgering. After all, who could possibly believe a feather-headed society miss would ever step out of the bounds of propriety to aid smugglers?

Father might suspect the worst after Lisbon, when she ran off without her chaperon, but suspicion wasn't proof. Clearly in hindsight, running away with Ian had been a mistake of monumental proportions.

Her only hope was to get to Alice before Father did. Hang waiting for word from Ian's brother Niall. They had to go and go quickly, first thing in the morning. They'd wasted too much time here already.

'That's a right pretty bride you've found yourself, Laird,' McKinly said, his deep voice carrying through the door. 'And a good lass from what I see, but delicate. 'Tis a shame about the limp. The Highlands is no place for the weak. You'll need to guard her well.'

'Aye,' Ian said, non-committally.

A burst of anger filled her veins. Whether it was because he made no attempt to deny her weakness, or because of the lies they were telling a man who had shown them nothing but respect, she wasn't quite sure. Either way it was only by clenching her fists that she managed not to open the door and tell them she could hear every word, thank you very much.

The voices reduced to a low rumble, probably moving on to other topics. There was no point in airing her grievances with Ian in front of one of his clan. She'd save her words for when they could be private.

She placed the candlestick on the table holding a ewer of water and a bowl and stripped out of her bodice, skirts and the breeches beneath, leaving on only her shift, washing herself quickly with the rag provided and clenching her jaw to stop her teeth from chattering as the cold water hit her skin. If Ian could wash in a cold stream out of doors, she could surely manage this, even if she was sure she could see her breath rise in front of her face.

She stripped the blanket off the bed and dumped

it on the small rug, then spread her cloak over the rough linen sheet before climbing in. Shivering beneath the thin covering, a sense of disappointment filled her. McKinly was right after all. She was not hardy enough for this life.

She watched the shadows from the candle dance on the rough ceiling and tried to stop the spasms of shivers by rubbing at her arms and legs to generate warmth.

Would her life ever return to normal? There would be no marriage, of course, no home or little Dunstan children, even if her visit to Alice was taken at face value. They'd all assume she'd jilted the young lieutenant. It would be the *on dit* in town for weeks. A man didn't suffer that kind of embarrassment lightly.

She'd have to start all over again, looking for the right kind of man for a husband. Strangely, the loss of Dunstan didn't bother her as much as she might have expected. Indeed, it was as if she'd been carrying an enormous weight and someone had lifted it from her shoulders.

Perhaps Dunstan hadn't been such a good choice after all. Perhaps she wouldn't marry anyone. The little bit of money left to her by her mother would allow her to live in independence, if not luxury.

She'd be an outcast. Considered odd. After she'd

spent all her time these past many years trying to fit in with society's expectations, too. All her hard work destroyed in a moment of madness. A moment of fear for a man she should have ignored altogether.

The voices on the other side of the door fell silent.

The door opened, the draught making the candle gutter. She sat up.

His gaze flicked down to her chest and back up to her face, his brows climbing.

Oh, right. She was wearing nothing but her shift. Heat flooded her face. She pulled the hem of her cloak up to her chin and opened her mouth to speak.

He pressed a finger to his lips and jerked his head towards the door, obviously not wanting McKinly to overhear their words. He closed the door and stared down at the blanket on the floor and then over at her.

She could not read his expression. 'We must talk,' she whispered.

He strode to the bed. He looked big in the dim light. Huge. In some way, he reminded her of a predator stalking its prey. In another, of a male standing guard over his female. In either case, it was imagination playing tricks. He no doubt regretted their wild flight as much as she did.

The thought made her feel hollow.

Ian sat on the edge of the bed. The ropes creaked and her body tilted towards him as if it sought the comfort of his heat and his strength. She resisted the pull, leaning away, gripping the fabric in her hands more tightly.

'I thought you'd be asleep by now,' he said softly. 'But here you are, waiting up for me.'

She gasped at the audacity of his words even as her insides melted.

He looked so beautiful, rugged, the haze of stubble darkening his jaw, his full lips curling in a half-smile that teased.

She drew in a quick steadying breath, determined to resist his allure. 'Why on earth did you tell McKinly we were married? I thought we were going to give a false name. Tell him I was your cousin.'

'He knows all my cousins. It was better than telling him you were my—' He shut his mouth with a snap.

'Your mistress?'

'That is one word for it.'

'He won't be pleased when he learns who I am and that we are not married. I feel bad about lying.'

His mouth tightened. 'We do have to talk about that.'

'We can't stay here. We must leave first thing in the morning. We have to reach Hawkhurst as quickly as possible.'

'We will wait to hear from Niall.' He touched a finger to her cheek. 'I was proud of the way ye helped the young lass there with the meal.'

A warm glow suffused her skin. Furious at herself, at the way she responded to this man, she jerked her head away. 'I did what anyone would do. Ian, listen, if I am to salvage anything of my reputation, I must get to Hawkhurst soon.'

His eyes turned hot. 'Your eyes are beautiful when you are passionate.' His low whisper strummed chords low in her belly.

A breath caught in her throat. Her heart stumbled. The glow turned to fire and she saw the answering blaze of heat in his face. And then his mouth was on hers and she was surrendering to the delicious sensations of the warm slide of his tongue, the feel of his large solid body under her hands.

Swept away by the passion he seemed to arouse in her so easily, she kissed him back. Whisky. She should not have had the whisky. It seemed to have muddled her head, taken away her will and left her longing for his touch, for the delectable sensations of the night before.

She dragged her lips free, felt the sting of regret. 'We must not.'

His glace flickered to the blanket on the floor. 'Ah, that is a hint, is it? It seems a little unfair when it is our wedding night.'

Blankly she stared at him, at the rueful twist to his mouth, the wariness in his eyes. And the regret.

A trick of the light? Or some sort of horrible jest? The kind his brothers had played on her that long-ago summer. Luring her on, then running away. Before he'd arrived and turned her world upside down. 'I don't think much of this joke.'

He reached out and forced her fingers free of the cloak. He frowned. 'Are you always this cold?' He enfolded her fingers in his and she felt his heat permeate through her skin. Seductive warmth.

She tugged at her hand, but he did not let go. His eyes regarded her intently. 'It is no joke. You see,' he said softly, 'under Scottish law, if a couple says they are married and act married, before witnesses, then that is what they are. We declared ourselves wed before we set foot in this house. McKinly is our witness.'

She uttered a cry of horror.

He quickly covered her mouth with his hand.

'Hush. Do you want to bring McKinly down on us?'

His hand was large and warm and gentle. She glared at him.

'Speak quietly,' he said.

She nodded and he released her.

'I am not Scottish,' she whispered. 'It was just a story, to…to protect my reputation. We can't possibly be married.' The pitch of her voice rose in panic.

An expression flashed across his face. Anger? 'The law applies to whoever is within our borders,' he spoke flatly, his face like granite. 'When McKinly questioned you, you confirmed it of your own free will. We are married.'

'Y-you tricked me,' she spluttered. 'You don't want to be married to me.'

Resignation filled his expression. 'We have no choice in the matter.'

Hurt by his obvious regret, she glowered. 'No one but McKinly knows. We can just pretend it never happened.'

His brows lowered, his expression became harsh. 'Just because I'm a Scot doesna' mean I have no honour. The law is the law.'

'What about the law banning smuggling?'

'That's different. It is an unjust law.'

'So you pick and choose the laws you follow?'

His lips pressed together. He shook his head. 'Don't you see, we dinna have a choice? You said it yourself. Your father will reach your friend before you do.' He stared at her for a long moment as if considering what he should say next. 'I'm not unhappy about it.'

'Nothing has happened between us.'

'We kissed,' he said softly, his blue eyes dancing. 'You slept beside me.'

And there it was again. The pull inside her. The longing to melt against him. The desire to give in and enjoy.

No other man had had this kind of power over her. If only she could truly believe he wanted this marriage. That he wouldn't regret it later.

Hadn't she already seen the regret in his face? Heard him agree with McKinly that she was not the kind of lass who could live in the Highlands?

'My father will never allow it. He will have it dissolved.' Could he?

His expression darkened. He muttered something under his breath in Gaelic. 'Let him try.'

This wasn't working. He wasn't listening. She touched his arm and felt a tingle in her fingers. Saw his arm twitch in response. She forced herself to ignore the sparks dancing between them and softened her tone. 'Ian, you don't want this. Neither of us does. Just get me to Hawkhurst and I will plan some way out of this from there.'

He shook his head. 'It is done.'

Done. Why did it sound like he'd been given a prison sentence? Because this was not what he wanted. No doubt he felt as trapped as she did. 'Alice will say anything I ask her to say. Even if Father reaches her first and she says she hasn't seen me, she will recant. She could say she was afraid for me and had me tucked away in her house all the time.'

'He would believe you walked there alone, no doubt?'

Did he have to be so practical? And was that hope she heard in his voice? The hollowness in her chest grew. 'I am sure I can come up with a plausible explanation. A ride with a carter.' She gave him a sweet smile and batted her eyelashes.

His brows went up. 'Days and nights on the road alone. Your reputation will still be ruined.' He shook his head. 'You helped me, now I will help you. Our being wed is the only option.'

Chapter Twelve

Ian had never seen a more beautiful woman. Her heart-shaped face was female perfection, her creamy skin translucent in the candlelight. However, her expression was determined.

For a moment, when he'd first mentioned marriage, he'd thought she seemed pleased, but her arguments said otherwise. Disappointing, but not surprising. His only option was to make sure the bargain was properly sealed, irrefutable.

He would have to mount a seduction. His blood warmed. He caressed her small palm with his thumb and felt her tremor in response. Her ruby lips, so lush and so delicately bowed, parted in a small gasp.

She was a passionate woman and her response to him was all in his favour.

'It doesn't matter what you say, lass. In the eyes of the world, we are married.'

She bit that lovely, full bottom lip with small, even white teeth. He wanted to bite it, too. He leaned closer, watching her eyes widen and sensing the movement of her throat as she swallowed. She straightened her shoulders.

And that was what he found so damnably attractive. Yes, she was tiny and delicate, but she had an inner resilience. She met life head on. She was just the sort of woman a man would be proud to call wife and not just because of her beauty.

'Come, now,' he cajoled. 'What do you say?'

She tilted her head, looking at him sideways, smiling just a little. 'I say I don't recognise this law of yours.' The tone was teasing, as if she knew she was defeated, but was fighting a fine rearguard action he couldn't help but admire, even as it infuriated.

It was as if the wild Scottish blood of his ancestors took over his body and his mind. He wanted to roar like a berserker and swing his claymore at his enemy—only there wasn't one, not one that could be seen. The problem was their history and that he couldn't change. His best weapons were logic and soft words, but he was having trouble keeping that in mind. 'You would prefer the wedding night wait until a minister can be found?' It wasn't a fair question. She was already flushed.

Already breathing fast. But he wasn't going to rush her. Tonight was too important.

She leaned back against the pillows, looking up, considering, gauging. 'Are you saying you would marry me against my will?'

'I did not take you for a fool, Lady Selina,' he growled, his voice like gravel, his body rigid with the desire he fought to contain. 'No man will have you after you ran away with me, especially since, without a word of protest, you played my wife. You have no choice but to wed me. Or I you.'

'How romantic you make it sound.'

He winced. Clearly he did not have a courtier's way with words, but the twinkle in her eye said she was playing with him. 'We are in this together whether we wish it or not.' He gazed at her lovely face, at the hint of the delectable body he'd held close and not touched. He lowered his voice, let his longing show on his face. 'Why should we not make the best of it?' He reached out and stroked his thumb across her cheekbone. 'Don't fight me on this, lass. We both know what we want.'

The shocking words tightened Selina's core.

She fought the desire inside her and gave him a soulful pout and a doe-eyed glance and let a teasing smile play about her lips. 'La, sir, you are indeed very forceful in your arguments,' she said in a whispery voice. 'but I am not so sure we will suit.'

His eyes flashed fire. 'Don't do that.'

Forcing herself not to recoil, she raised a brow. 'Do what?'

'Simper at me as if I am some Bond Street beau and we are engaged in a drawing-room flirtation.'

'Is it more than that?'

A muttered word in Gaelic ripped through the air. He rubbed the back of his neck. 'Of course it is. Your reputation is at stake.' His Scottish brogue seemed to deepen, become more darkly delicious. More him, yet the words were painful to hear. An admission that it wouldn't matter what woman had rescued him, he would feel honour bound to marry her.

So was he glad that it was she and not some other woman whom he found himself tied to?

'Our families are enemies.' She raised an arched brow as if they were discussing the latest fashion, instead of dire consequences. 'Your father would turn in his grave.'

He shook his head. 'I am not my father. Besides, a marriage between us can be a way to make peace between families. A way to move on from the past.'

Irrationally hurt by the cold of his reasoning, she closed her eyes briefly. It did make sense. As much, if not more sense, than an alliance with Dunstan's family. The Dunstans were old stock, but not particularly ambitious—one of the reasons she'd thought him such a good prospect.

Father might be brought to see the benefits of a marriage in time.

'Wouldn't a wife cramp your style? You would have to give up smuggling.'

His shoulders stiffened. 'That is my decision to make.'

Not about to be guided by a wife, then. Most men weren't, which was why she had been so careful in her choice of Dunstan.

Strangely, the thought of marriage to Ian made her heart pound hard—a much different reaction to the thought of wedding Dunstan. Dunstan was safe. Ian Gilvry represented all that was danger.

'The idea of marriage to you scares me.' The words flew out of her mouth before she could stop them.

A brow flew up. 'I see you as scared of nothing.' His voice was dark with amusement. 'You used to give my brothers as good as they gave.'

'Until you took their side.'

He inhaled a deep breath. 'And regretted it every day since.' He leaned forwards and brushed his lips across hers. 'You were such a brave little thing.'

He sighed. 'And you never told your father. He would have crushed us with a word from you, yet you never complained.'

'I'm no telltale.' She frowned. 'Which is why you should have trusted me enough to let me go home.'

'That had nothing to do with trust.'

And everything to do with the safety of his clan. She sighed. It was too late to worry about what might have been. He was right. Whatever she did now, she would be ruined. She'd been discovered missing from her bed. Not even Alice could protect her from such a scandal.

'What do you say, Selina?' he murmured, eyeing her mouth like a hungry wolf. He brought her hand to his mouth and brushed his lips across her knuckles. 'Do we consummate this legal marriage tonight? Or do we wait until we find a minister and I retreat to my cold hard bed on the floor?'

So, he'd thrown down the gauntlet. Likely a foolish thing to do with a woman as strong willed as this one, but he couldn't see any other way to proceed. He just wished she'd trust him to decide what was right or wrong. She saw smuggling as criminal, instead of a way of feeding his people. She had to learn to trust his judgement, as his clan did.

He stroked the hair back from her face, willing

her to understand that he had duties and responsibilities apart from pleasure.

Her skin warmed to his touch. Her eyelids fluttered, her lips were parted, ripe and ready for him,
and he took them carefully. Like last night, when
her response had been hungry and full of fire.
Only by dint of will had he left her as he had found
her. An innocent.

But not tonight. Tonight he was a married man.

A pulse of heat tightened his groin and he almost groaned aloud with the rush of pleasure. He
cupped her jaw and angled her head for better ac-
cess to her honeyed kiss. Her hand released its
death grip on her cloak and lay flat on his chest.

For one moment he thought she would push him
away, a last-ditch effort to deny him, but her small
palm caressed the contours of his chest, her touch
feathery light, but searing.

Then her arms crept up around his neck, pulling
him closer, melding against his chest where they
touched, her heart beating wildly, her breathing
coming fast and furious against his cheek. The
vibration of a soft moan in the back of her throat
sent a jolt of lust to his belly. Beneath the heavy
wool of his kilt he hardened.

Grim satisfaction filled him and he tasted her

whisky-flavoured tongue and the dark recesses of her sweet mouth.

He wooed her with his lips, his teeth and the hands gently stroking her chilly shoulders and stifled a groan of frustration.

Unless she accepted they were well and truly wed, he could do nothing about the lust gripping his body.

His mouth on her lips, his large warm hands on her shoulders plied her with unexpected gentleness. Sensual. Seductive. Heat trickled along her veins, searing her skin, leaving it tingling and burning. Her breasts, pressed against his chest, felt heavy and full. Her core ached and pulsed, begging for the pleasure he'd brought her before.

Her head swam at the battery of sensations rippling through her body.

Gentleness was not what she wanted. She didn't want to be the china doll upon the shelf, the spunglass ornament to be looked at, but not touched for fear of shattering.

His touch was delicious, achingly so, but it wasn't enough for the woman inside, the tempestuous female she had spent years battling into submission. The one who, left to herself, took risks. That woman, who wanted this big rough Scotsman who had carried her off to the hills. And that woman seemed to have taken control of her body.

Exploring his shoulders through his shirt, she was very much aware of their magnificent breadth and power as the muscles bunched and rippled beneath her hands. She raked her fingers through his silky-soft hair. Wound the strands around her fingers and tugged.

A hitch in his breathing. Surprise. A quickening of his heartbeat. More urgency in his kiss.

His tongue swept her mouth, then began to withdraw. What madness drove her, she wasn't sure, but she captured it with her teeth. He stilled.

She released him.

He drew back, breaking the contact between them, except for his hand on her upper arms and hers sunk deep in his thick dark hair. His eyes glittered and his chest rose and fell with each harsh breath.

Ah. It seemed she'd gained his full attention. Her lips were tingling, her face glowing from contact with his scruff of beard and she flashed him a saucy smile.

'So, Ian Gilvry,' she breathed in the little-girl voice that had brought the men of the *ton* to their knees, 'this is our wedding night.'

His gaze dropped to her mouth and then rose to meet her gaze. He smiled. 'It is, indeed.'

He sounded relieved, as if he really did want this marriage. She let her fears, her suspicions, slide away.

Her heart raced as if she had run a great race. His large body pressed against her chest as he leaned over her, the circling of his fingers on her shoulder, his breath against her cheek. Her chest felt so full of longing, she couldn't breathe around it.

'Well, the floor does look very hard and very cold. I could not let you spend such an uncomfortable night.'

His lips curved in a smile of pure seduction. His eyes lit up, gleaming like sapphires. Never had she seen him look so young or so boyish.

'So this surrender is all for my sake, is it?'

She grinned. 'Oh, I think it brings some benefits to me, too.'

He leaned in and bit her bottom lip. Pleasure raced through her body, settling deep in her core. She gasped at the wildness of it.

On a soft laugh, he thrust his tongue in her mouth commanding her to yield to him, pressing her down into the mattress as his body lined up with hers and his thigh pressed between hers. The weight of him melted her bones. She felt as if she could absorb him into her skin, as if they could fuse into one being. And all the while his lips teased hers and his tongue darted into her mouth, leading her on, encouraging her to follow.

Emboldened, she tried a hesitant lick. He captured her tongue with his teeth, then sucked.

Shivers of pleasure racked her from head to toe. Something deep inside her pulled tight. She gasped at the onslaught. He released her.

'You taste so good I might just swallow you whole,' he murmured and kissed the tip of her nose.

She nipped at his lower lip. 'Not if I eat you up first.' He chuckled as if she'd made a grand jest. She bit his rough chin, his cheekbone, his earlobe when he turned away. A quick hiss of his breath tightened the knot low in her belly. Interesting. It wasn't only what he did to her that felt good, but how he responded to what she did to him that made her body quicken and burn.

He captured her face in his hands, his thumbs gliding over her cheekbones, his gaze intense. 'I swear, from this day forth, I will honour you as my wife all the days of my life, in sickness and in health until death do us part.'

A wedding vow. It made her heart clench painfully, a kind of aching joy as it seemed constricted within her chest. 'As will I,' she managed, despite the tightness in her throat.

Then he was kissing her again. Through the haze of the delicious sensations produced by his mouth on her lips, she was aware of the sharpening need between her thighs as his knee forced them wider. The pressure of his hip against her mons felt both wonderful and tantalising.

A thumb grazed the underside of her breast, leaving a searing trail of heat, but his touch was still too light, too gentle. She made a sound in her throat, half growl, half purr, that he captured in his mouth. She wasn't even sure if he heard it. He must have. His hand moved higher, covering her breast, exploring and massaging.

She writhed beneath his touch and a sound of approval rumbled up from his chest.

His thumb teased her nipple through the fine lawn of her chemise. Another zing of shocking pleasure. She gasped. Shock had no place in this congress between them. They were now man and wife and she was melting and tingling all at the same time. Beneath her palms the vast plane of his back felt hot through his shirt. Her skimming fingers felt muscle and bone; the scent of him, soap and male, filled her nostrils and her heart felt full.

She was in the arms the man she'd always…

loved? She closed the door on that thought. It made her feel far too vulnerable. They were marrying for expediency, accompanied by pleasurable benefits.

He wrenched away from her, breaking the seductive spell. Slowly her mind cleared as he gazed down at her, his eyes hot, his expression hungry.

All her life she'd been running from men who looked at her with heat. Putting up barriers. He was the only man she'd ever run towards. What was done could not be undone. The consequences would be in the future.

He knelt up, pulled his shirt free of his belt and pulled it off over his head, tossing it to the floor.

She gazed at him with awe, just as she had the first time. He was glorious. Carved beauty. A god of war complete with battle scars and a bandage around his most recent brush with danger. Rather than mar, the silvery lines of old scars accentuated the purity of his form.

Not so the ruined flesh of her thigh. Would he find it as ugly as she did? Would he regret his offer to wed once he saw the damage her foolishness had caused?

With hesitant fingertips, she traced a scar slicing across two of his ribs. He caught her hand and brought it to his lips.

He slid off the bed and unbuckled his belt. 'We'll

have no secrets between us.' His voice was a low growl. And a challenge shone in his eyes. 'No uneasy coupling in the dark.' He let the kilt fall.

His phallus stood erect, dark and huge, aggressively jutting from its dark nest of curls. It was enormous. A pearl of moisture beaded on its tip.

She swallowed. Licked her lips, her mouth gone dry. Her face blazed with heat. She raised her gaze to meet his.

'Dinna be afraid, lass,' he murmured quietly. 'Not of me. I would never do aught to hurt you.'

'I'm not,' she assured herself in a whisper. Not of him physically, in truth. Mostly she feared what she might see on his face when he saw her body. Her scars. That she might see revulsion or, worse yet, pity.

'What troubles you?' he asked.

She must be wearing her fears on her face—something she never did as a rule. She took a deep breath. There was no going back. No changing the past, so she had best have it done with.

'No secrets.' She flung back the cloak, which had slipped below her waist along with the sheet. With a swift intake of breath, like the one taken before plunging into cold water, or before telling the truth when a lie would be easier, she hitched the chemise up to her waist and drew it off over her head.

Gooseflesh raced over her skin. Her nipples tightened with cold and with nerves. Determined not to flinch, she stared at his face, watching his reaction.

At first, he looked startled. He probably hadn't expected her to be quite so bold. Then, as his gaze swept downwards to her bounteous bosom, a bosom which had been the subject of more than one rake's ode, his expression softened to heavy-lidded appreciation.

He inhaled a long breath. 'Lovely,' he said.

She resisted the urge to cross her arms over her breasts. The males in London had, after all, seen all but the deep-rose peaks rising from her skimpy muslins and silks. They'd ogled her figure from the moment of her come out and must have had a pretty good sense of what lay beneath.

What she really wanted to do was turn on her side, hide her right leg with her left, but it was too late. His gaze had already reached her navel and was travelling to the nest of curls below the curve of her belly.

She knew when he took in the scars. His brows drew together and he glanced up at her face. Despite being ready, she averted her face and reached for the sheet to hide the ugliness, but his hand was already smoothing first down one thigh, then the other.

She dared a peek at his expression. No pity, just raw sensuality. Perhaps he hadn't noticed? She placed her hand over the ruined flesh, halting the soft swoop of his hand travelling upwards from her knee.

He glanced up as if surprised.

She felt her face heat. 'It is not a very pretty picture, I'm afraid. I was such an idiot and lucky I didn't injure anyone else. Hawkhurst saw the whole thing and managed to free the horses before they came to any harm.'

'Your friend's husband?'

His matter-of-fact tone made her feel a little less unsure. At least he wasn't reacting with horror. 'Yes. His quick thinking saved my leg. The doctors didn't think I would walk again.' She gave a casual flick of her fingers across the ruined flesh, hoping her voice did not reveal her embarrassment. 'If it disgusts you, we can blow out the candle. Or we can forget all about this.'

'Oh, *leannan*, sweetheart, is that what you think?'

He picked up her hand and kissed her palm. Heat shivered through her veins. He placed it on the scar on his chest. 'Do you find this unpleasant to look at?'

She swallowed. 'It makes you look like a warrior.'

A low chuckle vibrated beneath her palm. 'I thought so, too. I caught myself with a scythe when I was fifteen, but I told all the ladies it was a sabre cut.'

'Men are supposed to have scars. Women are supposed to be perfect.'

He shook his head. 'It is a part of you now. And just as perfectly lovely as all the rest.' His hot gaze swept up her body to her face.

He must have seen the doubt because he continued talking, his tone low and seductive. 'There is far more to a woman than mere physical beauty. There is the spirit too, you know. But you are just as beautiful to me here...' his fingers traced the jagged criss-cross of pink lines and the misshapen muscle, his touch gentle, almost reverent in its lightness '...as you are here.' He tickled the back of her knee.

Tears welled in her eyes, even as she smiled. Too much emotion. Too much gladness.

'Don't cry, darling,' he murmured. 'I promise to be careful.' He leant down to press soft kisses along the length of the wound.

Spun glass again. 'No,' she said, grabbing his shoulders, forcing him to look into her face. 'Don't treat me like an invalid. Or a doll. I am a woman. I won't break.'

A slow smile dawned. Blue heat flared in his eyes. 'Aye.' He nodded. 'A woman you are. All spit and claws.'

He took her mouth in a punishing kiss. Hard. Demanding.

Clenching her hands on his muscular shoulders, she made demands of her own. Pulled him closer, until he tumbled down on the bed beside her, parting her thighs to accommodate his weight in the cradle of her hips.

He broke free on a muttered curse, sliding down her body, trailing searing kisses and hot caresses with his hand. He stopped at the valley between her breasts, cupping them in his hands, drawing first one nipple into his mouth, then the other.

No gentleness. No featherlight brushes. His touch ravaged, as did his mouth. The touch of a man who loved the feel of her flesh in his hands.

He laved her nipple with his tongue, swirling heat, followed by sudden chill when he paid similar attention to her other breast.

His lips and tongue teased her breast as she watched from beneath lowered lids and clutched convulsively at his hair at each liquid tug on her insides.

While his mouth brought her exquisite pain, his hands stroked and kneaded her ribs, her hip, her belly, a slow downward slide of hot rough skin on skin so alive her mind seemed ready to splinter.

Chapter Thirteen

Permission to lose control? Encouragement to let the primitive beast out of its cage? Lust gripped Ian hard.

The urge to mark her as his, to brand her with lips and teeth, to let the force of his desire take him to mindless bliss, tempted him sorely.

Beyond reason.

The bite of her nails in his back and buttocks, the way she tasted his shoulder with tongue and lips and teeth, drove him mad.

Muffling a groan, he took one deep breath after the other. She had to be ready for him. He had no choice but to hurt her, but he would give her pleasure ahead of the pain.

Arching his back, resisting her pull, he took her mouth, the faint taste of peat-smoky whisky lingering on her tongue. And as their mouths melded and toyed with darting licks and sucking, his right hand palmed her mons, the curls damp, the flesh hot.

He pressed down with the heel of his hand and she whimpered her pleasure into his mouth. Her body arched into his hand, not knowing what it needed. Not yet.

Slow and easy he parted her delicate folds by touch, exploring her entrance, longing to see. Not this time. This was not his time. He slipped his little finger inside her, overawed at the tightness. At the barrier he could feel at her entrance.

She stilled. Her breathing hitched. He grabbed a deep but ragged breath through his nose and held still while she became accustomed to his intrusion.

He broke their kiss to look down at her face. Her eyes were hazy with passion, her lips red from his kisses, her cheeks, too, from the abrasive touch of his beard. It was a mark of sorts.

With his thumb he stroked in circles until he found that little nub that offered a pleasure all of its own. Her eyelids drooped. She looked wanton. Abandoned. His shaft pulsed its demand, dragging all thought from his head in the quest for completion.

He circled harder and faster. She gasped, her hips bucking wildly.

Her gaze flew to his face, her eyes wide with

shock and hazy with pleasure. Her breathing halted. Rigid, she hung on the crest.

And tumbled over in a climax of quivers.

Now. He plunged into her. Losing himself inside her depths, still feeling her wince of pain, even as the bliss roared through her blood and claimed her.

His own climax came on him fast. Out of control, not careful as he'd intended. His hips pounded into her and she clung to him with knees and heels and hands on his shoulders. And he rode her to completion as the clenches of pleasure of her core milked him dry.

Spent, and trembling like an exhausted stallion, he kissed her shoulder. He stared at that small bone with the silken flesh stretched over its delicate contour and was horrified to see the marks of his teeth.

So much for being in control.

He stroked her glorious mane of black curls back from her sweat-damp temples and kissed the pulse beat where the skin was traced with blue, then her lips.

'You are wonderful,' he breathed. 'My wife.'

'My husband,' she whispered in return, claiming him as he had claimed her. No one could separate them now.

He rolled on his side and held her tight to his body, reaching down to cover them with the sheet and her cloak. In a moment he'd get up and get that blanket. In a moment.

He closed his eyes and savoured the warmth flowing through his body.

Fists pounded on a door.

Someone yelling. 'Open up!'

McKinly's sleepy voice cursed.

They were found. Ian sat up, his mind racing. Had McKinly's lad inadvertently given them away? He leaped from the bed and hurriedly belted on his kilt, not bothering with a shirt.

'Who is it?' Selina asked.

In the pitch black of the early-morning hours, he could hear the worry in her voice, even if he could not see her face. 'I don't know. Get dressed and wait here.'

He opened the latch on the window and pushed it slightly ajar. 'In case we need to leave in a hurry,' he explained in a whisper.

She was already fumbling around for her clothes. No words, no panic, just getting on with what needed to be done.

He slipped out of the door and closed it behind him.

'Open up,' the voice yelled again.

Niall's voice. The tension in his shoulders eased.

He nodded at McKinly to open the door and the man raised the wooden bar. The door flew back.

'Ian!' Niall said, striding into the room with Logan close on his heels. He punched Ian's shoulder. 'Thank God we heard from you in time.'

'What is it, man?'

Logan went to the fire to warm his hands, his young face troubled.

For once, Niall's expression was sharp. And worried. 'Albright has the militia crawling the countryside looking for you. For smuggling and abduction. Finally the bastard has found a way to hang you. You'll have to leave. Go to France. America.'

Like hell.

McKinly's mouth was hanging open.

'Who am I supposed to have abducted?' Ian asked.

'His daughter. Logan said she was there on the headland. Now she's missing.'

Logan's eyes widened, staring over his shoulder.

Ian spun around. The door behind him had opened and Selina stepped out. Her black hair loose about her shoulders, the bright red of her skirts swirling around her ankles, with her flushed face and rosy lips, she looked like a woman well bedded.

Niall's jaw dropped. 'God, Ian, what have you done? We'll all hang.'

McKinly looked startled.

Ian pulled her close to his side, felt the stiffness in her shoulders. Fear, when up to now she'd been fearless. He gave her an encouraging smile.

'Lady Selina has done me the honour of becoming my wife.'

'Your—' Reading Ian's glare, Niall spluttered into silence.

Logan's eyes narrowed. 'You are a disgrace to the clan, Ian Gilvry. How could you? After her family stole our birthright?' His gaze ran over her, a bitter twist to his lips. 'I can understand you wanting to bed her. But marriage? Our mother will never forgive you.'

Selina gasped, tried to twist away from him. He held her fast. 'Mother will have to accept it. As will you.'

'Albright's daughter?' McKinly echoed. 'In my house?'

Ian shot him a glare, then directed his ire at his brothers. 'The lady is my wife. You will treat her with the respect that is her due.'

Logan opened his mouth to argue and Ian thought he was going to have to take him outside and pound sense into him. One thing a Laird could not allow was his men, any of them, to disobey a command. He should have known how it would be. If this was his brothers' reaction, the other clansmen would be worse.

He glared. 'I mean it, Logan.'

The lad put his hands up. 'All right.' He bent his head a fraction. 'I apologise to your lady wife.' Disgust dripped from his tongue and Ian still wanted to hit him.

Niall's expression was simply one of confused horror.

Selina's face paled, her lips tightened, yet she remained still at his side. He should have warned her how it might be, but he thought there would be more time.

McKinly sank down on the chair and scrubbed a hand across the back of his neck. Then one corner of his mouth kicked up. 'There is no crime in wedding a willing lass. 'Tis a fine plan for revenge you are having on Albright. Running off with his daughter.'

Another gasp from Selina. She looked up at him, a question on her face. 'You planned this?'

'You know very well I did not,' he said, angered by the note of accusation in her voice.

Niall looked thoughtful. 'You sly dog,' he said suddenly, a slow smile dawning on his face. He swung a punch at Ian's gut and missed when he jumped back. 'The keep. After all these years, Dunross Keep is back in the family.'

'It is?' Logan said, raising his gaze to Ian's face. Ian stared at Niall.

'Aye,' Niall replied. He looked at Selina. 'I heard from one of the lasses at Carrick's castle that she was betrothed to a *Sassenach* and the keep was part of the settlement. It will come to you now.'

His jaw dropped.

Selina slipped out of his grip, her expression wary. 'This was your clan business with Angus, wasn't it? This is the plot the two of you were hatching out of my hearing?'

Remorse stabbed him hard. Angus had put the idea of marriage in his head, but he'd known nothing about the keep. Guilt must have showed on his face, because her expression of outrage turned to one of disgust. 'I should have known,' she said, backing away. 'You are no better than Andrew. Cheating to catch yourself an heiress.'

The words were a slap in the face. Pride rose like a beast in his blood. 'I'm proud of any comparison with my brother.'

Logan and Niall ranged on either side of him, fists clenched. They looked ready to tear her limb from limb. A week ago he would have looked the same way himself.

Instead an overwhelming urge to protect her forced him to turn and face them as he thrust her behind his back, shielding her with his body. 'Enough,' he roared.

He turned to her. She glared at him, defiant as a kitten faced with a bull mastiff, claws ready to scratch. 'We are married, that is an end to it.'

Logan spun away. 'Wait until our mother hears this news.' With that he was gone out into the night.

Ian started after him.

Niall put out a hand. 'Let him go. He'll come to his senses soon enough.' He looked at Selina. 'He'll see the sense in it when his blood cools. As will our mother. And the clan. In one blow, you've solved all our problems.'

Selina's face was as white as a ghost, her eyes dark and accusing. 'You tricked me.' She turned on McKinly, who looked as if he could catch a fly on his tongue, his jaw hung so low. 'It is not true. We are not married, Mr McKinly. There has been no ceremony. No wedding.'

The repudiation hurt deep in his chest. A visceral sensation of loss. No. It was anger. She hadn't minded the idea of marriage an hour ago and now she was shaming him before his clansmen. And herself into the bargain. He wanted to shake her. He kept his fists balled at his sides, while he fought to contain his rage.

McKinly scratched at the night growth on his chin and glanced at Ian. 'Makes no nevermind what you say now, my lady. You said you were married, then you slept in my bed as husband and wife.'

Her cheeks fired bright red. Embarrassment. Shame. Hurt. It was the last that made Ian feel sick. 'I knew nothing about the keep. It may not come to pass.'

She drew herself up to her full height, staring down her nose with an arrogance he could not help but admire, even as her resentment infuriated him. 'That was why you went apart with Angus. He told you, didn't he? That's why you looked so guilty just now. That is why you tricked me into this marriage.'

'No.'

'I don't believe you. This marriage will never stand in an English court of law.'

'It will,' he said harshly. 'It always has. Deny we are wed and what does that make you?' Ian wished he'd held his tongue as she flinched.

'Selina,' he said more gently. 'It was done of your own free will. No one forced you.'

To his sorrow, tears welled in her eyes. He reached for her hand to pull her to his side, but she dodged out of reach.

He'd been wrong about the tears. Her eyes were blazing with anger. 'I hate you.'

Damn it all, if the clan sensed he was not in control of his wife, then there would be bickering among those who thought he was right and those who thought he was wrong. It would tear them apart. 'We will discuss this later. Leave us. I have business to discuss with my clansmen.'

She curled her lip. 'More secret talks.'

'Clan business. I will join you shortly.'

She glared at him, saw he was not going to relent and tossed her head. 'If you will excuse me, gentlemen, I never stay where I am not wanted.'

That had the sound of a threat. The way her eyes flashed in temper was magnificent, and the swirl of her skirts around her legs fired his blood as she headed for the bedroom door. And his bed.

'Spoilt little *Sassenach*,' Niall said, *sotto voce*, but not so quietly that she didn't hear. Ian knew by the way her spine stiffened. But he thanked God when she said nothing and closed the door with a sharp snap.

'I'll support your choice, lad,' McKinly said.

'She's no such a bad lass. Look at the way she helped my Marie Flora.'

Niall grinned. 'I think it is a brilliant move. The answer to all our prayers, you clever dog. I'll even drink to your health, if McKinly will part with a dram of his whisky.'

Brilliant. If he could only convince Selina to feel the same way. Seduce her again? His body hardened. Again.

He hadn't had this many jolting arousals since he was a lad. But he did not want an unwilling wife. Hell, he had not wanted a wife at all until he had the Gilvrys solvent. At least, not until this woman ran across his path again.

'We need to get back to Dunross and have a word with Albright,' he said. 'Without running into the militia. They seem of a mind to shoot first and ask questions after.'

Niall eyed his bandage and whistled. 'It seems they mean business.'

'So do I. Let's have that dram, McKinly.' He needed some fortification before he faced his wife.

The sound of mugs being set out and filled percolated through the bedroom door.

The truth was a bright sharp blade to her heart. No matter what he said, it was quite clear he had used her. Tricked her. She paced away from the door, striking her fist in her palm, her anger too great for calm acceptance. Anger and mortification. She felt like a fool—worse, she felt betrayed.

If only he hadn't kissed her in the cave. Only once before had a kiss overpowered her senses. And it ended with her getting hurt. Badly.

That kiss had been Ian's, too. He'd left her to join his brothers in their teasing. He hadn't thrown any rocks, but he had said she wasn't wanted.

It seemed she had not learned her lesson. Only this time the pain in her chest felt much worse.

She drew in a steadying breath. No point in moaning about what could not be changed. At least she knew the truth. Could work out her options.

She glanced at the open window. It wouldn't be difficult to leave and disappear into the night. And go where?

To Alice. Deny the marriage had ever happened for all she was worth? Or go home, bat her eyelashes at Father and pretend she'd been lost all this while and knew nothing of smuggling or smugglers?

But as she'd realised earlier, it was too late to save her reputation. Any hope of marrying Dunstan had flown the moment she'd set out to warn Ian. Was that why she'd done it? As a means of escape?

She squeezed her eyes shut. Tried to go back to the moment she had made the decision, to test her real intentions.

Had she really used it as an excuse to avoid marrying Dunstan? A form of running away. The way she'd run from Lisbon?

No matter how she looked at the situation she found herself in now, though, running was not an option. He'd taken her to bed. And she had been willing, because she thought they'd found something meaningful.

Bitterness rose in her throat. He'd tricked her into marrying him so he could regain Dunross Keep. How stupid could she be?

Tricked her with kisses and seduction.

And she'd fallen into his hands like a ripe plum. Or Dunross Keep had.

She groaned. Father was going to be so angry when he discovered she'd handed over the keep to the Gilvrys. And he must be worried. Why else would he have the militia out looking for her supposed abductor? A militia that seemed ready to shoot on sight. Her blood ran cold.

She flung open the door.

The three men around the trestle table gaped at her. Ian rose slowly to his feet, a frown on his face. 'Selina,' his said, his voice a warning.

'If we are going to Dunross, we should leave now,' she announced. 'Before it gets light and we are an easy target for some ambitious soldier.'

A smile spread across Ian's face. She glared at him. 'That doesn't mean I am happy about this situation. You've got your keep and a marriage of convenience.'

Niall gave her a narrow-eyed stare. 'You'd be a fool to trust her, Ian.'

Chapter Fourteen

To her surprise Ian had agreed they should leave right away. They'd bid McKinly goodbye and Selina left a message of farewell for Marie Flora.

She had ridden Beau, while the men had walked ahead, talking in Gaelic, excluding her from their conversation. How typical.

The sun was not very high in the sky behind a pall of grey clouds when they walked into the Barleycorn's courtyard.

Willy Gair came out of the stables and stared at them, his mouth agape. He looked at Ian, then at Selina and frowned.

Ian issued a sharp order in Gaelic.

The man seemed inclined to argue, then bowed his head and shot off.

Selina leaned over Beau's neck the better for Ian to hear her. 'I thought we were going to the keep.'

'All in good time.' Ian helped her down from the

horse and guided her into the inn. 'My first loyalty is to the clan. They will have been worrying.'

And did he think her father wasn't worried? Angry, yes, but worried, too. And right now she was feeling so guilty and so stupid she wanted to see him and beg his forgiveness.

While Niall saw to the horse, Ian guided her into the inn and seated her in a corner of the taproom.

Noisy footsteps trundled down a set of narrow stairs hidden behind a curtain at one end of the room. The curtain swept aside. A man peered into the gloom. 'We're closed.'

'There's a nice welcome, Ranald,' Ian said with the ghost of a smile. 'And here was me thinking you would like to offer me dram on the event of my bridals.' He spoke in English, no doubt for her benefit.

'Laird?' The innkeeper rubbed his eyes and looked again as if to ensure he wasn't seeing things. 'Are you mad? There are soldiers everywhere seeking you.' He peered over Ian's shoulder. 'And the lass is still with you? You'll hang for sure.'

'I don't think you heard what I said. Lady Selina has done me the honour of becoming my wife.'

Shock, followed swiftly by horror, chased across his face. His mouth opened and closed.

'Would you like some coffee, my dear?' Ian said, giving Ranald time to recover. 'If mine host can remember his manners, that is.'

'Tea, please.'

The man choked. 'Tea. Right.' He picked up a bottle, uncorked it with his teeth and took a deep swallow. He clung on to the bottle like a lifeline, staring at Ian.

'Tea,' Ian said.

'I'll have Bridie put the kettle on.' He put the bottle down and scurried behind the curtain. Ian went behind the bar and pulled a fresh bottle from the shelf. He poured a dram into the glass and looked at her with a wry twist to his lips. 'That went well, don't you think?'

'No.'

'It will get better, I promise.' He swallowed the whisky down and poured another glass. Then poured one for Niall when he came in the door.

Bridie, a plump, rosy-cheeked woman of about forty, brought a tray with a tea pot and milk. She gave Selina a hard look, but said not a word. She gave the same look to Ian and hissed something in Gaelic before disappearing behind the curtain.

'What did she say?'

He hesitated.

'I can go and ask her to repeat it in English.'

'She said he ought to be ashamed of himself,' Niall said. 'The words were different, but that's what she meant.'

Selina felt her cheeks go hot. 'I really think—'

Two men entered the taproom—Tammy and Colin Gilvry, the blacksmith, Ian's cousin. Both men were staring at her as if she was a nasty insect they would like to squash. A shudder passed through her body. She thought she had her dismay well hidden until Ian moved closer to her side.

She couldn't help but feel comfort at his closeness. She drew a deep breath and gave the men look for look. After all, having brought this on herself, she wasn't going to cower, now, was she?

After those two, other men arrived and soon the small parlour was filled to bursting with large vengeful Scots. She really wished he'd taken her up to the keep and met with his clan on his own.

Coward.

These were his people. His clan. If her husband wanted her here, then she didn't have a choice. She'd given up all her rights with this marriage. Her blood ran cold at the thought, but she met their dark glances with as much calm indifference as she could muster. And she could muster quite a lot, given her training in the ballrooms of London.

Most of them let their gazes fall away. Except

Willy Gair. He had a very strange expression on his face. Not horror, thought there was some of that, too—something more akin to fear.

Douglas McTavish grinned. 'I see you've dodged the soldiers, Ian Gilvry. Ye hae the luck of the devil himself.' His gaze slid to Selina and back, clearly demanding an explanation.

'A pox on the gaugers,' a man at the back cried.

Ian grinned. 'I'm glad to hear you all made it home safe and my thanks for ensuring the goods arrived safely at their destination. It will put coin in your pockets and enough food on the table to last the winter, too.'

'Good health to the Laird.'

'Aye, a toast,' someone yelled.

Ian put up a hand. 'There is another cause for celebration this day. Ranald, a dram all around,' Ian said. 'Then I'll offer you a toast.'

Niall looked up from the book he had pulled from his pocket when they entered. 'Are you sure you want to do this here and now?' he muttered in Ian's ear.

It seemed that for all his bookish ways, Niall took in more than one might guess.

He stood at Ian's shoulder as Ranald handed them both a glass.

'Lads,' Ian said, his face as hard as granite, 'let

me introduce my wife, Lady Selina. A toast to my bride.'

No one moved.

'Sold your soul to Albright, did you?' someone said. The eyes around the room glared at her. Hatred made the air in the room thick and acrid. Selina kept her chin high, but couldn't stop leaning closer to Ian's broad form. He put a protective hand on her shoulder.

'There's no need for insult,' he said. 'Lady Selina risked her reputation to help us all. Without her warning, there'd be no profit and most of us would be in prison.'

'Aye, well, grateful as we are, Laird, no one here wants an Albright spy in our midst.'

Willy Gair looked almost green. He turned and pushed through the crowd and disappeared through the door.

'Aye, and what would your grandfather have said?' another added.

She felt his sigh of disappointment. 'Accept her or find another Laird,' Ian said coldly.

The men's faces looked grim, unhappy, but not one of them flinched from Ian's steady perusal.

For some reason, he had not told them what the marriage meant with respect to the keep. Why was that?

Niall let his gaze wander the room. There was no mistaking his anger. 'Don't look to me. I'll not usurp title of Laird from my brother. Not now, not ever.'

Selina glance up at Ian, whose eyes were full of shadows, but also resolve. He'd known how it would be, yet he was not using his most persuasive argument.

The innkeeper looked at Ian; of all the men present, his gaze wasn't quite so unfriendly. 'What about the plans you had, Ian Gilvry? The promises. The mill. The...' He glanced at Selina and away. 'You know. The plan.'

'Aye, what about the plan?' Several voices joined the chorus.

They clearly didn't trust her enough to reveal what the nature of this plan was. And she couldn't blame them. She was an Albright and probably always would be in their eyes. Oh, why didn't he tell them about the keep? Surely it would make things better.

Ian gave the man who had called out a considering look. 'The plans haven't changed.'

The men looked uncertain. 'Your father-in-law is the magistrate. Don't tell me you have him in your pocket. I'll no believe it.'

'Her father does not yet know of our marriage. I

came here first. My loyalty is to the clan. Without your support, there can be no plan. No future.' He shook his head. 'You might convince Logan to stand in my place.'

'No. You won't.' Logan must have slipped through the door left open by Willy Gair. He pushed through the crowd to stand next to Niall. 'I'm not saying I'm happy about this marriage,' he continued, flushing red to the roots of his fair hair, 'but I'll respect his choice until it is proved bad for the clan.'

Some of the men nodded. Others shuffled their feet. A greybeard in the corner eyed the glass in his hand with longing. 'So the Laird married a *Sassenach*. Surely any man with a brain can see she's a right comely lass. The fact she's the land-lord's daughter can't be all bad. Can we no get to the toast? This whisky is evaporating before my very eyes.'

Chuckles rippled around the room.

'Any man who will not drink health to my bride, will put down his glass and leave now.' The command in Ian's voice was a force in the room.

No one moved.

'To Ian and his bride, Lady Selina,' Niall said.

'The Laird. Lady Selina. *Slàinte!*' The male voices were a deep rumble.

By sheer force of will, and their trust in his leadership, they had accepted his marriage. Her admiration knew no bounds.

Though nothing showed on his face, she sensed his relief. Niall, on the other hand, was grinning. 'That was a close-run thing, brother,' he murmured.

'I still had my ace in the hole,' Ian said.

'The keep,' Logan said, turning his back to the room. 'When will you tell them?'

Ian scanned the room. 'When it is settled. Who knows, my new father-in-law may try to wriggle out of the bargain.'

He couldn't. It was part of her mother's wedding settlements. The keep came to Selina on her marriage. Still, there was no reason to set his mind at rest—he'd find out soon enough.

'Well, I can tell you our mother is none too pleased,' Logan said.

'She'll see it differently when I have spoken to her,' Ian said.

'She won't have an Albright in the house, I'm afraid.' He nodded at Selina.

Ian saw Selina's face pale and her back stiffen.

'Right now it is her father I need to face. One battle at a time.' He raised his voice. 'Another round on me, Ranald. I'll settle with you later. Only one round, mind, and then send them home or they'll be getting no work done tomorrow.'

The innkeeper nodded. 'Don't worry, I'll see them away.'

'I'll borrow your gig, if I may.'

Ranald grinned. 'You'll want to make a good impression on your future father-in-law.' His face sobered. 'Do you have any idea who gave us to the gaugers?'

'None. But I will find out.'

'Aye. Let us hope so. We can't risk being caught again.'

Selina's eyes had narrowed in disapproval. Dear God, woman—not now, when the clan had barely accepted the fact of their marriage. They could make life very difficult if they thought she was trying to interfere in their business. He wanted them to get to know her and see her worth.

He hurried her outside before she could say anything, followed closely by his brothers. They watched Logan hitch a small brown mare to the gig.

'I hope I can manage my father as well as you managed your men,' Selina said.

He frowned. 'It is for me to manage your father.'

'I think not. I owe him an apology as well as an explanation.'

He looked at her for a long moment. 'Very well. I will let you speak first, but let it be clear between us that you are now my responsibility, not his.'

No doubt he thought of her like a chattel or a burden. 'He is my father.'

He closed his eyes, briefly, as if he regretted his harsh words. 'I just want you to remember you are my wife. It is my duty to keep you safe.'

Her insides softened at the protective note in his voice. The back of her neck prickled. Then she let go a breath. He had married her to get back by stealth what his family had been unable to reclaim by force. How else would he sound? He wanted to protect what he had won.

No doubt he thought she should be grateful he would let her speak to her father at all.

'Ready to go,' Logan said.

Ian turned to Niall. 'You two stay here and make sure things stay calm and reasonable.'

'You aren't going up to the keep by yourself,' Logan said, his face shocked.

'I am.'

'What if he strings you up out of hand?'

'This is the nineteenth century,' Selina said crossly. 'Not seventeen hundred. My father would never do such a thing. And without evidence, there can be no trial.'

Logan didn't look convinced, but shrugged and stepped back beside Niall. 'You're a fool to trust an Albright. It wouldn't surprise me if he wasn't involved in what happened to Drew.'

Ian's expression darkened. His lips narrowed. 'Don't you be a fool. His death is no one's fault but mine.' Pain filled his voice and his expression. Guilt, too. And deep sadness. He set the horse in motion, leaving his brothers to turn back and enter the inn.

Selina gazed at him curiously. 'What did you do to Andrew?'

He inhaled a deep breath and let it go slowly, as if planning what he would say. 'I made him board a ship for the New World. I sent him to see if there was somewhere the clan could settle should we be forced off this land.'

'Because of my letter?'

'I would not have known, if you hadn't written, to be sure.' He clicked his tongue at the horse to encourage it up the hill. 'But what he did to that young woman was wrong. It brought dishonour to our name and so I told him.'

She winced. Hadn't he just done the same thing with her? Perhaps it wasn't as dishonourable to trick an Albright as it was to trick a perfect stranger. Drew had been awful to Alice, pretending to love her when all he really wanted was her money. He'd pretended he was wealthy and seduced her to ensure she could not refuse to marry him. Worst of all, he'd circulated gossip about it as a sort of insurance.

Alice had refused to be blackmailed, and when Selina realised just who it was who was breaking her best friend's heart, she'd written to Ian and asked him to intercede with his brother. Drew had left town within the week.

'He didn't want to go. I had Carrick force him onto that ship. When months passed with no word, I assumed he was still angry. Then we got a letter. He had joined a group exploring new lands. They never returned. Drew always was reckless. He couldn't resist the adventure, I suppose. He went off to see more of the country instead of undertaking my commission. An acquaintance wrote and told us how it was. My mother blames me for his death.'

'That is hardly fair.'

'I should not have sent him away. He was my younger brother.'

'What he did was heartless.'

'Aye, but with the best of intentions. But I never told anyone it was you who let me know what he was up to.'

'Oh.'

'And nor should you.' His expression was fierce. 'They will never forgive you.'

Chapter Fifteen

The sound of galloping hooves behind them had Ian turning in his seat.

He cursed.

Selina turned to look and her heart sank at the sight of red uniforms and glittering accoutrements, the jingle of which drew ever closer.

Ian stopped the horse. 'We don't want to give them the idea we are running away,' he said wryly. 'One bullet wound in a week is enough for any man.'

More than enough. She steeled herself for the coming meeting.

The horses passed them and then circled around. Their leader broke rank and brought his horse close to the carriage. Lieutenant Dunstan, of course.

Dunstan's blue eyes had dark circles beneath them and his face looked weary. The pistol in his hand pointed at Ian's head. He bowed. 'Lady

Selina. Ian Gilvry, in the name of the king, I arrest you for the crime of abduction. You will come with me quietly or risk further charges.'

'And just who am I supposed to have abducted?' Ian asked.

Dunstan glanced her way. 'This lady.'

'This lady is my wife.'

Dunstan frowned. His cheekbones flushed pink. The pistol lowered. He looked at Selina again. 'Is this true? Are you married?'

'Yes.'

The pink turned to red, the pistol coming up again. 'Under duress?'

This was her chance to be rid of a husband who had tricked her into marriage. Ian was looking at her, waiting for her to deny him, but it was too late for that. No doubt he'd haul witnesses in who would say exactly what she'd done. She shook her head. 'Not under duress.'

Beside her Ian relaxed. Good Lord, had the man planned to make a fight of it?

The expression of anger on Dunstan's face dissolved into one of disappointment. He returned the pistol to its holster. 'I see.'

She felt terrible. 'I'm sorry.'

For a long moment he just looked at her and then he bowed. 'I, too, am sorry.'

Sorry he'd lost her dowry, no doubt. There wasn't a pin to choose between him and Ian. She felt a bit like a bone between two dogs. One a foxhound and the other a wolfhound. She had no doubts about which one would win.

Ian shifted in the seat beside her and she glanced at him. He was glaring at Dunstan. A bone indeed.

'We were just on our way up to the keep to see my father,' she said.

'My men and I will accompany you,' he said. 'To ensure you arrive safely.'

'I am quite capable of driving half a mile to the keep,' Ian said grimly.

'And a great deal farther, I am sure,' Dunstan said in arctic tones. He gave a brief order to his sergeant and the men fell in behind the carriage. Dunstan walked his horse alongside Selina.

'I gather your courtship was of the whirlwind variety,' Dunstan said after a few moments.

Ian made a sound like a growl low in his throat. A warning.

Selina nudged him with her elbow. The lieutenant could easily take it into his head to arrest him for some trifling offence, given the opportunity. 'Indeed, lieutenant,' she said, batting her lashes. 'A positive tornado. Although Mr Gilvry and I have known each other for a very long time. It wasn't until we met again that we realised our affections were still engaged.'

Not a bad story. Romantic. The kind of thing the *ton* might forgive after they recovered from the scandal.

Not that the *ton*'s opinion would matter, living here in the wilds of Scotland. But they did matter to her papa and Dunstan made a good sounding board for its effect.

He seemed to take it in stride, because he continued to smile even if his usually warm blue eyes seemed more like a wintery grey.

She slanted a glance at Ian. His expression was thunderous.

He probably preferred her to remain silent. She leaned a little closer to Dunstan. 'Were you able to catch the smugglers?'

The soldier flushed. 'You know I did not. I did hear there was a woman involved. Quite the adventuress, some are saying. I doubt it myself.' He raised a brow.

Was he trying to trick her into saying it was her?

Ian shot her a look that would make a lesser woman quake, but not one who had learned how to deal with the barbs issued by the ladies of the *ton*.

She shuddered. 'I can't imagine any lady doing such a thing.' She smiled up at the lieutenant. 'It is very kind of you to take the time to escort us when these criminals are still on the loose.'

Ian snorted what sounded like a muffled laugh.

Dunstan glared at him and let his horse fall back.

'You will get burned if you play with fire,' Ian muttered.

'He tried to trip me up.'

They passed through the heavy wooden gate into the keep and Ian drew the horse to a halt on the cobbles. The soldiers halted behind them in a clatter of hooves.

What had Ian said the day he brought her home last time? Oh, yes. He would not enter the gates while the keep was owned by another. Well, soon it would be his.

Dunstan once more brought his horse alongside. 'One question for you, Gilvry.' His voice was sharp, his hand on his pistol. 'How did you manage a wedding in less than two days?'

Ian looked over his shoulder. His eyes narrowed. She turned to look at the soldiers guarding the gate behind them. There was no way out. Oh, dear, they were effectively trapped. She glanced at Ian in consternation.

He raised an arrogant brow and looked at the other man. Was he planning on fighting for her, after all? If Ian was him, he would have. He held the other man's gaze. 'Scottish law doesn't require banns or a licence.'

Dunstan frowned. 'There are some formalities, though, surely?'

'All addressed and very nicely, too.' Ian's smile widened and his eyes showed a knowledge the other man would instantly understand.

Selina blushed.

The horse beneath Dunstan pranced sideways at a sudden tightening of the reins.

A palpable hit, Ian thought. Not quite a bullet to the arm, but close enough. Ian turned his attention to the portly gentleman coming down the steps into the courtyard. Albright. His father-in-law.

His colour was an unhealthy red. He rushed to the gig and helped Selina down, holding her in a tight embrace.

Something rushed through Ian's veins in a hot tide. He forced himself to step down slowly and walk around the front of the horse and stand behind his wife.

Albright held her away from him, his gaze travelling over her. 'Thank God you are safe. You gave me such a scare.'

Tears brightened Selina's eyes. 'I'm sorry, Father.' Scarlet rose in her cheeks.

Ian waited for her introduction.

Was she ashamed to admit her newly married state? He would not be surprised if she was. A little disappointed, perhaps even a trifle pained, but not surprised.

Albright became aware of his presence. His frantic gaze went to Dunstan, who hung back with his men. 'Arrest this man. He is a smuggler. He abducted my daughter.'

The blond soldier curled his lip. 'There has been no abduction, I am sorry to say, my lord. He has cleverly ensured your daughter cannot give evidence with regard to the charge of smuggling.' The starchy prig gave a stiff nod. 'If you will excuse me, my lord, I will be about the king's business.' He brought his horse's head around and moved off.

Selina frowned.

Ian held his breath, waiting for her to realise what Dunstan meant. For her to realise his real purpose for the marriage. The one thing he could not deny.

Her puzzled gaze followed the soldier, then comprehension filled her eyes, followed swiftly by fury as she turned on him. 'So that was part of your game, too. You really are despicable.'

His anger flared. 'Tell your father our news, Selina,' he said harshly, 'or I will.'

Her shoulders sagged as she turned back to the old man also watching the soldiers leave, his jaw slack with astonishment.

She took a deep breath. 'Father, I would like you to welcome my husband, Ian Gilvry.'

'What?' he said, his mouth opening and closing, his jowls wobbling. 'What?'

Ian thought the old man would drop dead on the spot of apoplexy.

'I married Mr Gilvry.'

'No.' His gaze shot to Ian. 'It is not possible. There hasn't been enough time.'

'Under Scottish law it is quite possible,' Ian said. He was getting quite weary of explaining his country's laws.

Albright's wife came running down the steps, her face full of happiness. 'Selina, dear. You are safe.'

'Apparently not,' her father said. 'She has married this fellow.'

He didn't like being called a fellow, either.

'My ancestry in the Scottish nobility goes back far longer than yours does in the ranks of the English,' he said. 'You can address me as Gilvry, or Laird. But I do not answer to fellow or you or lad.'

Albright reared back. 'You are insolent, sir.'

'Sir is all right, too.'

'Father, Papa,' Selina said in soothing tones, her voice light and breathy. 'I am married to Ian Gilvry. There is nothing anyone can do to change it.'

There went the twang of his conscience again. It wasn't as if she'd been asked for her hand and had accepted. Not in the sense a young woman of her rank would expect to be asked. He'd tricked her, just as she'd said. Not that she hadn't been a willing participant in the resulting seduction, he thought darkly.

'May I say how pleased I am that Lady Selina accepted my suit,' he said politely.

The old man looked ready to explode. He kept his face fixed on Selina. 'Why? When you could have had so much more?'

'It is too late for regrets,' she said, but regret showed on her face.

Ian wanted to hit something.

'You could have had a duke or an earl.'

'Before the accident, Father.'

'I would have settled enough on you to make it happen. I told you that. But you said you wanted Dunstan. And now this? A criminal. And Scottish to boot.' He glared at Ian. 'What have you done to my daughter?'

'Melville,' his pretty wife whispered, putting a hand on his sleeve. He looked at it and seemed to gather himself. It stopped his tirade at any rate.

Selina's eyes filled with tears. 'I'm sorry, Father. It was all my own doing. There was really no other option.'

So she wasn't going to tell her father how he'd tricked her.

Albright's face reddened further. 'You should be ashamed.'

He'd had enough of listening to the father casti-gate his wife. 'Whatever your opinion of me, my lord,' he said stiffly, 'your daughter is now legally my wife. As is usual under these circumstances, I believe there are certain settlements to be made.'

The colour drained from the old man's face. And from Selina's too, he saw. What? Did she think he wouldn't insist she receive her dowry? Did she think he would allow her to live in poverty?

'Very well,' Albright said. 'Come to my study, Gilvry. Take your spoils.' He glared at his wife. 'Lady Albright, be ready to leave in an hour. As for you, daughter, I would prefer not to look on your face before I depart.'

She reached out a hand. 'Papa, can you not un-derstand that this could be a good thing?'

Her defence surprised him, but he could see it was hopeless.

'I see nothing of the sort.'

The stricken look in Selina's eyes gave Ian a pain in his gut.

Albright, his arm linked through his wife's, turned and walked heavily up the steps. 'Come now or come not at all, Gilvry.'

Much as he would have liked to stay and comfort Selina, he had to get this business done. He gave her a quick hug. 'Wait here.'

She looked ready to argue.

'Wait.'

Chapter Sixteen

Selina stared up at the old stone walls that were about to become her home. Permanently.

Years ago, dazed by his kisses, she'd dreamed of this. Now the dream of a foolish schoolgirl had come true. But not in the way she had imagined. There was no love involved. Just advantage.

What a fool. One smile, one look at his face and the defences she'd built up over the years had instantly crumbled.

What if Father never forgave her for this last piece of folly? What if he refused to see her ever again?

Perhaps Chrissie could soften his anger.

She looked up at her father's study window. No doubt her husband and father would be engaged for a while. She ran up the steps and headed for Chrissie's chamber with hope in her heart.

She passed through the chamber with the oriole

window overlooking the courtyard that would have once been the lord's chamber and now served as Chrissie's sitting room and into the bedchamber where she heard sounds of movement.

Chrissie was directing her maid with the packing.

She looked up at Selina's entry with a small gasp. 'Oh, Selina,' she said, looking sorrowful. She glanced at the maid and walked into the sitting room before speaking. 'Your father was out of his mind with worry. And now this?'

'I know he's upset and disappointed, but perhaps in time he will forgive me, don't you think?'

Chrissie looked at her. 'Not for a long while, I think. His heart is wounded, he had great hopes of Dunstan.'

It was more likely it was his pride she had wounded. A footman knocked. 'Come for the baggage, my lady.' They remained silent as he carried out Chrissie's trunks and boxes, the maid following along behind admonishing him to be careful.

'Will you write to me?' Selina asked. 'Tell me how he fares from time to time?'

'If he does not forbid it.' Chrissie smiled her sweet smile. 'But then, I will not ask his permission, I shall assume it. And I will speak to him on your behalf, when he comes down from the boughs.'

It was time to say farewell. Selina held out a hand. 'Oh, Chrissie, I am truly sorry for spoiling your visit to Scotland.'

Chrissie shook her head a little ruefully. 'It has certainly been a good deal more…exciting than I expected.'

Chrissie clasped her hands together and paced to the window, then swung around to face Selina. 'I wish I'd never asked Melville to bring us.'

'Me, too,' Selina said. She couldn't help her sigh. 'I thought I had the future so carefully planned.' And she had given it all up for a devil's kiss.

A noise at the open door brought her head up. She winced as she saw Ian standing there looking like thunder. 'I thought I told you to wait,' he said.

'I wanted to bid Chrissie farewell.'

'Well, do it now. Her ladyship's carriage awaits.'

Tears glinting in her eyes, Chrissie threw her arms around her and hugged her close. 'I'll speak to him for you.' Head down, not looking at Ian, she whisked out of the room.

Ian's hard expression softened. 'Your father doesn't like this wedding any more than does my family. We can only hope they both come around.

Come.' He held out his hand. 'We will watch them depart from the ramparts.'

He tucked her hand under his arm and walked her along the corridor to the door that opened onto the winding staircase that led up to the small platform behind the tower's crenellation.

The narrow steps meant they had to go single file. She pressed the latch on the door at the top and stepped outside. She hadn't been up here for a very long time and gasped at the strength of the wind and the way it buffeted against her ears. Her father's carriage was already passing through the arch.

Gone without so much as a farewell and certainly no blessing. She had the sense she might never see him again. Prickles stung the back of her eyes. Her vision misted. She swallowed the lump in her throat and stared at the receding carriage, wishing with all her heart things could have been different.

Had she known what would come of her attempt to help, would she have rushed out into the night? The answer wasn't quite as clear in her mind as she thought it should be.

Ian looked at her straight back and the way the skirts of that shockingly red skirt clung to her slender legs, held there by the wind, and didn't know what to say as she watched her father's coach disappear.

He wanted to offer comfort, but her straight back and stiff body shut him out. He had the feeling whatever he said would be wrong.

He was married, but somehow, at this moment, he felt lonelier than he'd ever felt during all his years as Laird. Being in charge of his people was a duty he could not share with anyone else. Except a wife, perhaps. The right sort of wife.

In the past he'd made decisions he wasn't proud of, made mistakes, too, and those were his burdens to shoulder. But he'd always imagined that marriage would give him someone to share in his joys and, damn it, his sorrows in a way that brothers or clan members could not.

But the clan didn't seem at all ready to accept her. And they could be cruel to outsiders. A shudder passed down his spine as he recalled what his brothers had said to her when they were younger.

He would do all he could to protect her from their anger. In time they would come to accept the idea. They must. While this marriage had not started off on the best of feet, surely it could only get better from here.

He put a hand on her shoulder. She stiffened beneath his fingers, but then turned to face him.

His gut lurched. She'd been crying. He could see the moisture in her eyes.

An emotion he hadn't expected rose in his gorge. 'Are you so sorry for losing Dunstan, then?'

Damn, why did he have to ask that?

She looked at him for a moment, blinking back her tears before she spoke. 'He would have made a perfect husband. He was my choice.' She bit her lip and turned her face away as if appalled at what she'd said.

The words shouldn't hurt, because they were honest, but they did.

He let go a sigh. It didn't matter what she wanted. She was stuck with him now.

She looked so beautiful with strands of her dark hair whipping around her face. And so vulnerable. He wanted to kiss away the shadows in her eyes. Allay her fears. If she would let him. He offered her a smile of encouragement. 'It will be all right. You will see.'

Her expression softened for just a moment, her lips parting. He leaned closer, inhaling her scent, feeling her breath on his jaw. This was their common ground. This was where he would win the battle.

She frowned. 'Why didn't you tell the men at the inn about the keep being part of the settlement?'

This was a trap. No doubt about it. He'd need to tread warily. 'I wasna' sure your father would give me the same terms as Dunstan.'

Her mouth turned down in a bitter grimace.

Wrong answer, he realised. He opened his mouth to say more, but she tossed her head back and looked at him full on, her gaze hard and cold.

'It seems you got everything you wanted.' She swept an arm around to encompass the surrounding hills. 'Let me go. To Alice. As we planned.'

The words landed on his chest like one of the stones from the castle wall, hard, cold and heavy. 'You are my wife.' My wife. It sounded like ownership. It sounded medieval. He was feeling pretty medieval right at that moment as a primitive urge to claim her blasted though his veins.

'In name only.' She spoke so calmly, she might have been discussing the weather. She smiled then, a brittle little curve to her lips. 'You don't need me. You have what you Gilvrys have always wanted. Dunross Keep.'

'Your place is here.' Och, now he *sounded* medieval. He reached for her hands and almost cursed when she tucked them behind her.

'Give it three months,' he said. 'If you are still of the same mind then, I'll let you go.' If he could not win his wife in three months with the kind of passion they shared, he did not deserve to keep her.

She didn't look happy. Because she knew he would win, he thought with a surge of triumph.

'A week,' she said.

Oh, yes, she knew he would win. He shook his head. 'A month. No less, or we will forget all about this nonsense.'

She glared at him. 'It isn't nonsense to want to leave a place where everyone hates you.'

'They need time to become accustomed to the idea.' And in the meantime, he would do his best to make sure she never wanted to leave.

Anger followed by determination chased across her face. 'Very well. A month.'

Now why did he suddenly have the feeling the trap had closed? He reached out a hand. 'Then we have a bargain.'

She took it. Instead of shaking her hand, he brought her small cold fingers to his lips, turned them palm up and kissed the inside her wrist. He felt her shiver, slight though it was, and saw the flush of heat in her face. He smiled. He was worrying for nothing. A month would be plenty of time. He released her. 'Let us go down.'

She made to push past him.

He barred her way. 'Let me go ahead, lass. The stairs are steep and twisty.'

'You might be wiser to give me a good hard push from behind. Perhaps I'd obligingly break my neck, then you can marry someone of whom your clan will approve.'

Red veiled his vision. He caught her arm, held her immobile while staring into her flashing dark eyes, noting the petulant set of her full lower lip. She tipped her chin in defiance. Taunting him. Daring him to prove his baseness. Winning her might not be as easy as he thought.

He took a deep breath and smiled with what he hoped was calmness and not quite the grimace he felt on his face. 'As long as I have breath in my body, you will suffer no harm from me.'

'No more harm, you mean,' she said with an overly sweet smile of her own.

He wasn't going to pursue that, not now. 'Come, let us go down, supper will soon be ready.'

And then would come the night and the battle would commence in earnest. His body hardened. This war between them definitely had its compensations.

He headed down the stairs, holding her hand fast in his all the way.

Chapter Seventeen

Supper was done and cleared away, the candles and the fire were lit, and they were alone in the old solar, the room off the bedroom Chrissie had used. Across the blackened wooden planks of the ancient trestle table, Ian sprawled in a carved wood chair, sipping his whisky like some medieval knight and watching her from heavy-lidded eyes.

As if she was some choice morsel he had yet to taste.

He'd got his precious keep. Why did he have to want her, too? Thank God she hadn't blurted out foolish professions of love the previous night. That would have made him impossible. She just had to survive a month of him and then she could go her own way.

It was even a better arrangement than she would have had with Dunstan. They would have lived together. With Ian, she would have freedom and respectability. She should be feeling pleased, not miserable.

There was no reason to feel miserable. Not once had he indicated he cared for her no more than he might care for any other woman. Attraction, yes. Lust, yes. But nothing more. And look how quickly he'd agreed to let her go in a month if they did not suit. No doubt he wanted to make sure the marriage could not be disputed. But for that, he would have let her leave with her father.

Not that Father would have taken her. She didn't quite understand why he'd been so angry. She could have understood disappointment, but it was as if there was something of importance riding on her marriage to Dunstan.

Ian rose.

Her heart beat faster. Her mouth dried. She felt flustered. Unsure.

In London, this would be the moment when she would retire to the drawing room for tea and he'd take his port in some male dominion. His study, if he was alone, the dining room if he had company. But this room was the domain of the lady of the keep. She had nowhere to go except to her bedroom.

He held out his hand. 'Come. We will sit by the fire.'

Two deep chairs flanked the merrily blazing hearth.

So he intended to prolong the evening. Continue the pretence of married bliss. No doubt for the sake of appearances, with half his clansmen now employed in the keep. With a sigh she rose to her feet and strode for one of the chairs.

Before she could sit, he swept her up in his arms and sat down with her on his lap.

'What are you doing?' she gasped.

'Enjoying a pleasant evening with my wife.'

The way his deep voice caressed the word 'wife' sent a shiver down her spine. She stiffened against the traitorous trickles of heat that sparked in her veins.

She gazed at the fire, trying to pretend she felt nothing, that the strong arms holding her against his chest were not warm or protective. That the feel of his heartbeat against her shoulder didn't send little thrills of anticipation through her body.

But she was his wife. And she could not deny him her body, a little voice whispered with a bit too much glee and excitement.

'I'm tired,' she said. 'I would like to retire.'

'Bed sounds like a good idea.' Amusement coloured his voice, along with desire.

Heat rushed through her. Anger. Defiance. 'It

has been a long wearing day. Surely you will not force yourself on me tonight?'

She winced at the brittleness in her tone. Clinging to her anger was not easy when cradled so softly in his arms. But his utter stillness said her barb had reached its mark.

His chest rose and fell with a long breath. A man trying to hold on to his patience. Perhaps if she made him angry enough, he'd let her go sooner than later.

Fingers calloused by work grasped her chin with gentle force and brought her face around. Blue eyes dancing with the light of the fire gazed into her face. He didn't look particularly angry. Indeed, he looked as he always did, handsome, alluring, manly.

Then a seductively dark smile curved his lips. 'That's better,' he said. 'Your face is lovely by firelight. I have not yet looked my fill.'

He wasn't the first man to praise her beauty, but his softly spoken words warmed her more than any before. Somehow the power she'd always drawn from her beauty leached away in his presence. He made her feel weak. Needy.

Needing anyone was a mistake.

She returned his smile with one of her own. 'La, husband, you flatter me.'

His gaze darkened a fraction. 'It is not flattery to speak the truth.' His lips descended on hers, gentle, wooing, teasing.

She tried to resist, to pretend his kisses did not make her dizzy, did not rob her of reason. Indeed, she even went so far as to place the flat of her hand on his shoulder to push him away, but instead her fingers closed on the lapel of his coat, clutching as if she would hold on to him. Her lips parted and his tongue stroked with a soft silken slide. And she was lost.

Lost in passion. Her body clenching at the thought of the pleasure to come.

A soft groan rumbled up from his chest as her tongue tangled with his in a shocking dance of intimacy she'd learned only one night before, yet now seemed to know the steps by heart. The give and take of pleasure.

Her hands cradling his head, the silk of his hair brushing her skin, she pressed into his hard wall of chest, while his hands wandered across her back, her buttocks, her thigh. Beneath her, the evidence of his desire pressed against her.

She let the passion carry away her fears and her anger, let physical sensation fill all the corners of her mind. Her body trembled at the sensual on-slaught of his mouth, his hands, his body.

Heat rolled off him in waves. His scent filled her nostrils, the clean smell of the Highlands, the tang of soap, but more powerful yet, his essence.

And then he stood up, rising from the chair with her in his arms as if she weighed nothing.

Released from the magic of his kiss, she scrambled to pull herself back together. 'What are you doing?'

'Taking my wife to bed.' He gave her a wicked grin that curled her toes in her slippers. 'That was what you wanted, was it not?'

'Not quite,' she managed, though it was hard enough to breathe, let alone speak with any sense.

He cocked an arrogant brow. 'Tell me I did wrong after it is done, lass.' He strode for the bedchamber, kicked open the door and deposited her gently on her feet.

Now was the moment to tell him to leave, before she succumbed to him utterly. Before he stole her sense of self.

The resolve in his face, the determination in his eyes said he would not be gainsaid his rights as a husband. Nor did she want to gainsay him. Damn it. In the matter of attraction, of physical desire, it seemed they were of one mind. Yet she still resented the way he'd played her for a fool.

Well, she was a fool no longer. And she had her

own arsenal of weapons. As long as she shielded her heart, as long as she kept him at a distance, she would be safe.

He had proposed the bargain, and in all honour he had no choice but to keep to it, just as she'd had no choice but to agree to this marriage. She would enjoy her month of married life and at the end of it she would walk away.

Without regret. Or very little.

She stood on her tiptoes, twined her arms around his neck and drew his head down. His eyes widened with surprise and flared with banked heat.

Then she tasted him in a slow measured kiss, teasing his lips with her tongue, nipping with her teeth. His hands skimmed her body as if they knew just how to touch and where so her bones would melt and her mind turn to mush.

One large warm hand came to her breast, gently circling and teasing, while the other explored the shape of her hips and her buttocks.

With each stroke of his tongue, each caress of his hand, he stoked the fires within until her body took on a will of its own, melding into him, demanding more.

Flames of desire leapt within her, heat flushed through her and the tension within her tightened.

When he broke the kiss to pull at the laces of her bodice, she fumbled with the buttons of his coats.

When he knelt to remove her stockings, she fought with the knot of his cravat. When he untied the strings of her petticoats, she undid the buttons of his shirts. Urgency made each article of clothing a barrier to be conquered.

Finally she stood before him in nothing but her chemise. And he was naked. Beautiful. An aroused pagan warrior.

He stood still and proud and let her look. The sight stole her breath. Too bad she had to let him go. A pang twisted her heart.

He stepped towards her. 'Selina,' he murmured and there was comfort in his voice, along with the husky rasp of lust.

Now was not the time for comfort. That was not what she needed from him. It came too close to emotions she would never admit to. Not ever.

She undid the ties of her chemise and let it slip down her shoulders and slither its way to the floor. She could not hold back her smile as his hot dark gaze followed its progress, stopping only for a second to linger at her breasts and belly and finally the heart of her femininity.

On a groan he pulled her close, his mouth coming down hard on hers, ravishing and plundering and pleasuring.

She gave herself up to the pleasure of his hard strong body pressed against hers and rejoiced when he eased her back onto the bed, never breaking the kiss for a moment.

This was all she needed. All she would ever accept. She wasn't a child any longer and he would not break her heart again.

She stroked her hands over his shoulders, across the plane of his strong wide back. He felt lovely beneath her palms, skin like silk, muscle like bands of iron rippling beneath her hands. His soft indrawn breath let her know he enjoyed her touch as much as she enjoyed his. Perhaps she wouldn't be the only one to suffer loss when she left.

The thought pleased her. Gave her a surge of confidence, returned a little of the feminine power she had always relied on.

When he finally broke the kiss, he raised himself up to look into her face, as if he had noticed something different and was puzzled. She smiled at him.

He swallowed. '*Leannan,*' he breathed. 'My lovely wife.' There was awe in his voice.

It was nothing new, her beauty, or male admiration, but there was something of awe in the way he said the words that seemed to caress a soft place in her heart.

She didn't want tenderness. She reached up and clasped her hands around the back of his neck, drawing herself up to tease his lips with her tongue and her teeth. A soft groan filled her ears and he pressed his thigh between her legs. She shifted, parting her thighs, welcoming him into the cradle of her hips, telling him she was ready for their joining and the pleasure she had learned it would bring.

'Selina, love,' he rasped against her mouth. 'Slow down. You'll unman me.'

'Is that a bad thing?' she asked with a teasing note in her voice.

He took a deep ragged breath. 'It might be.' And then he was pressing hot kisses to her throat, licking the rise of her breasts, laving her nipples with his tongue, making her writhe and squirm beneath him as the pull of tension tightened within her.

His hand went to the apex of her thighs and he parted the soft folds and she felt his fingers slide within her slick passage. She cried out as a shudder of desire swept through her as he teased her with his touch.

She wanted to curse him, when he stopped and raised his head to look into her face with a dark smile of satisfaction. She let her hands slide down his back to the rise of his buttocks and pulled him tight against the heart of her that ached with a need for his flesh against hers.

The expression on his face tightened to one of painful intensity.

To see the effect of her actions on his face jolted through her like lightning, a hot spark of lust that darkened the edge of her vision and brought her close to the edge of bliss and yet keeping it just out of reach; she wanted to scream her frustration.

The inner core of her fluttered and tightened and she lifted her hips, wrapping her legs around his waist. And then, as if in obedience to her will, he drove home. Deep within her, he filled her and remained utterly still.

On a moan, she twisted her hips, fought to find the deeper pleasure waiting just beyond reach. One large hand went beneath her, bringing her body tight against his. The other curved around her breast. He bent his head and took her nipple in his mouth.

And then he suckled.

The sharpest sweetest pain she could ever imagine pierced her to the core.

He drove into her again and again as she shattered in a fiery burst of light behind her eyes as her core pulsed around his shaft. A deep sound in his throat and the convulsive shudders of his body heightened her bliss.

It seemed like hours before her heartbeat returned to normal and she noticed the hot weight of him on her body. It could not have been more than a moment or two, but the warmth went on and on, waves of it making her languid and content. When he eased off her and pulled her close against his chest, she felt replete and complete.

Dangerous, she thought, but undeniably wonderful.

After a week, Selina's life at Dunross Keep settled into a rhythm. Tumultuous passion at night, followed by long, hellishly boring days.

Tonight, as usual, her husband sat with his dram of whisky beside the hearth, reading the news from London, while with a stomach tied in knots she pretended to read a book.

From beneath her lowered lashes she couldn't help but watch him, the way he sprawled in his chair, his long legs stretched out before him encased in a pair of buckskins, his shirt closed by a practical stock, rather than a cravat, and his shirtsleeves rolled up. He'd discarded his coats because of the warmth of the evening.

He looked handsome, relaxed and very much the Laird of Dunross.

He belonged here. Unlike her. There was nothing for her here. No society. No friends. No purpose. She was nothing but a china ornament to be admired and caressed and put away at the beginning of each day.

Three more weeks and she'd be free to leave. No matter how he wooed her in the bedroom, she was determined to make him stand by their bargain.

Chapter Eighteen

Ian had tricked her into thinking there was more between them than there was, and she wasn't going to pretend it was otherwise.

Every day he left her alone and went off to the mill. Each day, she carefully erected reasons why she should not give herself to this man. And each night it was ridiculous how easily he tore down those objections with his lovemaking.

She had no illusions about why they had married, and he might torment her body each night until she cried out with the pleasure of it, but he was not going to touch her heart. Not a second time.

He must have sensed her looking at him, since he glanced up.

She bit her lip.

'Out with it, lass,' he said quietly. 'What troubles you?'

'How do you know something troubles me?'

'There's an expression you get on your face.' He shrugged. 'I can't quite explain it.'

'I am troubled by the idea that you are smuggling again. Not that I care if you endanger yourself, understand, but I think the people of Dunross deserve better.'

His lips twisted wryly. ''Tis kind of you to worry, but the people of Dunross are my concern.'

'Don't you think I have a right to know if you are involved in a criminal activity? Something that might bring the law down on my head, too?'

He folded his paper and put it on one side with a sigh. 'We are turning the mill into a commercial still,' he said quietly.

'An illegal still, you mean. Are you mad?'

He grimaced. 'My family, my people, have been making whisky for centuries. It is our right.' He gave a hard laugh. 'Anywhere else in Britain, apart from the Highlands, what I am doing would be perfectly legal.'

'How so?'

'When they passed the law delineating the Highlands, the English Parliament also passed a law that no still beyond that line should have a capacity of less than five hundred gallons. Anything less is outside the law.'

'And that is what you are building?' She felt a

flicker of relief. Not for him, he could do just as he wished, she assured herself, but for the people of Dunross.

'That,' he said flatly, 'is well nigh impossible. We can't grow enough barley for a still of that size.'

'Surely if the farmers all got together?'

He nodded. 'We might come close. But if we don't, we are still taxed as if we did. And even so, we can only sell what we produce in the Highlands. Pointless, when every man worth his salt makes his own. We are being penalised for the sins of our forefathers.' He frowned. 'Not to mention that distillers in England don't like the competition because they know our whisky is better than any geneva they can make.'

'Why make whisky at all? Or is it your dearest wish to go to prison?' Or worse.

'You don't understand.'

'I understand well enough that you are taking risks with other people's lives.'

A crease formed between his brows. 'You were out today. Where did you go?'

Changing the topic, because her opinion mattered not one wit.

'I went for a ride. What else is there for me to do?' She winced, knowing she sounded like a sulky child. 'I rode to Balnaen Cove. Topaz needed the exercise.'

He frowned. 'You should not go so far from the keep.'

'Why? Are you afraid I might see more smugglers?'

He cast her a dark glance. 'We still don't know who betrayed us to the gaugers. Or whether they intend more mischief. If you wish to exercise your horse, you will do it in my company.'

'You are never here during the day.'

A seductive smile curved his lips, his eyes becoming heavy-lidded and lighting with a wicked gleam. 'Are you telling me you are missing me during the day, lass?'

Heat flashed through her. Unwelcome little stirrings trickled through her blood. She stiffened against them. 'Certainly not. I am telling you I do not intend to sit inside these walls all day long with nothing to do.'

He frowned. 'You have things to do. The running of the household.'

'It pretty well runs itself. It isn't as if we have a vast number of servants and nor do we have guests to entertain. I tried visiting your mother, but was turned away at the door.'

His gaze shuttered. 'You know she isn't well.'

'I thought to ask her to live here at the keep. She would be more comfortable. She could have her own suite of rooms.'

''Tis kind of you, lass,' he said and there was warmth in his expression, but he shook his head. 'She's still not used to the idea of our marriage. You have to give her more time.'

'Not used to it? She hates it.' She shrugged. 'It doesn't matter to me. I'll be gone soon enough.'

The warmth in his eyes fled, replaced by a look of hurt. Or was she mistaken, as she was mistaken in so much about this man? For now it was determination on his face. His gaze dropped to her breasts and then rose again. Heat flooded through her.

Her body tingled.

She fought the sudden rush of desire. To no avail. He was already rising to his feet, a hand held out for hers. It seemed that conversation was over.

Ian wanted to curse as he looked at his beautiful wife. Every day she grew less and less happy. A woman like her should be dancing at balls, be the centre of society instead of stuck in a backwater like Dunross.

What had he expected? That she would be happy here, because she was with him? Four weeks she had given him. And every night he did his best to bind her to him. And every morning he knew it wasn't working.

Yet.

A Gilvry never gave up.

Sitting with her after dinner in her sitting room always helped him relax. Made him forget the day's worries in the anticipation of the night to come.

But his guilt over Andrew was always there, a looming shadow between them. He didn't blame her for what he'd done. She'd only asked for his help. The urge to win her gratitude had made him act against his brother more harshly than was warranted.

Thank God no one else knew what he had done. Nor would he ever let her influence him that way again. He would not let her twist him around her little finger. He was the Laird of Dunross and she would abide by his decisions as did the rest of his people.

Even so, he was gnawed by guilt, a feeling in his gut, that Drew had died so Ian could have everything he ever wanted. Dunross. Selina.

Except he didn't really have Selina. She clearly still had every intention of leaving. He should just let her go. It would be easier on them all. But the thought of her returning to her London friends, a married woman, free to do as she pleased, drove him to the madness of trying to win her.

And God knew they were compatible in bed. Blissfully so. Not that she came like a lamb. Each night he had to woo her anew. But the pleasure was not all one sided. Not in the least.

Lust surged through him. And something else. A kind of softness he did not want to examine too closely. He was already weak enough when it came to this woman.

He swept her up in his arms, gazed down into her face and saw her eyes were the colour of whisky. No shadows now. Only desire. Whatever the differences between them, in their desire for each other they were equally matched. And that was enough for him. Wasn't it?

It had to be. It was more than he deserved.

Heat raced through his veins and he strode for their bed.

'What are you doing?' she said, clearly knowing very well what he was doing, but bedevilling him none the less.

'I've had enough of arguments for one night. And talk of leaving.'

He set her down on her feet and pulled her into his arms, kissing and nibbling at her full lush lips, teasing them with his tongue until he felt her body start to melt beneath his hands, the way she always did. He just wished that once she would initiate their lovemaking. His body hardened to granite at the thought and he almost groaned aloud just imagining such a thing.

Sometimes she did things with her hands and her mouth that sent him far too quickly over the edge and he wondered if it was intentional. But he doubted it. She was too angry with him for tricking her into this marriage for her to care about his pleasure. He wasn't sure she would ever let go of that anger, but he would continue to attempt to convince her. As long as she'd let him.

Just as he would try to make her forget Dunstan.

He plundered her mouth with his tongue and she slipped her arms around his neck in sensual surrender. Perhaps tonight would be the night he'd win more than her body.

The next morning it was pouring with rain so Selina was surprised when a grim-faced Angus brought a message to the breakfast table that Mr Tearny urgently wanted to see Ian in the hall.

'Is something wrong?' she asked.

'That is for the Laird to say.' Angus didn't like the land agent, who was employed by both Carrick and the Dunross estate, and had remained after her father left. As Angus had. By choice.

Ian put down his knife and fork. His face took on hard lines as he rose from the table. 'I had better see him right away.' He followed Angus from the room.

Selina frowned at her toast. He hadn't asked her to join him. Nor had he said she should not. And Angus's grim countenance had aroused her curiosity.

It was a large space, once used by the Laird for his men-at-arms and the keep's servants. It still had the raised dais at one end where in the old days the lord and his family would have taken their meal. Now the space was primarily used for storage.

Her father had also used it when in residence as a place to fulfil his responsibilities as Justice of the Peace. It seemed that Ian was doing the same. A solitary chair and small table held the centre of the dais and Ian was already seated by the time Selina reached the bottom of the stairs behind him.

She remained in the shadows. Silent. Watching. It was the first time she had seen him in the role of Laird. He looked stern, perhaps even harsh, where the light from a window high in the wall cast his face in shadow.

Tearny stood before him with a firm grasp

around the arm of a young lad. A brace of rabbits lay at his feet. The boy brushed his russet hair out of his green eyes with defiance. There was a large red mark on his face, like a recent blow from a fist. Selina had a sense of recognition, yet she did not think she knew the lad.

'Well, Tearny?' Ian said without expression. Strange how both Scotland and Ireland spoke Gaelic, yet neither could understand the other in their native languages. It meant they had to resort to English.

'Caught young McKinly poaching, Laird,' Tearny said, his Irish lilt unmistakable.

McKinly. Selina stifled a gasp and pressed a hand to her chest. This must be the older boy she had not met. That was why she thought she had recognised him. He had the look of Marie Flora.

The land agent pushed the rabbits with his foot. 'He didn't deny it.'

'On whose land did you catch him?' Ian asked.

What did it matter whose land? No one cared about a few rabbits.

'He was on your land, Laird, when I caught him. But he could have caught them Carrick side. He won't tell me.'

Carrick's land abutted theirs to the south.

Ian frowned at the McKinly boy. 'What do you have to say for yourself?'

'My wee brother Tommy has been sick with the ague. Grannie McDonald said he needed a broth to make him well.' He glowered at Tearny. 'I only took what we needed for a stew.'

'Who hit you?' Selina asked, then winced as all eyes turned on her. She held her ground as Ian gazed at her with lowered brows.

He gestured to a stool beside his chair. 'Lady wife, you are welcome to watch the proceedings, but please do not interrupt.'

She flushed, but, shoulders straight, she climbed the steps up on to the dais and perched on the stool.

'Who hit you?' Ian said gently to the boy.

'I did,' Tearny said before the lad had a chance to reply. 'He kicked me in the shins, trying to escape. He knew he was in the wrong.'

'You hit me before I kicked you,' the boy muttered.

Ian looked at the rabbits. 'If they were discovered on my land,' he said, looking at Tearny, 'then we must assume they are my rabbits. Unless you have evidence to the contrary?'

The Irishman shook his head. 'Doesn't matter whose land. He stole them. If he wants rabbits, he should go to the common land and hunt them there.'

'The common land no has a rabbit to be seen,' the boy said.

Tearny glared at him, then turned to Ian. 'There's gratitude for ye. I told you it would do no good to give them free land for grazing their beasts. They just want more.'

Ian's eyes narrowed. 'Poaching is a serious crime, young man.'

Selina couldn't repress her gasp at the severity in his tone. 'It is only a few rabbits,' she said.

Ian glared at her.

'Well, it is,' she said. 'We could do with a few less of them, too. They make holes everywhere.'

'It seems my wife has no fondness for rabbit holes, Tearny.' His voice held a touch of wryness.

Selina frowned. Was he referring to the time she'd twisted her ankle in one of their burrows? The first time he kissed her. She flushed red. If not for that rabbit hole, it was unlikely they would ever have spoken at all.

She glared at him. He raised a brow in response, then turned back to the matter at hand.

The bruise on the boy's face was turning purple. It wasn't right for a man Tearny's size to strike a boy.

'Ye need to make an example of him, Laird,' Tearny said heavily. 'They'll be clearing the land of game birds next.'

Anger, hot and wild, rose up inside her. She shot to her feet. 'What are you suggesting? That he be hanged? Or transported?' She turned on Ian. 'He's only a child. He needed meat for his brother. You can't do such a wicked thing.'

The young lad's mouth dropped open. Tearny looked shocked, then looked at Ian with a sneer on his lips.

Ian's face darkened to thunderous. 'Be silent, woman.'

She rose to her feet. 'I'll not sit here and listen to such…such inhumanity.'

'You will sit and listen to my judgement,' Ian said quietly, and there was more danger in that quiet tone than there was in all of Tearny's bluster.

But she didn't care. What he was doing was wrong. Blindly she leapt down from the dais and hurried out of the chamber into the courtyard and the driving rain. She didn't care what kind of sentence Ian imposed, she was going to find a way to send the boy back to his father, before anything bad happened to him.

Ian half-rose in his seat, then realised he'd have to let her go. Tearny thought him weak enough already with the concessions he'd given to the clan, without him chasing after his wife, a woman who had just flayed him with her tongue. He could almost imagine a strip of skin a yard wide ripped off his back.

So much for wifely respect. Somehow he would have to make her understand that it was important that they present a united front to the world. In private, they could argue. The clan would turn against her completely if they thought she was trying to rule the roost. It was the way they were. She needed to give them time to become used to her, to see her as the wife of the Laird, not an outsider, before she handed out her opinions.

It was a discussion they would have later, behind closed doors. Right now he had a more important matter on his mind. One that would set the tone with the clansmen for the future.

'Well, lad,' Ian said sternly, 'what do you have to say for yourself?'

'We are not like thieving Irish,' the boy blurted out.

Ian focused in on the boy. 'Say what you mean.'

The boy darted a glance at Tearny's dark frown and shook his head.

Ian switched to Gaelic. 'I am your Laird. You

must answer the question. Be a man. If you have right on your side, no harm will come to you.'

The boy straightened his spine. 'Everyone knows Tearny—'

'In English, lad,' Ian said.

The boy took a deep breath, glanced at Tearny, then started to speak. 'Everyone knows Tearny sells grouse and snipe to a butcher in Wick and pockets the money.'

'Is this true?' Ian asked.

The Irishman shuffled his feet. ''Tis one of the perks. Lord Albright gave me permission. As does the Carrick. It has no bearing on him stealing rabbits.'

'I am Laird here now and I did not give you permission,' he said quietly. 'The estate requires the income from all the birds it raises.'

'As you wish. But I'm not the one on trial here. The boy is.'

Ian turned his gaze back to the boy, who shrank a little.

Stone-faced, Ian leaned back and folded his arms across his chest, regarding the man and boy before him. He had to make the right decision here, prove he was the Laird in truth, not just in name.

The boy squirmed a little, but held his gaze. Tearny, on the other hand, looked anywhere but his face. For some odd reason he had the feeling the man was out to make trouble.

'I suppose the boy should count himself fortunate you didn't shoot him first and ask questions afterwards.' He kept his voice neutral.

Tearny grinned. 'Aye, but question him, Laird. You'll find the father knew what he was up to. Encouraged him. He's the one who should be standing before ye.'

'No!' the boy yelled. 'Pa didn't...' He looked at Ian, then flushed bright red. He pressed his lips together.

'But you did hit the boy?' Ian asked mildly.

'Gave me some lip, kicked me, then tried to run off.'

Ian nodded. 'Mr Tearny, I do not approve of grown men striking boys.'

Tearny's fists clenched. 'Very well, Laird. I'll remember that in future.'

'In fact, I don't approve of any of your methods. I think it is time Dunross dispensed with your services. You will attend me in my office in one hour when we will settle matters between us. You may go.'

Tearny's face turned brick red. His jaw worked as if he would argue, but he must have thought better of it because he gave a jerk of his head. 'As you wish.' He glared at the boy. 'Be assured Lord Carrick will not welcome your trespass, boy. So make sure you do not stray onto his land.' He spun on his heel and stomped out of the hall.

The McKinly boy grinned and made a rude gesture at Tearny's departing back.

'Enough,' Ian said grimly. 'Why have you no been attending the school at the tythe barn?'

The boy shrugged. 'I'm too old for school.'

'No man is too old to learn something new,' Ian said. 'As your punishment for not asking permission to trap rabbits on my land, you will attend every afternoon after you have finished your chores for your father. Now get those rabbits home.'

The boy ducked his head, obviously relieved. 'Yes, Laird.' He picked up the carcases and ran for the door.

'Oh, McKinly,' Ian said. The boy stopped and turned, anxiety written all over his face.

'No more than a brace every two weeks, do you ken? And that goes for everyone else or they'll be no rabbits left this side of Edinburgh.'

His face brightened. He shot out of the door and was gone.

Ian let go a long sigh. Now he had to deal with his angry wife. It made him feel a little sick to know that she thought so badly of him that she thought he would harm the boy.

He went out into the courtyard. Rain splattered his face as he glanced around.

Angus, talking to one of the grooms, gestured with his chin towards the stables. With a heaviness in his chest he hated, he ducked into the barn. It took a moment for his eyes to adjust to the gloom, then he saw her in the stall with her gelding, rhythmically stroking his glossy coat with a brush. What would he give for that kind of attention from his wife?

He strode towards her and she turned at the sound of his footfall. A frown appeared and she turned away to continue her brushing.

'Planning on going somewhere?' he asked and was aware that there was an edge of anger in his voice, despite his attempt to sound pleasant.

'I thought I might go for a ride.'

'And when were you intending to come and ask me to go with you?'

She kept on brushing. 'I was going to ask Angus.'

Another nice hit to his pride. Of course she'd sooner go with his steward.

'And where were you planning on going? McKinly's croft, by any chance?' This time he made no effort to keep the bitterness from his voice.

'Perhaps.'

'To what purpose?'

'To tell him that his son is here. That he should come and…and…speak for him. Rescue him. Something. Couldn't you see the boy was terrified out of his wits?'

'You ran off before I was done with him.' The insult to his integrity rankled.

'I thought I should go to his father, at once.'

'Then why are you still here?'

She swung around and glared at him. 'Because Angus wouldn't let me leave without your permission. It seems I'm a prisoner.'

Tears welled in her eyes, and he felt like a tyrant. 'It is for your own safety. I told you that.' He let out an impatient sigh. He had intended to let her believe the worst, let her think he was hardhearted as she seemed to think, and let her find out on her own that he wasn't. But that would put her in a very embarrassing position. And he could not do it.

'I let the boy go with a warning,' he said.

She flattened herself against the stall, as if she didn't trust her legs to hold her up.

'I turned Tearny off,' he continued. 'He's too

harsh. I've no truck with men who hit boys. You should have known that, Selina. You should have given me the benefit of the doubt. I'm not your father. These are my people.'

Her face paled. She looked down at the brush in her hand and back up at his face. 'I…I am sorry.'

He gave her a grim smile. 'I am sorry I could not explain my intentions, but I do expect you to support me, at least in public, if you want the clan's acceptance.'

'I see.'

He wished he was sure she did see. There was still a stubborn set to her jaw. 'We can talk about this later. Right now I have Tearny waiting in my office.'

Selina stood looking after him long after the door closed. Feeling deflated. Empty. Very much in the wrong. Because he was right. She should have known he wouldn't do anything to hurt McKinly's boy. She'd just wanted to believe the worst because it fed into her determination not to trust him. If she trusted him, then other softer emotions would creep under her guard and take her unawares. She could not allow it. It would become too easy to give in, to easy to give him her heart and let him trample it.

She stroked Topaz's nose. 'I don't think we'll be

going riding today.' She sighed. 'But I will swallow my pride and ask him to go with us tomorrow.' After all, she couldn't live in a state of war with him. He didn't deserve it.

Chapter Nineteen

The next two weeks passed quickly. Too quickly for Selina's peace of mind. Each morning they sat in the solar taking breakfast, reading their letters, planning the day's activities. Like a happily married couple.

The time was coming when she would leave and she was wishing she had given him the three months he had asked for. Not because she wouldn't leave—she would not go back on her word—but because she was learning so much about the Highlands and its people.

She and Ian rode out together on the days he wasn't busy at the mill, riding through the village and around the estate, visiting outlying crofts. The welcomes she received were rarely effusive, but the clansmen were polite in Ian's presence.

She couldn't help feeling that he would have been much better off marrying one of the local women. Some of them were quite lovely. And they all spoke Gaelic. Although she had learned a few more words, she could not follow any of the rapid conversations Ian had with his tenants so she always had to ask him what was said as they rode away. She had the feeling he only told her the parts that wouldn't upset her.

She certainly hadn't made any friends, unless you counted Marie Flora McKinly. So without their nights of passion, she might have gone mad with no one to talk to but the cook, who came in from the village every day and with whom she decided the menus, and her occasional conversations with Angus about the supplies she needed for the household.

She glanced at her husband on the other side of the breakfast table. So handsome. The longer she stayed the more affection she felt for him. He was a kind and just Laird. And she could only admire him.

Right now he was frowning at a letter he had received that morning. He'd seemed more abstracted than usual the past couple of days. More remote.

Ian looked up and caught her watching him. 'What troubles you?'

Did he have to pretend he cared? These gentle enquiries of his always disarmed her. In one more week she would leave. She could not afford for him to see any chink in her armour. 'Do you like this way of arranging my hair? I saw it in one of the fashion plates Chrissie left behind.'

His frown deepened. 'You sighed. Twice in the last ten minutes.'

Had she sighed? 'I was just tired of your head being buried in that letter. Is it bad news?'

He glanced down at the paper. 'No.' He shook his head as if trying to convince himself. 'It just isn't as good as I had hoped.'

She waited for him to say more. Not that he usually did. He told her not to worry about clan business. He had it all in hand. She was like a porcelain doll, all right to look at, but easily broken.

An expression of horror crossed his face. 'I'm sorry, I forgot.' He pulled a crumpled letter from his pocket. 'Logan brought it up from the post this morning. I meant to give it to you right away.'

'But you became engrossed in your own letter, which contains matters of little importance.' He looked at her blankly and she wondered why she bothered.

He slid the note across the table and her heart lifted at the sight of the familiar crest on the seal.

'It is from Alice!' She couldn't keep the excitement from her voice, but then remembered it was probably better not mentioning Alice. Her name always made him grumpy. Probably because it brought back memories of Drew. The man's shade seemed to hang over them enough as it was.

She broke the seal and read eagerly, filling her mind with images of Alice and Hawkhurst and the recent addition to their family. She chuckled at Alice's description of Hawkhurst rowing his son around the lake and playing pirates. He had been a pirate once. Or at least a privateer, which was as close to a pirate as one could come these days. He had captured the ship on which she and Alice were returning to England from Lisbon. In the end, he was the one who had ended up in irons. But the war was over and all that was behind him.

When she finished, she had a smile on her lips. She looked up to find her husband watching her intently. The expression on his face was carefully blank.

'Your friend is well?' he asked in a non-committal voice.

'Yes. She writes of her son. Nursery stories. She begs me to visit.'

'I can't take you now, or any time soon.'

In one week's time she had the right to choose whether to leave or whether to stay. 'I will visit them later, after we...' She shrugged as his lips thinned to a straight line and his jaw hardened.

He glowered and picked up his letter.

'There is nothing to keep me here, Ian,' she said, feeling the need to explain when she saw hurt in his eyes. Deep hurt. Something she thought she had glimpsed from time to time when she spoke of leaving. This time she was sure of it. If only he would say something. Tell her what he was thinking. 'Ian?'

He pushed to his feet. 'Since being my wife isn't a reason to stay, what more is to be said? Excuse me. I have a busy day ahead of me and must cancel our planned ride this afternoon.'

He strode out, leaving her staring after him. It was all in her imagination. If he wanted her to stay, if there was anything beyond their physical attraction, surely she would know by now? He would have said something. And after all, what did he have to feel hurt about? He'd got everything he wanted out of this marriage. She was the one who had been tricked. She was the one who had lost everything she valued because she'd tried to help him.

Sometimes, at night, when they were alone, when he was making love to her, she sensed he cared for her more than he would say—but if that was the case, why did he shut her out of the rest of his life?

No, it was Dunross he had wanted, not her. And now he had it.

Their marriage was purely for convenience. His. He had established the rules and she had abided by them. Now it was coming to an end. A few more days and she could head south as he had promised.

Something twisted in her chest.

'Did you hear what I said, Ian?' Niall's voice was sharp with impatience.

Ian shook his head. 'I'm sorry, I was thinking about something else. Say it again.'

Niall huffed out an impatient breath. 'I've let everyone know to bring their harvest to the mill over the next two days. The weather looks ready to hold fair for at least a week. We could take in some from farther afield if they can bring it in.'

'They know to bring it at night?' Ian asked, looking down at the two drawings of two stills Niall had spread out on a bench in the stables. Designed to fit one over the other, it might fool the authorities if they didn't look too closely.

Niall nodded. 'I gave them all the trails being watched by the gaugers. They know to avoid them.'

Logan grinned. 'And the militia are watching the coast after my visit to the tavern at Wick.'

Ian nodded. Dunstan wasn't a complete idiot,

but since he expected them to smuggle brandy, he seemed ready to believe his eyes and ears. Still it would not do to underestimate the man. 'Have Tammy keep an eye on Dunstan and his men over the next couple of days. Once the barley is in, things should be quiet again until it is time to distil.'

Niall glanced down at the drawings. 'It is too bad we can't apply for a licence and do all this legally.'

It was too bad. But five hundred gallons at a time was beyond their meagre resources.

'We can't. Not with the law as it stands. I heard from Carrick the other day that, even with Lord Gordon's support, there is no hope of the English Parliament changing its mind. We proceed as planned.'

The sound he had been listening for, the reason for his abstraction, came to his ears. Coach wheels on cobbles. He straightened his shoulders. Saying goodbye to her was going to be the hardest thing he had ever done. But after careful thought, he had decided she would be safer with her friend. If she wanted to go, it was better she went now, before they ran the still, then she could claim she knew nothing if he was caught. She would be tainted enough as his wife; he would not want her to witness his disgrace.

And the clan didn't want her here. No matter how often he defended her and no matter how often he argued, there were still some who blamed her for the last fiasco. Her presence undermined his authority.

Their marriage was doomed from the start. Their worlds were too far apart.

He glanced up to see her walking down the steps dressed for travel. Her trunks were already at the bottom of the stairs. Even though he'd steeled himself for this moment all morning, her appearance came as a shock.

What, had he thought that when it came to it, she wouldn't go, when he wasn't the man she wanted?

The slight hesitation in her gait as she descended caused a painful tug in the region of his chest. She looked so beautiful and calmly remote, yet he knew she was vulnerable, fragile, and the need to protect her overcame regret.

The coachman and his guard hurried over to load her luggage in the boot. He joined her at the bottom of the steps.

'You are making an early start,' he said, for something to fill the silence between them, when he wanted to ask her to stay. Oh, that would be a fine sight for his men, the Laird begging his wife not to leave him. Especially if she went anyway. And he had no doubt she would.

'I don't wish to make more stops on the road than necessary.' Her voice was cool, emotionless, light.

As loneliness stretched before him, he gazed at her face. There was a glittering brittleness about her determination this morning. The same brittleness she'd used to keep the world at a distance at Carrick's ball, and when she fell from her horse. It dazzled, like her beauty.

It left him in awe and feeling rough and awkward. The way he'd felt as a lad, when he'd found her stoically hopping her way back home after she had fallen in a rabbit hole and twisted her ankle.

He had never seen such a pretty girl. Or heard one talk so boldly. He'd been unable to resist her pretty full lips and had stolen a kiss. How many times had they met that long-ago summer? Four. Five. They all blurred together in one happy memory he thought he'd forgotten. They had all come crashing back the moment he got her letter about Drew. Along with the guilt. When his brothers had come across them on the beach he'd been ashamed of being caught consorting with his family's enemy. He'd said some pretty cruel things. At least he had stopped his brothers from throwing rocks at her as she ran off.

An urge to tell her he needed her here, with him, rose in his throat. Angry at himself, angry at his inability to think logically when it came to this woman, to be the Laird he was raised to be, he cut himself off from his feelings and focused on what had to be done.

He opened the door and held out his hand to Selina. No gloves. Her hand nestled in his like a small broken bird. He had broken her. He saw it on her face, in the shadows in her eyes. He had taken away her freedom to choose and now he should be pleased to give it back, instead of feeling as if someone had reached into his chest and plucked out his heart.

A flash of understanding hit him hard.

While he had been busy trying to woo her, he had fallen in love, not with her beauty, though he dearly loved that, too, but with her courage and spirit, her caring heart.

Love. Was that what all this turmoil in his chest was about? Apparently it was a brutal taskmaster, for it turned a sensible man into a fool and had him wanting things he couldn't have. Like her loving him back.

How could she? He'd crushed her dreams to further his own. Well, he would not do it any longer.

So while it went against every instinct he had—

indeed, he found that his hands were actually shaking as he helped her into the vehicle—he closed the door.

She sat back against the squabs.

A man ran down the steps from the keep. Angus. 'Fire!' he yelled. Breathless, his chest heaving, he struggled to speak. 'At the mill,' he panted. 'I was up on the battlements looking out for yon chaise when I saw a pillar of smoke. It can be nothing else. You need men down there right away.'

Everyone looked at Ian, their mouths agape. 'I'll take Beau to the Barleycorn and gather as many as I can there. You go on down in the chaise, Niall, please. Take Logan with you. Do what you can until we arrive.'

His brothers were already leaping onto the roof of the coach as he finished speaking. The coachman swung the carriage around as Ian ran for his horse. He glanced over his shoulder.

Damn it. Selina was in there. And in for a rough ride. He just had to hope she would understand this was important.

As the carriage rocked to a stop and the three men leaped down, Selina peered out of the window at the mill. Stunned, she watched as smoke poured from under the eaves and rose up for a few feet, only to be whipped away by the wind.

Two figures, one small, one large, ran up from the stream to throw the contents of their leather bucket through an open door into the heart of the blaze. Greedy red flames.

The coachman yanked the door open as Niall and Logan rushed to help. 'Out you come, my lady, in case these beasts panic.'

Heart racing, she jumped down. 'Go. I'll be fine.'

Outside, the roar of the fire was overpowering and so was the smell of smoke. She glanced around, wondering what she could do to help. More men were pouring over the hill and women from the village. They carried buckets of all shapes and sizes, running to form a chain from the stream to the mill. Another chain formed beside the first. Selina joined it, squeezing in beside a small girl who was sobbing with the effort of passing the heavy containers.

Selina added her strength to the child's and they soon had a backbreaking rhythm of lift and heave and pass, until her back ached.

The supply of water-filled buckets stopped for a moment.

Were they winning? She stood and stretched

her back, looking towards the head of the chain. Flames licked around the doorframe. A familiar figure ran inside. Ian? She hadn't seen him arrive, but he must have been with the rest of the men. What on earth was he doing?

One of the younger boys, his face covered in soot, ran towards the stream with several empty buckets. And the woman behind her tapped her on the back. The rhythm started again. A pause several buckets later gave her another chance to look up. Ian and several of the other men were rolling barrels out through the doorway, wet jackets pulled over their heads for protection. Spirits. They were risking their lives for smuggled liquor?

Again.

She might have guessed. Anger stirred in her stomach. How could they be so stupid?

At any moment, the militia might see the smoke and ride up and arrest the lot of them. They should have let it burn.

The child beside her tugged at her hand. 'My lady?'

Beneath the soot and the tears tracking down the child's face were thousands of freckles. 'Marie Flora? What are you doing here?'

'Pa brought his barley. Then the fire started.'

Selina turned to take the next run of buckets from the woman behind her and the backbreaking work began again.

'It's out,' someone yelled.

Cheers rang out.

Selina looked up. Smoke, acrid and choking, still swirled around the cobbled courtyard, but it was lessening, being cleared out by gusts of wind.

'Keep the water coming,' someone shouted. 'Just to be sure.' She passed on the next few buckets until there were no more to grab and walked out of the line.

Marie Flora ran off, no doubt looking for her father.

Selina surveyed the damage. Part of the roof had fallen in, but most of the stone building remained intact. The fire had been confined to the end where the waterwheel turned the great millstones.

Thank God they had arrived in time.

She glanced around. There was no sign of Ian. Or the barrels. Then she realised the coachman was whipping up his horses.

It was leaving without her? As the coach moved off it revealed Ian on the other side of it, sooty-faced and with a hand raised in farewell.

Blast them. No doubt the coach was full of their precious barrels. Her stomach sank. She wouldn't be leaving the village tonight, after all. She wasn't sure if she was sorry or glad. Glad, damn her soft heart.

Chapter Twenty

Looking as wild as some ancient warrior, Ian set the men to shoving the ashes outside where the women poured water every time they saw smoke rising.

A tug on her skirts drew Selina's attention away from the work. 'Tommy's gone,' Marie Flora said.

For a moment the words didn't sink in. 'Your brother, Tommy?'

'I told him to wait beside the stream while I helped my father. He's not there.' Ignoring her aching back, Selina crouched down so she was eye to eye with the child. 'Do you want me to help you look for him?'

Relief flooded her wide eyes. She nodded. With a groan Selina rose and took the child's hand. 'Show me where you left him.'

Pray Heaven the little lad hadn't fallen into the stream.

She walked along beside the child, heading up-stream from the mill, aching all over from the unaccustomed heavy work, limping more than usual.

'There,' Marie Flora said, pointing to a flat rock. 'I told him to sit there with Milly and wait.'

'Milly?'

'Grannie gave him one of her chicks. Pa didn't know he had it until we were halfway here.'

'How did you get here?'

'We borrowed Grannie's cart. It is in the barn. We were going to walk to the village after, to visit.'

The barn lay on the other side of the courtyard, but a small door led out the back on the side facing them. The door was ajar. 'Do you think he would be hiding in there?' It didn't seem likely even as she said it. The place would be full of smoke. Or not. The wind was blowing in the other direction.

'If he's hidin', Pa will warm the seat of his breeches,' the girl said.

As one they marched down the hill to the open door, two angry women ready to do battle with one recalcitrant little boy. Selina was already feeling sorry for little Tommy.

She pushed open the door.

'Tommy,' Marie Flora called. 'Get out of here. Wait till I tell Pa.'

No answer. Just the soft noises of animals in their stalls.

'Tommy,' Marie Flora called again and there were tears in her voice. She was afraid he wasn't here.

'Tommy, come out now,' Selina said, 'and we will say nothing to your Da.' She stepped deeper into the barn, her eyes adjusting to the dim light streaming in from this door and the opening to the courtyard.

She could see the cart and the donkey. And the pony Ian had hitched to the cart he had brought her home in when she fell off Topaz.

Something scuttled across the floor. A rat? She squeaked a protest.

'Milly,' Marie Flora said, diving forwards to catch the chick. 'Tommy,' she shouted. She rattled off something in Gaelic, but the scold in her tone made translation unnecessary. The warm breeches again, no doubt.

Peering into the gloom, Selina expected at any moment to see Tommy step out of hiding with a sneaky little grin on his face.

Holding the chick close to her chest, Marie Flora spun around. 'Tommy.' Now she sounded furious.

Little bits of straw floated down from above to fall on the child's shoulder and in her hair. Some landed on Selina's face. She looked up. A loft! A ladder rested against an opening in the upper floor.

She touched her fingers to her lips and pointed upwards, then at the ladder. Comprehension filled the girl's eyes. She pursed her lips and lowered her brows.

Oh, dear, Tommy was going to be in trouble.

'I suppose he is not here,' Selina said loudly. 'We shall have to look elsewhere.'

'He'll catch it when Pa finds him,' Marie Flora said, with quick understanding. She tucked the chick in her grimy apron pocket.

They stomped their feet and opened the door as if they were leaving, then crept to the ladder.

Marie Flora clambered up quietly and her head disappeared, then the rest of her. Selina followed more slowly, her skirts hampering her movements. When her head cleared the opening, she stopped in shock.

Both children were staring at her, their eyes wide and terrified in the light streaming in from the gable window. A knife glinted wickedly. The breath left her lungs in a rush and she grabbed for the edge.

The man who held the children in one arm, tight against his chest, and the knife in his hand against Marie Flora's throat, smiled.

'It seems luck is with me, after all. Do come right up, Lady Selina,' Tearny said.

Ian stared around at the mess. The fire had been quite deliberate. Yet who on earth among those who knew about the still would want to see it damaged? Even if the success of the mill hadn't meant good money for the clan, no Highlander in his right mind would want to see good whisky go up in flames.

He could imagine them stealing it and drinking it, but not this. He ran his gaze around the courtyard. Everyone here was covered in soot and working hard to clean up the mess.

Niall joined him, also looking around. 'Anyone hurt?'

Ian shook his head. 'No. And the damage is minimal. Whoever set the fire must not have realised that it is not the mill where we have been putting all our efforts.'

'Do you think Albright might be behind it?'

He took a deep breath. His father-in-law had seemed more saddened than angry, though he had been that, too. 'I don't know, but it doesn't make any sense. What good would it do him?'

'Revenge.'

Ian glanced around for his wife. The last time he saw her she was passing buckets of water.

A group of women stood nearby, washing up in a bucket. He tapped the nearest one on the shoulder. 'Have you see Lady Selina?'

The woman smiled. 'Aye, Laird. Going up the hill behind the barn with the wee McKinly girl, not more than five minutes ago.'

McKinly wandered over then; his face was grim. 'The mill should nae take too much to repair. We were lucky to save my whisky.'

'Aye, lucky. But how the hell did it start?'

''Tis the oddest thing. My wee lad said he smelled the smoke of a pipe when we pulled up. I ne'er smelled a thing. I unloaded the barrels as you'd instructed and took the sacks of barley into the stable to unload it there when my wee Tommy yelled fire from outside.' He rubbed at the back of his neck. 'The mill door was open. I could have sworn I barred it behind me, but I'm that bluidy tired from harvesting… I'm sorry, Laird. It must have been a spark from the donkey's hooves, or maybe my boots. I canna think of aught else.'

Had the other man been smoking and was now trying to lay the blame elsewhere? The clear gaze meeting his showed no signs of guile. A spark from a hoof hardly seemed likely, though.

'Did Tommy see anyone?'

'I didna' ask him. I sent the bairns off to wait up the hill and ran for water. It took hold verra fast. Almost seemed like it had started in several places at once. I just thank God the barley is safe in the barn.'

Ian clapped McKinly on the shoulder. 'And I thank God you acted so quickly. I can never repay you.'

The other man smiled a shy smile. 'Glad to do it, Laird.' He looked around. 'But now I can't find Marie Flora. I told her to care for her brother. Next thing I see her passing buckets.'

'Apparently she is with the Lady Selina. Come, man, we will find them together.'

The hillside behind the barn was deserted. Ian frowned. 'One of the women said she saw them head in this direction.'

McKinly pointed to a flat rock. 'This is where I told her and the boy to wait.'

Forced at the point of a knife to stand in a corner with the children, Selina watched Tearny scatter straw from a pile of bales all over the floor in little heaps. Her body was still trembling with the shock of seeing the knife held to Tommy's scrawny little neck. She tried to swallow the lump in her throat.

Tearny laid his knife down at his feet and pulled out his tinderbox.

Dear God. Her stomach roiled. 'You fired the mill.'

He smiled with terrible triumph. 'Indeed. I told Gilvry when he paid me off he'd have his just deserts one of these days. The best of it is it comes with a reward. A good one.'

'What are you talking about?'

His answer was a grin. He struck flint against steel. The click sounded terribly loud in the strained silence.

Tommy turned his face into her skirts. Marie Flora was looking up at her expectantly, relying on her to save them.

The tinder didn't spark. She breathed a sigh of relief.

Tearny fiddled with the flint.

Selina eyed the distance to the knife and knew it was too far. Somehow she had to distract him.

'Come, Mr Tearny, whatever grudge you hold against my husband, you surely do not wish to harm a woman and two children.'

'Mr Tearny,' he mimicked. 'How are you today, Mr Tearny? You never expected an answer, though, did you, you haughty bitch. I saw how pleased you were, though, the day he gave me notice. You married the wrong man, my lady.'

This wasn't making any sense. 'I don't see what my marriage has to do with you, Mr Tearny.'

'No, I'm sure you don't. Ian cock-of-the-walk Gilvry shouldn't have brought you here today. You can blame him for this.'

His gaze went back to his tinderbox. 'He should never have got his hands on Dunross.' He struck the flint against the steel. Again no spark.

A horrid thought entered her mind, one she didn't want to believe. 'Are you doing this on my father's behalf?'

He looked surprised, then he sneered. 'This has nothing to do with your father. Still, I won't be sorry to know he'll also be grieving his loss.'

Her heart stopped at the callousness of his words. 'My father won't care one way or the other.' She slid one foot forwards.

'Do you think not? It is not the impression he gave me when he thought you were abducted. What a slut, going off in the night with Gilvry and letting everyone worry.' He shot her a glare. 'If he'd been picked up by the gaugers that night, we would all have been better off.'

'Someone paid you to betray him.'

'Quick, aren't you?'

She inched forwards another step. 'Thank you. Who was it?'

His glanced up, his eyes gleaming with cunning. 'Wouldn't you like to know?'

Blast the man. 'As soon as you walk out of here, they will know you are to blame. Let us go and I'll say nothing.'

His lip curled. 'No one saw me come and no one will see me leave. I might not be a Scot, but I know my way around these hills better than most.'

Two more steps and she'd be close enough to dive for the knife—if she could just keep him talking. 'Don't I have the right to know who is behind my death?'

He struck the flint again. The straw caught.

Little Tommy cried out. Tearny's eyes snapped to the child. He picked up the knife and waved it. 'Enough talk. It is time I was finished here. I have a purse to collect.' He tucked the knife in his waistband.

Her heart pounded. Her voice shook. 'If it is me you want to hurt, let the children go.'

He glanced at Marie Flora. 'Well, little girl? Would you know me again?' He spoke so kindly, so mildly, he sounded almost harmless.

'Aye. I know you,' Marie Flora said, her curls springy with defiance. 'You are a bad man.'

Selina groaned. Wrong answer, child. Not that she believed the right one would have done them any good. Tearny had made up his twisted mind.

He crouched and blew gently on the spark. The small pile of straw between his knees smouldered, then flared. He picked up the bundle and backed down the ladder, until all they could see was his face like some grinning devil emerging from the pit of hell. He touched the flames to the straw encircling the hole in the floor and tossed the bundle at them, making them back up. In that brief second, they lost any chance of getting out.

'Scream all you want, Lady Selina,' he said. 'Hopefully Gilvry will rush to save you and it will be the end of him, too.'

As he disappeared, she rushed for the opening. The heat of the flames drove her back. While she whirled around, looking for another way out, the flames spread, racing outwards. The dry timber of the floor started to catch.

Smoke filled her mouth and her nose. It was hopeless.

Chapter Twenty-One

Ian and McKinly had walked a good distance up the hill and still no sign of Selina or the children.

'She's a grand lass, your wife,' McKinly said. 'Marie Flora has done nothing but talk about her since she left. How she peeled the tatties and mended my shirts. And the way she joined the women on the buckets, you would never know she was a lady born. You should be proud of her.'

'I am,' Ian said. Proud enough to realise she was far too good for the likes of him. His biggest fear right now was her being caught here by the gaugers or the local militia. He had to get her away. 'Where in hell's name did they go?'

McKinly glanced back down the hill towards the mill and froze. 'Dear God, not again,' he muttered. 'The barn is on fire.'

Startled, Ian turned.

Wisps of smoke were curling up from the roof.

He cursed. 'Fire,' he roared racing downhill. He had to get the animals out. And the barley, or all of their earlier efforts wouldn't mean a damn thing.

'I don't get it,' McKinly panted, jogging alongside him. 'The smoke is from inside the roof. Perhaps we should have looked there first.'

Holy hell. 'You think the children are in there?'

The look of terror in McKinly's eyes was answer enough.

Ian increased his pace. If the children were there, then… He didn't dare finish the thought.

He ducked through the low-arched door as a male figure ran out through the open double doors into the courtyard opposite. He hesitated, looking around.

'Up there!' McKinly yelled. Two small legs dangled from the trapdoor where the ladder should have rested. It lay on the floor. A moment later, the rest of Tommy appeared, in his shirtsleeves, his hands above his head, dangling far above the floor.

Ian and McKinly ran beneath the opening where Selina's head and shoulders were now visible. She was holding the lad, her hands gripping the boy's elbows, smoke writhing around her. 'Let him go,' Ian called. 'I'll catch him.'

She raised her face, the effort of holding the boy

etched on her features, along with the flash of re-lief when she realised help had come.

The boy dropped with a screech. Heart in his throat, Ian caught him and handed him off to his father. He heaved the ladder up against the edge of the opening and dashed up.

Heat hit him in the face like a wall. Nearby, bales of hay were on fire. The floorboards were smoul-dering. Somehow Selina and the child were stand-ing in a small area free of flames, the remains of a singed boy's coat in her hands. They were cough-ing and gasping, the fire crowding in on them. She batted at the flames with the coat.

He grabbed the child and handed her down to her waiting father behind him on the ladder, then, without really quite knowing how it had happened, he had Selina on his shoulder and was making his way down to safety.

As he reached the floor, men were running in with buckets of water. Another was leading the animals out of the barn and others were manhan-dling the sacks of barley. It looked like they'd be in time.

He carried Selina out and up the hill away from danger. Away from the flames to safety. This was where he wanted her. Safe in his arms.

He set her down, inspected her hands, her face

covered in soot, her reddened bare arms, saw the singed hem of her gown and a bone-deep shudder went through him. Another few moments and it might have been too late.

He pulled her close against his chest. 'Tell me you are all right.' His heart was beating so hard he thought it would make a hole in his chest.

She struggled against him and he loosened his grip. 'I'm all right,' she said, gazing up at him, her eyes full of shock. 'The children.'

'They are in fine fettle,' McKinly said from right behind him. 'Tommy, don't tell me you did that?'

Ian whirled around to stare at the cringing boy.

'No,' Selina said. 'It was Tearny.'

The man he'd seen running out. He'd all but forgotten him in the haste to get to Selina.

Anger burned in his veins at the danger she'd been in. Fury hotter than the flames in that loft. There was only one way to be rid of it. He raked his gaze over the courtyard and saw no one who looked like his erstwhile land agent. He pushed Selina towards McKinly. 'Take care of them.'

'Ian, wait!' she called out. 'He's dangerous.'

He couldn't help the smile that came to his lips. 'So am I, lass.'

Leaving her with McKinly, he went in search of Tammy McNab. 'Did you see Tearny pass you by?'

Tammy looked puzzled. 'He ran up towards the road. To get more help, he said.'

The rodent was running back to his burrow. Ian would catch him long before then. He lengthened his stride and headed up the cart track leading to the road. It wasn't long before he saw his quarry bent double, catching his breath a few yards from the main road. So he thought he'd escaped.

A smile touched his lips.

The other man must have sensed he was not alone, because he straightened, turning to look back. His jaw dropped. Shock. Horror. He put his head down and ran, but with his paunch, he was no match for Ian's long stride. Realising his danger, he cut off the road and headed downhill, no doubt thinking to lose Ian among the heather. In his haste, he stumbled over the rough terrain, his feet catching in tussocks that in places were up to his knees.

Within moments, Ian was upon him.

Tearny pivoted, pulling a knife, holding it in front of him, his chest heaving, his eyes wild.

Ian put a hand to his sock and pulled out his dirk. 'Give it up, Tearny. You can't get away with it.' He lunged.

Tearny dodged, then slashed out with the knife. It sliced through Ian's shirt. It stung like the devil.

Blood ran warm down his chest. A quick glance showed little more than a scratch, but the man was quick with a knife. He would have to be more careful.

Tearny grinned. 'How good of you to come after me. I can finish what I started.'

None of this made any sense. 'What are you after? I paid your wages in full.'

The man's grin didn't falter.

'Did Albright put you up to this?'

'The answer won't matter to a dead man.'

Ian lunged again. If he could get behind his opponent, he could get an arm around his neck.

Tearny twisted away, thrusting with his blade as he went. He missed. His eyes turned wary. Then his gaze shifted. He looked past Ian. His jaw dropped. His eyes widened.

An accomplice? Ian backed around to see what had caught the other man's attention.

He groaned at the sight of Selina running towards them. Alone. The strength of purpose in the set of her shoulders made him feel proud. And angry. The word wait didn't seem to exist in her vocabulary.

But she wasn't alone. McKinly appeared over the brow of the hill, followed by Tammy. He turned to Tearny. 'Seems you are outnumbered.'

The man turned and fled.

Idiot. There was nowhere to go. Ian raced after him and stared in surprise as the man tripped and went flying. He almost felt sorry for him as he lay in the grass, too stunned to get to his feet.

He didn't move when Ian reached him. Warily he turned the man onto his back by the shoulder. His eyes were wide open and full of pain.

For a moment, Ian didn't understand. Then he saw the hilt of the knife sticking out of his chest. He'd fallen on the blade. Ian's gut churned. He dropped to his knees.

Tearny's gaze focused on Ian and he seemed to rally. 'It is not over, Gilvry. You'll see. I've paid my debt, but yours awaits.'

'What the hell are you talking about?' Ian said, pulling off his jacket, thinking to somehow staunch the wound.

Tearny's breath rattled in his throat and then his eyes were staring sightlessly up at the sky.

Selina came up behind him. He rose and blocked her view of the body as the other men arrived. 'He's dead. By his own hand.'

Selina turned her face away, her expression full of doubt.

'I swear it. I did not touch him.'

'I know.'

Then why the doubt?

Her gaze dropped to his chest. 'You are hurt.'

'A scratch.'

'Did he say who was behind him in this?' she asked.

'No.' Ian didn't want to give voice to his suspicions.

'He admitted to me it wasn't my father.'

Could she read his mind?

'I asked him, just before he left us in the barn. He thought my question a great joke. But he wouldn't say who it was.'

Ian pulled her close and tipped up her tear-streaked face. 'Then we have something to be glad of, right?'

She nodded and gave him a wobbly smile.

Tammy was staring at the man on the ground. 'He used to come in the Barleycorn. None of us could understand why he came night after night. It wasn't for the company. We rarely spoke anything but the Gaelic. Stupid Irishman never could understand a word.'

Selina lifted her head. 'He threatened Tommy McKinly in Gaelic. I heard him.'

Tammy looked scandalised. 'He never once showed he could speak the Gaelic.'

'I think his mother was Scottish. He was some

distant relative of Carrick's. He recommended him to my father,' Selina said.

Tammy turned pale. 'The scoundrel. He must have overheard us talking. He betrayed us to the gaugers.' His face crumpled. 'Laird, I never guessed he understood a word.' He cursed.

'One mystery is solved,' Ian said, glad it wasn't one of the clan. But Tearny wasn't working alone if his last words could be believed. The back of Ian's neck prickled. He wished like hell he'd been able to get more out of the man. 'Whoever was behind him might try to strike again. We will have to be careful who we trust. I hope he was paid well, because he has paid the ultimate price.' Yet the threat was still there. Selina might have been killed, for the sake of whisky and his clan. And if Tearny had told the truth, the danger wasn't over.

It was good that she was leaving. Going somewhere she would be safe.

He turned and gestured to the corpse on the ground. 'Tammy, get him back to the village. We'll need to inform the coroner. I'll be back in time to speak to him.'

'I'll fetch the cart,' McKinly said.

Ian put an arm around Selina's shoulders, wanting to hold her and offer comfort, and take it, too, in the knowledge she was safe, though he knew it was the last thing he should be doing.

She shivered, not from cold, but from the blaze of awareness between them. He felt it course through his blood. 'The chaise should be back any moment,' he said.

She didn't answer.

He slowed his walk, waiting for McKinly and Tammy to get a little ahead of them. He stopped and swung her around to face him. 'Tearny could have killed you. It is not safe here.' As he looked down into her face he found himself catching her nape and seeking her lips. A farewell kiss. It was probably the last time he would see her.

She turned her head at the last moment and his kiss landed on her ear. Ears were good. And even though he could smell the smoke from the fire on her, he could also smell the perfume she favoured. Something light and floral.

He glanced over her shoulder and saw the carriage a few yards away, waiting. He had to let her go. It was the right thing to do. He caught her chin between thumb and finger and turned her face.

Anger glowed in her eyes. 'No, Ian. I won't let you do that to me again.' Her lips thinned. 'It was always about Dunross. I wish you joy of it.'

Startled, he stared at her. Then he realised the truth. It really was over.

He clenched his teeth hard. Balled his hands at his sides. His heart twisted with the knowledge of how badly he had used her. He'd had his chance; if she no longer responded to his kisses, then he had nothing to offer. 'I'll walk you up there.'

He took her arm and walked her slowly up the hill to the waiting chaise. His heart felt as heavy as lead. He wanted to say something to fill the silence, but the longer it went on, the more difficult it became, as if the closer they drew to the carriage, the greater the distance between them.

The gap had always been too wide to conquer, even when they were younger.

Once settled on the squabs, Selina leaned forwards and lowered the window. He let himself imagine that she was having trouble leaving.

'I really do wish you well, Ian,' she said softly. 'I wish it might have been different.'

Over the past few weeks he'd watched her smiles become brighter, heard her laughter become more and more brittle. And if it was Dunstan she wanted, then no matter how he felt he must make things right. He must.

Looking at her now, the smudges of soot on her cheek, the wild tangle of jet hair around her beautiful heart-shaped face, she didn't look at all out of place here in the wilds of the Highlands, but he had tricked her into this marriage for the sake of his clan. He owed her a debt he could never repay, but, as much as he wanted her to stay, he wanted her happiness more. Since he could not change the past, he had to let her choose how to live her future. He had to give her that gift.

A band tightened around his chest. The pain of loss. But she deserved better than a penniless Laird. She deserved to shine among her own people. To find love. He rubbed at a smudge on her lovely cheek. 'You look like you've been to hell and back.'

Her smile was blade sharp. 'I'll repair the damage when we stop to change the horses.'

She couldn't wait to be gone.

He had only himself to blame. He shouldn't have let his weakness for her, his desire, influence his decision the night she came to warn him. He should have left her at the keep and trusted her to keep silent.

'You'll find a welcome at my hearth any time you choose to seek it,' he said, his voice sounding hoarse. He hoped he didn't sound as pathetic as he felt.

Her gaze searched his face. 'Thank you.'

He fought the urge to drag her from the coach and kiss her into staying, seducing her into forgetting how he'd played her false. Passion was the one thing they had between them that was honest. But passion only lasted until the morning. In the cold light of day he'd once more be faced with the truth.

He made her unhappy.

He covered the small hand gripping the window with his and found it chilled to the bone. She was so fragile, so delicate, so incredibly strong.

'Are we to leave then, gov?' the coachman called down from the box.

'A moment more,' he said as she began to withdraw into the carriage. There was one thing more to tell her, one gift he had to give, no matter how it tore him in two. He drew in a deep breath. 'There is something I must tell you.'

She raised a brow.

Was that hope he saw in her eyes? Hope for what? He shook the thought aside. Hope had no place in what he was about to say. 'I'm sorry I tricked you into marrying me. Our marriage was…well, it is on pretty shaky ground, even for Scotland. We could probably have it annulled.'

She gasped. Looked shocked.

'I know.' He shook his head. 'It might not work. But a divorce is not out of the question, either.'

Her face looked pale beneath the grim of the smoke. 'You said nothing of this before.'

'No.' He'd kept hoping she would want to stay. But he'd been thinking only of himself. 'I'll talk to a solicitor as soon as I can and send you word.'

Her gaze clashed with his and he thought he saw regret in the depths of her eyes. He hadn't expected that. Was that cause for hope?

'I see,' she said coolly. 'It would have been a whole lot easier if you had let me go the same day my father left, as I suggested.'

Never had he heard her sound so cold. And now he knew the reason for her regret. 'Yes. I'm sorry. I will set up an account for you at Coutts's Bank. Draw on it as you find the need until things are settled. I will write and let you know the details.'

She nodded gravely and for a moment she was the large-eyed sprite he'd fallen in love with as a boy and, feeling like a knight in shining armour, had carried home to his castle.

So soft and sentimental. So weak when it came to this woman. And he'd let his weakness bring her harm.

He stepped back.

'Promise me you will be careful.' He heard tears in her voice, but when he looked into her eyes, they were clear and dry.

Too full of emotion to say more, he raised a hand and walked to the front of the carriage.

'Drive carefully,' he warned the coachman. 'Or deal with me.'

The coachman touched his hat with his whip. And the carriage moved off. He watched the dust rise behind it until it was only there in his imagination. He was doing the right thing for her. She could change her mind any time she wanted. He'd always be here, waiting.

He smiled wryly. Love was a very strange thing. It made you do the one thing you didn't want to do, so the one you loved could be happy. And it hurt like hell.

Now he knew how Drew must have felt when he'd forced him to get on that ship for America. Loss. Despair. Anger. Unending loneliness.

Just deserts, then.

Chapter Twenty-Two

Selina had been at Hawkhurst for two weeks and was sitting with Alice in the drawing room dandling her friend's four-month-old son and heir, David, on her lap.

'He is such a good child,' Selina said.

'At the moment he is.' Alice, her freckles more noticeable than ever, smiled her quiet smile. 'At three in the morning, he turns into a hungry monster and reminds me of his father.'

Selina tickled the satin-soft cheek and he smiled sleepily. So adorable.

'You must marry again as soon as you are divorced from that dreadful Highlander,' Alice said. 'You should have children of your own.'

The note of censure in her friend's practical voice caused her to stiffen. Words in defence of Ian hovered on the tip of her tongue. She kept them behind her teeth. Alice was only reflecting her own anger. The hurt she'd poured out into her friend's ears when she'd arrived at Hawkhurst's front door.

The anger had gone, but the hurt still remained at being his dupe.

But did she really want to sever all ties? Her marriage to Ian hadn't caused much of a stir. It seemed that Dunstan had said little or nothing about the end of her understanding with him and nothing about Ian's criminal activities had come to light so far.

She and Ian wouldn't be the first married couple to live estranged, each going their own way. It wasn't as if he needed an heir. He had his brothers for that.

The thought reminded her of something. 'Oh, I meant to tell you, Chrissie is expecting a happy event. Perhaps my father will finally get his son.'

Alice, like the good friend she was, let her change the subject. 'Please give her my congratulations when next you write. How is your father?'

'In alt. Very proud of his accomplishment, according to Chrissie. She asked me if I would like to visit them.'

Alice looked at her sharply. 'With your father's agreement?'

'Apparently so.'

'That is good,' Alice said with a smile. 'Families belong together.'

And Ian wasn't family, was he? He was her inconvenient husband. She just wished she didn't miss him.

She held back a sigh. Ian had his own family. They also only wanted Dunross. They were welcome to it. She just wished she could be rid of the ache in her chest.

Time. It would take time for the wound to heal.

She just wished she didn't have the feeling that she would never feel whole again.

The door swung back. A tall dark-haired man strode across the room to kiss Alice on the lips.

'Back so soon?' Alice said fondly.

'I invited Jaimie to tea,' Hawkhurst said, greeting Selina, then taking his son from her arms and lifting him high above his head. 'And how is my feisty son?'

Two more men entered the room at a more leisurely pace. Alice's father, Alex Fulton. He wasn't a well man, but there was joy in his eyes as he watched Hawkhurst kiss his grandson. The other man was Hawkhurst's cousin, Jaimie, Lord Sanford. Fair haired, slender and impeccably dressed, he spent most evenings with the

Hawkhursts when he wasn't in town, Alice had explained.

'That child is ready for a sleep,' Alice scolded her husband.

'Let me take him,' Alex Fulton said.

Hawkhurst handed the child over to his grandfather and watched him leave the room. 'Your father is having a good day today,' he said to his wife.

Alice's expression became sad. 'They are few and far between these days, but he seems happy.' Alex Fulton had suffered badly from his overindulgence of alcohol, but in the last few years he hadn't drunk a drop of liquor. It was only that abstinence that had prolonged his life.

Simpson, their butler, who had once been Hawkhurst's steward at sea, carried in the tea tray, set it beside Alice and left, his rolling-seaman's gait still in evidence.

Jaimie brought Selina her cup and sat down beside her, balancing his cup and saucer precariously on his knee.

'May I say how ravishing you are looking today, Mrs Gilvry,' he said. His green eyes were warm with admiration. He'd been engaging in a mild flirtation with her ever since she had arrived. He was quite the rake, according to Alice, and Selina had felt just a little flattered by his attentions.

She'd enjoyed their verbal sparring. It stopped her from thinking about Ian. At least for a few hours in the day. Her nights were a very different story.

She missed him all the time, but at night, when she was alone with her thoughts, she felt the full force of her misery.

'You are very kind to say so, Lord Sanford.' She gave him a brilliant smile. 'Is that a new way of tying your cravat?'

'Don't encourage him,' Hawkhurst said. 'He's already far too dandified.'

The sound of someone pounding on the front door echoed through the house.

Alice glanced at her husband, who rose to his feet.

'What the devil?' Hawkhurst said.

Jaimie went to the window. 'I don't recognise the horse, but it's a fine bit of blood and bone. Probably some irate shipowner from your past,' he said to Hawkhurst.

The butler scurried in. 'There is a barbarian at the door, my lord,' he said, all out of breath and mopping at his brow. 'Shall I fetch your shotgun?'

The pounding started again.

'Are you saying you left this man on the door-step?' Sanford asked.

'He looks ready for murder,' Simpson replied.

'What do you mean, a barbarian?' Hawkhurst asked frowning.

'He is wearing some sort of skirt.'

Heart pounding, Selina rose to her feet. 'What does this barbarian look like?' She found she could hardly get the words out, she felt so breathless.

'As to that, my lady, it is hard to tell, for he has a black beard covering most of his face.'

A beard. That didn't sound like Ian, then. Her heart dipped. Perhaps he'd sent one of his men with a message. Perhaps he was in trouble. 'What colour is his kilt and plaid?'

'My lady?'

'His skirt.'

'I didn't notice the colour, my lady, but he was demanding you come to the door if I wouldn't let him in.'

It had to be someone from Ian. Her mouth dried. 'Perhaps we should at least find out what he wants?'

''Tis a good thing your doors are solid,' Jaimie observed, returning to his seat beside her. While he seemed insolent enough—indeed, he seemed very much the fop—there was a lethal quality about his movements that occasionally made her wonder if he wasn't more than the man milliner his cousin often called him.

The butler looked to his employer. 'Shall I set the dogs on him, then?'

'Certainly not,' Alice said, her gaze on Selina. 'Send him up.'

Hawkhurst's brow lowered and he sent his wife a considering look.

She shrugged and he said nothing, but walked to the hearth and leaned one elbow on the mantel, watching the door.

Selina clasped her hands together, sure it couldn't be Ian and praying nothing had happened to him. Like being arrested. Or deported. Or, bile rose in her throat, hanged.

If so, she hoped his people were suitably grateful, she thought with a surge of bitterness.

The door burst open.

She gasped. The man towering in the doorway indeed looked like a ruffian. 'Ian,' she choked out.

Never had she seen him look so dreadful. A beard covered his jaw beneath gaunt cheeks. Purple smudges beneath sapphire eyes snapping with fury made him look as if he had not slept for days. His blazing gaze honed in on Sanford.

'Are you the lordling trifling with my wife?' he asked in a dangerous voice.

Jaimie aimed a brief glance at Hawkhurst, who hadn't moved, and shrugged, his mouth mocking. 'Since we haven't been introduced, I'm not sure which one of the ladies I'm trifling with is yours.'

Ian clenched his fists. 'She is sitting beside you, you little cur. Outside with you, so I can teach you some manners.'

'How very rustic, old chap.' Jaimie pushed to his feet.

Selina leapt in front of him. 'Ian, stop it, this instant. No one is trifling with me. Where on earth did you get such a notion? And besides, if they were, why would you care?'

His gaze left Jaimie and focused on her. 'Because you are my wife.'

'Dear Lady Selina, did you really marry such a dreadful boor?' Sanford drawled. He raised his quizzing glass and inspected Ian from head to toe.

'Enough, Jaimie,' Hawkhurst commanded, moving into the centre of the room.

Ian turned and looked surprised, as if he hadn't seen Hawkhurst until that moment. And then he took in Alice. Some of the rage in his face lessened. 'I beg your pardon. I was under the impression that this...this dandy was alone with my wife.'

Jaimie picked a piece of lint from his sleeve and watched it drift to the floor before meeting Ian's gaze. 'Does that mean you don't want to engage in fisticuffs on the lawn?'

Ian's eyes narrowed. He looked at Selina. 'It means I'm reserving judgement, so don't be going anywhere just yet a while.'

He sounded so very Scottish when he was angered. The sound of those rolling *r*s and the lilting cadence made her feel weak inside. Not to mention the way he was looking at her as if he wanted to eat her whole.

'I believe introductions are in order,' Hawkhurst said mildly. 'Followed by an explanation.' Once more his gaze drifted to his wife, who was looking suspiciously innocent.

Selina stared at her. 'Alice?'

Alice shook her head.

Hawkhurst continued on as if Selina hadn't spoken. 'I am Hawkhurst.' He stuck out a hand. He was as tall as Ian, but nowhere near as broad, but he didn't look the slightest bit intimidated, whereas Selina could feel her knees wobbling in the strangest way.

'This is my wife, Lady Hawkhurst. We don't tend to stand on formality, so Michael and Alice will do.'

Ian bowed over Alice's hand and did it with such grace and charm that Selina felt proud.

'This young reprobate is my cousin, Jaimie, Lord Sanford,' Hawkhurst continued. His lips curved in a hard smile. 'I can assure you he would not be welcome in this house if his manners to my wife's guest were anything but impeccable.'

Ian shot a glance at Alice. 'It is not what I am hearing.'

'Nevertheless,' Hawkhurst said in a tone that did not brook argument, 'it is the case.'

Jaimie raised a brow and held out a languid hand.

Ian glared at it, then clasped it with his own. 'Sanford.' Then he grinned. 'You've a firmer hand than I expected.'

Jaimie bowed very slightly and made as if to return to his seat beside Selina. Ian glowered and he smothered a laugh and strolled to the chair at Alice's right hand.

'How can we be of service?' Hawkhurst asked.

Ian looked blank.

'I am assuming,' Hawkhurst drawled, 'you came with some purpose in mind?'

'I would have conversation with Lady Selina.'

'By all means,' Hawkhurst said, gesturing to the sofa.

'Alone,' Ian said. 'If you don't mind.'

'That is up to the lady, surely?' Hawkhurst said.

All eyes turned on her. Heat crawled up her neck and into her cheeks, where it stung painfully.

She swallowed the lump in her throat. 'I am not sure there is anything to say.'

'I have something to say,' Ian said. And he sounded very determined to get it off his chest.

'Very well. I will hear it.'

He glared around the room. 'What I have to say does not need an audience. I would like to be alone with my wife, if you do not mind.'

'I, for one,' Jaimie said, 'fear for the lady's safety. What assurance will you give us that you will not try to bully her when we are gone?'

'Or trick her,' Alice added.

Ian flushed.

Selina winced. He might not be pleased to learn she had been so frank with Alice.

'I give you my word,' Ian said, his gaze fixed on her face.

She didn't actually have the right to refuse him. He was her husband, but she was glad to see he did not force that issue. Though she had the feeling he might, if she turned him down.

'It is all right, Alice,' she said. 'Mr Gilvry has given his word. If he has something of a private nature to discuss with me, I am quite willing to hear it.'

Hawkhurst bowed and brought his wife to her feet. 'We will be in the library, just down the hall within calling distance, should you have need of us.'

'Such a pleasure,' Jaimie said, with a slight inclination of his head. 'Lady Selina, I look forward to seeing you at dinner tonight.'

Ian looked ready to strangle him as he followed his cousin Hawkhurst out of the door.

'Well, Ian,' she said, glad that the thump of her heart in her chest did not affect the calm of her voice. Or at least she hoped it did not. She was shaking much too hard to be sure.

He gestured to the sofa. 'Please, sit down.'

She sat. He did not. He towered over her, looking down with narrowed eyes as if he wanted to assure himself she was still in one piece.

Heat travelled up from her belly. Answering heat flared in his eyes.

But that had always been the best part of their marriage.

She took a quick breath. 'You wanted to speak with me. What was it you wanted to say?'

He straightened his shoulders. 'Did you want a divorce?'

Pain seized her heart and twisted it cruelly. She lowered her gaze to her hands, kept them fixed on her fingers so he would not see how his words wounded.

She forced a smile before she looked up. 'Is that why you came? La, sir, surely a letter to your solicitor or even to me was all that was necessary?'

'He's the kind of man you should have married. That young puppy who just left here. Another drawing-room dandy.'

'He is a well-bred young gentleman, to be sure.'

'What happened to Dunstan? I thought you wanted him.'

'No.' Was he accusing her of something?

He spun away and paced the carpet in front of her. 'When your friend wrote to me last week saying how unhappy you were and how you ought to be free as soon as possible because there was a gentleman...' he paused to glower at her '...another gentleman, with an interest, I thought I'd come here and take the high road, offer you your freedom if that's what you wanted. But the closer I got, the less noble I wanted to be.'

'Alice wrote to you?' A feeling of betrayal rippled through her. 'I suppose she meant for the best.' Only right now she wanted to strangle her friend.

He stopped pacing and looked at her. 'I thought so, too.'

Her heart no longer seemed to be beating at all. It still hurt, but didn't seem to be working. 'You did?'

'So I will ask you again,' he said harshly. 'Shall I set the wheels in motion for our divorce?'

Should he? 'And Dunross?'

He took a deep breath. 'It goes back to you.'

She stared at him. 'It was the only reason you married me.'

He gave her a long look. 'It was not.'

'This is part of the settlement, isn't it? The arrangements you made with my father.'

He shook his head. 'Your father made Dunross over to me, free and clear. But I'm no that kind of cur, Selina. Yes, I wanted Dunross. Gilvrys have always wanted Dunross, but I never expected to get it. I wanted you, too, but I never expected to get you either. I do not deserve a woman as fine as you. And I'll not be robbing you of your dowry.'

It was a pretty long speech, but something in the middle of it was pretty important. 'What do you mean, you always wanted me?'

He let go a long sigh. 'I believe I fell in love with you when I was eighteen, though I never would admit it, given the history between our families. It was my own stupid pride that made me turn from you when my brothers came along that day at Balnaen. I was ashamed for not doing my duty and hating you the way they did.' He gave a short laugh. 'I have never done my duty where you are concerned. You muddle every proper thought in my head.'

She knew just what he meant. He only had to look at her to muddle her brain. 'Did you say you loved me?'

Red stained his cheekbones above the disreputable beard. He took a deep breath. 'Aye. I. Love. You.'

No mistaking that. Something like joy bubbled in her chest. And hope. 'Why did you never speak of this before?'

He stilled, looking at her, and in that startlingly blue gaze she saw his hope. Only it was stronger than hope. It was longing.

Mingled with dread. 'Would ye have believed me? Would it not have seemed a mite too convenient? And besides, you told me you loved Dunstan.'

Not exactly. 'I told you I had chosen him.' She had a bit of confessing to do on her own account. 'I picked him because I knew my heart wasn't engaged. I knew he couldn't hurt me the way you had.'

He blinked. 'When I saw you again at Carrick's ball, I wanted to hate you. Because of Drew.'

'You blamed me.'

'I blamed myself for wanting to please you. I vowed I would not let you twist me around your finger again.' He gave a short laugh. 'So you tied my heart in knots instead.' He inhaled a breath so deep she thought the seams of his jacket might split asunder. A ragged-sounding breath. 'Well. Is it to be a divorce?'

She shook her head.

'If you are to stay as my wife, then you will have to live as my wife. I'll not have it any other way. And I'll do all in my power to prove my love. I promise you that.' His voice ended on a low seductive note.

Heat raced under her skin as the thought of the benefits of being his wife came to mind in full force. But she wasn't quite done torturing him yet. After all, he had offered to divorce her and let her stay here for almost two weeks when all the time he'd known he loved her. 'And where would we live?'

His face twisted in a grimace. 'Wherever you prefer.'

Oh, the delicious sound of his *r*s as they vibrated all through her body and down to her toes. But did he mean what he said? 'In London, then?'

His expression became stoic. It reminded her of

the time she had dressed the bullet wound in his arm. He was determined not to let her see how the thought irked him. 'If that is what you want.'

'Whatever I want?'

He nodded, albeit a little stiffly. He sat beside her and took her hand lacing and unlacing their fingers. 'I missed you.'

She almost didn't hear the words, he said them so softly.

'I couldn't sleep,' he said louder. 'Couldn't force a mouthful of food down my throat. All I could do was work and try not to think. Try not to wonder if things would have been different, if I had found the courage to tell you the truth of how I felt.'

'Oh,' she said, her heart lifting a little more than was seemly. 'And you did find the courage.'

'Aye. I did. For there was no denying it, no matter how hard I tried.' He brought her hand up to his lips and kissed it with a gentle kind of reverence that was so out of character for this big rough man, except around her. Her insides quivered with longing.

'I missed you,' he said. 'I missed your smiles and I missed your laughter. I even missed your frowns. My chest ached like a great rock was pressing down on it.'

His symptoms sounded much like hers.

'Oh, Ian. I did not mean to hurt you.'

'It was not your doing.' He stood up. 'Where you are concerned I have no strength at all.' He dropped to one knee. 'Selina, *leannan*, please, come back to me. I know I treated you badly. I did indeed trick you into marriage, but it was for your sake as much as mine. I swear to you I did not know about the dowry. You have to believe me.'

As he gazed into her face, she knew he did not lie. 'I believe you.'

'Then you'll come back to me?' He took another of those deep shuddering breaths and gazed into her eyes with longing and hope and a vulnerability that caused her poor heart to contract in the sweetest way. 'I love you, Lady Selina, and I will spend the rest of my life trying to make you happy. This I swear.'

The lump in her throat turned into hot prickles behind her eyes. She tried to breathe and the tears welled over.

A fierce grimace twisted his lips. 'Now I've made you cry. I'm sorry.'

He made to get up, but she flung herself at his chest, clinging fast to his neck. 'You are a fool, Ian Gilvry,' she sobbed into his cravat. 'An idiot.

I love you, too. I always have. I was afraid to tell you, in case I lost you. And it seemed that I had.'

Tentatively, his big hands came around her back, circling and patting. 'Aye, it would seem I truly am an idiot,' he said softly.

She pulled herself together with a small laugh, but he didn't let her go. Oh, no, the brute lifted her arm and sat down with her on his lap.

He gave a sigh of contentment. 'This is where you belong.'

She sat with her head on his chest while he dried her tears with his handkerchief. He kissed the tip. of her nose. 'You always loved me?' he mumbled.

Feeling terribly shy, she smiled up at him. 'It was why I could never bring myself up to the mark. Every time I got close to accepting a proposal, I remembered our kiss, that little touch of your lips to mine and the thrill I felt. No other man ever made me feel that way, so I always backed out.'

'Until Dunstan.' His voice was harsh.

'Poor Dunstan. He was my forlorn hope. I had to marry someone. I could no longer live with Father and Chrissie. It was too painful to watch their love grow and know I would never have the same.'

'You will and you do. More.' He stroked her arm.

'I know that now.'

'I kept hoping you might be with child. My

child,' he added quickly. 'I would have had you back, then.'

'I suppose we will have to try again.' She gave him a soft smile.

He captured her mouth in a kiss. 'I can't wait to get started,' he said when they finally came up for air.

'So you will take me to London?'

He nodded grimly. 'If it is what you want.'

'And who will look after Dunross and the people there?'

'Niall and Logan.' He sounded quite worried, but determined. 'Though I must tell you, after the fire, the people have been asking after you. It seems they miss their lady.'

She stared at him astonished. 'And your mother?'

'Not quite so much. I dinna understand it. She's not a vindictive woman. I am sure she will come around.'

Her mind drifted on dreams of the future. 'Ian, do you think we could have a proper wedding? In a church?'

'In St George's, Hanover Square, I suppose.' Again the stoic face and she had to force herself not to laugh.

Then she imagined the ceremony and the pomp and the *ton* all coming to gawk. 'No. I'd like it in the village church in Dunross. With those of your family who will come. And the McKinlys. And the rest of the clan, too, as long as they won't throw stones.'

'They wouldn't dare.' He looked deep into her eyes. 'Are you sure?'

'Yes. I've been talking to Hawkhurst about that law—you know, the volume of stills in Scotland. He thinks it is very unfair. He knows all about the smuggling and didn't express a bit of concern.' She frowned. 'Not about the brandy, but about moving whisky from Scotland to England. He said he couldn't see any other way of dealing with such a stupid law. He likes whisky.'

Ian gave her a quizzical look. 'If I'm not mistaken, Hawkhurst also thinks it's all right to be a pirate.'

She grinned. 'Privateer. And he's given it up. I'd be happy for you to give up smuggling, too, but not until Dunross's people are secure.'

He looked at her intently. 'Are you telling me you want to come back with me to Dunross? We still don't know who was behind Tearny, or whether they will strike again. I am not entirely sure I can keep you safe.'

She took a deep breath. 'I love you, Ian. Dunross

is where you belong and it is where I belong as your wife. But only if you don't shut me out. My father shut me out of his life when my mother died. And again when he married Chrissie, though Chrissie tried to prevent it. You kept me at a distance too, and I won't be locked out of your life. Whatever we do, we do together.'

He gave a soft groan and kissed her mouth, long and slow and lingering. It felt like a promise. And when he was done, he set her back on the sofa and once more went down on one knee. 'Lady Selina, to thee I plight my troth for ever and always and from this day forth will share with you all that I am, if you will do the same.'

She cupped his beloved rough-bearded face in her palms and pressed a kiss to his lips. 'I will, Ian,' she whispered.

'You know you have made me the happiest man alive, *leannan.*'

She took a shaky breath. 'I'd like to invite Alice and Hawkhurst to the ceremony.'

He nodded.

'And my father.'

'Invite the world, love. I want them all to see my beautiful wife and what a lucky man I am.'

He leaped to his feet. 'And now to get you home where you belong.'

Belong. It sounded like such a sweet word to her ears. And he was right. She did belong there, with him.

'You came on Beau?' she asked.

'Aye.'

'Well, since it is too far to ride on your saddle bow, I think we need to ask Hawkhurst for the loan of his carriage. And since it is too late to set out today, I think perhaps you should stay the night. We can set out in the morning.' She cast him a wicked look.

His blue eyes danced with amusement. 'Only if you have room for me in your bed.'

'What, before we are married, sir?'

She laughed as his face fell comically and rose up onto her toes and put her arms around his neck and pressed a kiss to his lovely sensual mouth. 'I have missed you so much, my dearest Ian. I waited for you for years and years, even though I didn't realise that is what I was doing, and I am not going to wait another moment.'

He picked her up. 'Thank God for that. Now, which way to the bedroom?'

She let out a squeak of surprise, as he carried her out of the room to the staircase, but she did not

hear the door down the corridor open or the whis-
pers and laughter from the library.

She was too busy looking at the love shining in
her husband's eyes and trying to kiss his lips, while
he took the stairs two at a time.

* * * * *

'I'm glad I reached you in time.'

A groan broke in his throat. 'Me too.' His hand came to her jaw, cradling her chin, angling her head the better to kiss her back.

His lips firmed over hers, testing and teasing. Thrills ran amok in her body, making her gasp with shock at the pleasure of such an intimate touch.

Heavenly sensations coursed through her veins and turned her bones liquid.

His parted lips matched hers, and open-mouthed they melded and moved in a harmony she hadn't expected. Tentatively, she tried a taste of her own. Their tongues met and danced and played, at first gently, carefully, and then with wild fervour.

Dizzy, breathing hard, she lay in his arms. The magic of his kiss took her out of her body. Whereas she'd been floating before, now she was flying, soaring, released from the chains of the world.

Inside she trembled.

Never in her adult life had she lost her sense of self so utterly as now, as if some part of them had fused and become something different altogether. It exhilarated. And terrified.

Fear made her struggle.

He drew back, breathing hard, looking into her face with a jaw of granite, with eyes the colour of midnight, hot and demanding.

AUTHOR NOTE

You first met Selina in CAPTURED FOR THE CAPTAIN'S PLEASURE. Selina was so different from Alice I found their friendship intriguing and I wanted to find out more. I didn't expect to discover that, like me, Selina had spent part of her youth in the Scottish Highlands. Despite everything she told herself, she could never quite forget the place—or the young man who caught her youthful fancy. Ian is as rugged as his country and equally hard to get to know. I hope you find their story as much fun to read as it was to write.

It seems that Scotland has fought against the odds over the centuries, and the Regency was no different as the clearances continued. Illegal whisky stills and smuggling were a matter of survival for many—and aren't we glad they persevered? Dunross and its people are figments of my imagination, but they are drawn from history and I hope you enjoy your visit. If you would like to visit me, you can find me online and at my website: www.annlethbridge.com. Drop me a note—I would love to hear from you.